THE HORN

THE HORN

by John Clellon Holmes

CREATIVE ARTS BOOK COMPANY / BERKELEY

c.4

CREATIVE ARTS BOOKS
ARE PUBLISHED BY DONALD S. ELLIS

JUL 8 '81

The incidents in this book are not intended to reflect the factual history of jazz music during the 1930's and '40's; nor are the characters intended to depict the actual men and women who made that history.

The book, like the music that it celebrates, is a collective improvisation on an American theme; and if there are truths here, they are poetic truths.

For
Shirley, who listened
and for
Jack Kerouac, who talked

Contents

If, then, to meanest mariners, and renegades and cast-aways, I shall hereafter ascribe high qualities, though dark; weave round them tragic graces; if even the most mournful, perchance the most abased, among them all, shall at times lift himself to the exalted mounts; if I shall touch that workman's arm with some ethereal light; if I shall spread a rainbow over his disastrous set of sun; then against all mortal critics bear me out in it, thou just spirit of Equality, which hast spread one royal mantle of humanity over all my kind! Bear me out in it, thou great democratic God!

HERMAN MELVILLE

Music is your own experience, your thoughts, your wisdom. If you don't live it, it won't come out of your horn. They teach you there's a boundary line to music. But, man, there's no boundary line to art.

CHARLIE PARKER

INTRODUCTION

The first chapter of THE HORN was written in five exhilarated sessions in the late summer of 1952. I was in the midst of a divorce, and living in a twenty-five-dollar-a-month walk-up on 49th Street in New York, and I had never written so easily before. The joy of it was keen. The chapter was based on an idea I'd had for four years (and failed to execute), called *The Afternoon of a Tenor Man*. The next chapter came equally easily the next year when, married again and living on 26th Street, I started to glimpse the book that lay, nascent, in that beginning — a man's life as remembered by those who loved and envied him. The rest of the novel came with difficulty after the death of Charlie Parker in 1955, which provided me with the end I felt was necessary both to my urge to attempt a book about jazz, ignorant though I was, and my growing awareness that I was trying to write about the artist-as-American. The book was first published, entire, by Random House in 1958, got respectable reviews, and slowly slipped from sight.

Jazz music has haunted America for seventy years. It has tempted us out of our lily-white reserve with its black promise of untrammeled joy. We grow up with it, into it, out of it. My father, shaving, when I was thirteen, yelled at Jimmie Lunceford's *White Heat*, "Turn it down, for God's sake!" — he, who had danced indefatigably to good bands in the 20's and 30's. I gave up trying to learn the guitar after hearing Charlie Christian and Django Reinhardt in the early 40's, and became a buff rather than a musician. I made the arduous transition from Dixie to Bop with the help of Jack Kerouac and Bird in 1948, and the seed-idea for THE HORN came that same year.

Some books accrete things to themselves like a magnet. The writer risks sterility by subjecting the mysterious power of imagination to the devices of mere comprehension. So I let THE HORN write itself; I let it find its own tone and language — lyric, wordy, continually verging on the legendary. Some critics had pedagogic fun with that aspect of the book. But I had been in a seethe of excitement during its composition, discovering that the quintessential American artist was the Black jazz musician, discovering as well my own limited adequacies to deal with Black experience and Black music, yet deciding, nevertheless and early on, to go with my love for both, and let the flaws justify themselves by my passion and sincerity.

I had dealt myself a tough hand. I wanted the book to function on three levels: fictional characters — Edgar Pool, Geordie Dickson, Wing Redburn; plus the musicians whom rumor and hearsay had already made fabulous to those of us who cared — Lester Young, Billie Holiday, Diz and Bird; and the writers of the great American

Renaissance of the 19th Century, who had defined, in their personalities and their works, the situation of the artist here — Melville, Whitman, Poe, Emily Dickinson. The epigraphs to each chapter, added with some trepidation after the fact, are clues to who is who.

Beyond all intellectual considerations, however, it was the music that mattered most — beauty, lift, swing wrestled out of sordidness, the miraculous concatenation of African rhythm and European melody in an America still uncertain of its soul. It seemed a story worth the telling. At times, pencil pushing along the page, I fancied that I knew what it was like to be them.

These twenty-odd years later, I occasionally read back in THE HORN, and am embarrassed by its flat-out earnestness, its overflow of language, its obvious musical flaws. But I recall, too, the thrill of writing it, the stubborn hope for our future that sometimes made the afternoons of writing pulse. I've never regretted the book. To have it in print again is a personal satisfaction. Jazz, the illegitimate child of our "peculiar fate" as black and white Americans, provided for this then-young writer the first word that announced the intention of the finished work.

Consider. At the very least, consider these people, these sounds, without which we would all be less alive.

—John Clellon Holmes
March, 1979
Fayetteville, Arkansas

THE HORN

CHORUS:WALDEN

> "*Men will lie on their backs, talking
> about the fall of man, and never make
> an effort to get up.*"
>
> THOREAU

Consider that it was four o'clock of a Monday afternoon,
and under the dishwater-gray window shade—just the sort
of shade one sees pulled down over the windows of cheap
hotels fronting the sooty elevateds of American cities
where the baffled and the derelict loiter and shift their feet
—under this one shade, in the window of a building off
Fifty-third Street on Eighth Avenue in New York, the wiz-
ened October sun stretched its old finger to touch the dark,
flutterless lids of Walden Blue, causing him to stir among
sheets a week of dawntime lying down and twilight getting up had rumpled.

Walden Blue always came awake like a child, without
struggle or grimace, relinquishing sleep in accordance with
the truce he had long ago worked out with it. He came
awake with a sparrow stare, fast dissolving as the world

3

was rediscovered around him unchanged for his absence. He lay alone—without moving in the way a man used to waking beside the body of women will move, either toward her or away; lay, letting his water-cracked ceiling remind him (as it always did) of the gullys of shack roads back home where he would muddy his bare black feet when a child, and where, one shimmering cicada-noon, he had stood and watched a great lumbering bullock careen toward him, and become a Cadillac-full of wild, zoot-suited city boys, pomaded, goateed, upending label-less pints, singing and shouting crazily at everything, "Dig and pick'-ninny! Dig the cotton fiel'! Dig the life here!" to bump past him, gape-faced there in the ruts, and plunge on around the bend of scrub pines, where he had once mused over an ant hill in the misty Arkansas dawn—for all like some gaudy, led-astray caravan of Gypsies, creating a wake of rumor and head-shaking through the countryside.

Walden Blue slid long legs off the bed, and for a moment of waking reflection—that first moment, which in its limpid, almost idiotic clarity is nearly the closest human beings come to glimpsing the dimensions of their consciousness—he considered the polished keys and the catsup-colored neck of the tenor saxophone which, two years before, had cost him $175 on Sixth Avenue, becoming his after an hour of careful scales and haggling and of the gradual ease which comes to a man's fingers when they lose their natural suspicion of an instrument or a machine which is not their own, but must be made to respond like some sinewy, indifferent horse, not reluctant to be owned but simply beautiful in its blooded ignorance of ownership. For on this saxophone Walden Blue made music as others might make love a kind of fugue on any bed; Walden made music as a business, innocent (because love of it was what kept him alive) of just what others meant by their "business," implying as that might some sacrifice of most that was skilled and all that was fine in them. He considered his saxophone, in this first moment of waking, without pleasure or distaste, noting it with the moody, half-fond stare of a man at the tool he has spent much time, sweat and worry to master, but only so that he can use it.

Looking at it, he knew it to be also an emblem of some inner life of his own, something with which he could stand upright, at the flux and tempo of his powers—as others consider a physical feat an indication of manhood, and still others, a wound. To Walden the saxophone was, at once, his key to the world in which he found himself, and the way by which that world was rendered impotent to brand him either failure or madman or Negro or saint. But then sometimes on the smoky stand, between solos, he hung it from his swinging shoulder like one bright, golden wing, and waited for his time.

"Hey there," he said to himself reproachfully, dangling his feet in an imaginary brook, for it was nearing three-thirty, which meant the afternoon was slipping by; and so he got up, stretching himself with the voluptuous grace some musicians give to any movement, and went about coffee-making. The electric plate was dead in one coil, the pot itself rusty from weeks of four o'clock makings; and without troubling his head about it, he used yesterday's soggy grounds. Coffee had no taste or savor to him at that hour: it was merely hot and black. He started his day with it, and as though it poured something of its nature into him, by the swirling night hours, amid smoke and roar, he would be like it: hotter and blacker, if anything. The second scalding cup was as necessary to the beginning of the day as the second shot of bourbon or the second stick of tea was to its blissful morning end someplace uptown, where, for sociability and personal kicks, he would blow one final chorus for himself, with a rhythm section of hardy, sweating souls collected from a scattering of groups around town, and then, packing up, go home empty of it all again. He drank his coffee back on the bed, lean shanks settled down on it, naked as a child; and each gulp reestablished him in the world.

His mind was clear; in these first moments, scarcely a man's mind at all, for he had no thoughts, just as he rarely dreamed. One afternoon in L.A.—back nine years ago, when bop was an odd new sound, and a name for the jazz many of them had been blindly shaping, and something else as well (a miraculous, fecund word, because no one then really understood its meaning, only somehow knew)—he had sat on a similar bed over his first cup, just like now, and out of the sweet emptiness of his morning head a thought had come: that he was a saxophone, as bright and shiny and potential as that, and the night and his life would play upon him. Some afternoons since then, he recalled recalling this thought, and often giggled secretly at its foolish accuracy. But never troubled his head.

But this afternoon something else was there. This morning—three or four o'clock at least, up at Blanton's on 125th Street, where, in the back, and after hours, they served coffee, and the musicians gathered to listen or play or talk that shop talk without which any profession in America would be thwarting to Americans—Edgar Pool had been inveigled to sit in with the house group (nothing more than rhythm upon which visitors could build their fancies), and as everyone turned to him in the drab, low-ceilinged room, giving him that respectful attention due an aging, original man whom all have idolized in the hot enthusiasm of youth, something had happened. And now Walden remembered.

There are men who stir the imagination deeply and uncomfortably, around whom swirl unplaceable discontents, men self-damned to difference, and Edgar Pool was one of these. Once an obscure tenor in a brace of road bands, now only memories to those who had heard their crude, uptempo riffs (their only testament the fading labels of a few records, and these mostly lost, some legendized already, one or two still to be run across in the bins of second-hand jazz record stores along Sixth Avenue), Edgar Pool had emerged from an undistinguished and uncertain musical environment by word of mouth. He went his own way, and from the beginning (whenever it had been, and something in his face belied the murky facts) he was unaccountable. Middling tall, sometimes even lanky then, the thin mustache of the city Negro accentuating the droop of a mouth at once determined and mournful, he managed to cut an insolently jaunty figure, leaning toward prominent stripes, knit ties, soft shirts and suede shoes. He pushed his horn before him; and listening to those few records years later, when bop was gathering in everyone but had yet to be blown, Walden, striving more with his fingers than with his head at that time, first heard the murmur of the sounds they were all attempting. Edgar had been as stubbornly out of place in that era, when everyone tried to ride the drums instead of elude them, as he was stubbornly unchanged when bop became an architecture on the foundation he had laid.

He hung on through fashions, he played his way when no one cared, and made money as he could, and never argued. One night in 1938, in a railroad bar in Cincinnati, where the gang men came to drink their pay with their dusky, wordless girls (something in them aching only for dance), he sat under his large-brimmed hat and blew forty choruses of "I Got Rhythm," without pause or haste or repetition, staring at a dead wall; then lit up a stick of tea with the piano man, smiled sullenly, packed his horn and caught the train for Chicago and a job in a burlesque pit. Such things are bound to get around, and when Walden saw him a year or so later (on another night at Blanton's), the younger tenors had started to dub him "the Horn," though never (at that time) to his face.

Edgar Pool blew methodically, eyes beady and open, and he held his tenor saxophone almost horizontally extended from his mouth. This unusual posture gave it the look of some metallic albatross caught insecurely in his two hands, struggling to resume flight. In those early days he never brought it down to earth, but followed after its isolated passage over all manner of American cities, snaring it nightly, fastening his drooping, stony lips to its cruel beak, and tapping the song. It had a singularly human sound—deep, throaty, often brutal with a power that skill could not cage, an almost lazy twirl on the phrase ends: strange, deformed melody. When he swung with moody nonchalance, shuffling his feet instead of beating, even playing down to the crowd with scornful eyes averted, they would hear a wild goose honk beneath his tone—the noise, somehow, of the human body; superbly, naturally vulgar; right for the tempo. And then out of the smearing notes, a sudden shy trill would slip, infinitely wistful and tentative.

But time and much music and going alone through the American night had weakened the bird. Over the years, during which he disappeared and then turned up, blowing here and there, during which, too late, a new and restless generation of young tenors (up from the shoeless deltas, like Walden, or clawed out of Harlem's back-alley gangs) discovered in his music something apt and unnamable— not *the* sound, but some arrow toward it, some touchstone —over the years which saw him age a little and go to fat, which found him more uncommunicative and unjudging of that steady parade of eager pianists and drummers that filed past behind him, the horn came down. Somehow it did not suggest weariness or compromise; it was more the failure of interest, and that strain of isolated originality which had made him raise it in the beginning out of the sax sections of those road bands of the past, and step solidly forward, and turn his eyes up into the lights. The tilt of his head, first begun so he could grasp the almost vertical slant of the mouthpiece, remained, the mouthpiece now twisted out of kilter to allow it; and this tilt seemed childishly fey and in strange contrast to his unhurried intent to transform every sugary melody he played and find somewhere within it the thin sweet song he had first managed to extract, like precious metal from a heap of slag.

Walden felt Edgar Pool threaded through his life like a fine black strand of fate, and something always happened. When he first heard him in the flesh—sometime back in 1941, in the dead center of war, after learning those few records by heart, after finding his own beginnings in Brahmin Lightcap's big band that came in with a smashing engagement in Boston, and went out six months later, a financial bubble, when the trumpet section grumpily enlisted in the Navy and most of the saxes were arrested on narcotics charges—after this, after waiting to hear Edgar, missing him in L.A. by a lost bus connection, getting hung up in Chicago, Walden had come into Blanton's one night, and heard a sound, and there was Edgar, horn at a forty-five-degree angle to his frame, playing behind Geordie Dickson as she sang "What Is This Thing Called Love?" with a tremble in her voice then that made you wonder. Something settled in Walden that night, and he decided to get out of the big bands, the bus schedules, the dance halls, the stifling arrangements; to get off the roads for a while; to stick around New York, which was his adopted pond after all; to give himself his head. (It wasn't Edgar actually—just that aura of willful discontent around him: wanting a place, but not *any* place.)

Since then Walden dug Edgar whenever he was around,

puzzled and disturbed, but not until this morning in Blanton's had anything come out clear. Edgar had played with weary and indifferent excellence, noting neither Cleo —who played piano with Walden at the Go Hole every night but never got enough and, like so many young musicians (he was only eighteen), seemed to have no substantial, homely life but jazz, no other hours but night, and so hung around Blanton's till dawn with untiring smiles of expectation—nor the others who wandered in and out, listening to every other bar, gossiping and showing off their latest women. Edgar stood before them, down among the tables, for there was no proper stand, sax resting on one thigh, and Walden studied him for an instant with that emotion of startling objectivity that comes only when a man least expects or desires it. And for that moment he forgot his own placid joy at the night narrowing down to an end and to this hour among his own sort, at the sight of someone so inexplicably isolated from it all, though generally accepted as one pivot on which it turned.

Edgar fingered lazily, ignoring Cleo's solid, respectful chords, one shoulder swinging back and forth slightly, his chin pulled in. His hair was long over his large collar, he padded up and down on exaggerated crepe soles, and between solos he chewed an enormous wad of gum soaked in Benzedrine. They said he had "gone queer," but instead there was something soft and sexless about him. Then he smeared a few notes over a pretty idea—a crooked smile glimmering behind the mouthpiece, all turned in upon himself, all dark; and Walden alone seemed to catch the sinister strain of self-ridicule behind the phrase, behind the sloppy, affected suit, the fairy hip-swinging; and at that moment the presence of a secret in Edgar reached him like a light.

For if jazz was a kind of growing Old Testament of the Negro race—and of all lost tribes in America, too—a testa-

10

ment being written night after night by unknown, vagrant poets on the spot (and so Walden, reared on a strange Biblical confusion, often thought of it), then Edgar had once been a sort of Genesis, as inevitable and irreducible as the beginnings of things; but now, mincing, chewing, flabby, he sounded the bittersweet note of Ecclesiastes, ironical in his confoundment.

But just then Geordie Dickson flounced in with her cocker spaniel under one arm, two smirking white men guiding her, half-tipsy, between them. The sweaty faces around the room pivoted, and someone whispered hoarsely. For this was almost the first time in the ten years since something unknown had separated them that they had been in the same room. Their lives were fatefully, finally intertwined, for Edgar had found her singing in a ginmill in Charleston (no more than sixteen then) and, probably with only a clipped word of command, had taken her away and brought her North—a sturdy, frightened, bitter girl, one-quarter white, raped at fourteen on a country lane by two drunken liquor salesmen, thrown into reform school where she was chained to an iron cot while her child was born out of her dead, finally released to find her family vanished, thrown back for pickpocketing in colored churches, released again in the custody of a probation officer who tried to get her into a whorehouse, and trying to keep off the streets with her voice when Edgar first saw her. He taught her some sense of jazz, got her the initial jobs, backed her on the records that followed, and took money from her when, all overnight, she became a sensation to that dedicated breed of lonely fanatic which jazz creates. Walden, among the others, had often stood in the vest-pocket clubs on Fifty-second Street during 1942, as the lights faded away and one spot picked her out—mahogany hair oil-bright, over one ear the large red rose still wet from the florist's, candle-soft eyes, skin the sheen of waxy, smooth wood—and heard the opening chords, on grave piano, of "I Must Have That Man"; and also heard, with the others, the slur, the sugar, the pulse in the voice, and had known, without deciding or judging, that it was right; and been dazzled too.

People turned wherever she went (although not anticipating a scene, as they did at Blanton's that morning), because she had the large, separated breasts of a woman who has spent hours leaning over her knees, working or praying; breasts that would be tipped with wide, copper-colored nipples; breasts that would not be moored; made for the mouths of children, not of men. In all her finery (off-the-shoulders gown, single strand of small pearls, the eternally just-budded rose), her flesh and the heavy-boned grace of her body alone had any palpable reality. There was a breath-catching mobility to her—nothing fragile or well bred, but that extraordinary power of physicality which is occasionally poured into a body. The deep presence of fecundity was about her like an aroma, something mindless and alive; that touch of moist heaviness (suggestive of savagery, even when swathed in lace) which is darkly, enigmatically female. She was a woman who looked most graceful when her legs were slightly parted, who appeared to move blindly, obediently, from some source of voluptuous energy in her pelvis; whose thighs shivered in brute, incomplete expression of the pure urge inside her.

Edgar did not indicate by even the quaver of a note that the excitement and apprehension in the rest of the room had reached him. He played on, as if in another dimension of time, when she took a seat not ten feet from him, the spaniel squatting in her lap, wet nose over the edge of the table, eyes large. Neither did *she* look, but went about settling herself, nodding to acquaintances, chatting with her companions. She was arrogantly drunk, opulently sensual as only a woman in the candor of dissipation can be; and beside her Edgar looked pale, delicate, even curiously effeminate. She had always been strangely respectful of him, even when swarms of white men had fidgeted at her elbow, pleading to fasten her bracelets, even when easy money had turned her life hectic and privileged; she had looked at him, even then, with a tawny, resentful respect, like a commoner with a sickly prince.

Now she was drinking heavily out of a silver-headed, leather-jacketed pocket flask; her eyes grown flashing and wet. The spaniel lay on her thighs, subdued, and she poked and patted and cooed to him loudly, as if trying to goad him into a bewildered bark.

Edgar finished his chorus and gave it to Cleo on the piano, who never soloed, for whom the dreadful spaces of thirty-four open bars held no terrors, but small interest either; and then he slowly turned his back on her, a dreamy, witless grin weakening his face as he muttered nonsense with the drummer.

His absolute lack of recognition in these first moments was the surest sign to Geordie that he was electrically aware of her movements there in the room. Something in him was indestructible, some merciless pride with which he chose to victimize himself. Only he could smash or break it. Some said, after all, that he had gotten her on the morphine habit she threw only when, at the height of her glittering success, she had begun to miss engagements and ruin tunes; other rumors went that love between them had been a stunted, hot-house pantomime, always lurching on the shadowy edges of sensations—as queer and deformed as Edgar himself.

She began to chatter with vicious affectation when he took his reed into his mouth like a thumb and blew a windy yawp—trapped into the chatter as into everything else, because his placid, punishing indifference (not only to her but to all the real world) was yet another symbol of some incalculable superiority. Her mouth, as it snarled and quivered, was indescribably, cruelly sensual, as though she was about to faint from some morbid and exhilarating thought. But only her mouth had learned the tricks of contempt, brittleness and sophistication. Her eyes glowed steadily with something else, and as Walden looked at her, in these first moments that seemed supercharged with tension and thus unendurably long, he saw (as this morning he seemed fated to see everything that had been under his nose for years) the nature of that something else—saw that her long, shapely neck had started to wrinkle, that she had expensive powder in her armpits where there should have been soft, dark hair—and knew there was a flaw now where there had been none before, a flaw developed by a life that had carved a black cross on her forehead; and then sensed again the woman in her flesh, now gone slightly stale, and remembered that some said even the dog had licked it.

Edgar chose this moment to blow sweet, as a final passionless mockery of the auspiciousness or sentiment others might be feeling in that situation. His sound was disarmingly feeble, earnest, but meant to prove, by some inmost private irony, that he was, if so he chose, a timeless man. The limpid pathos of his song was somehow a denial of the past, a denial of any power over him but his peculiar self-abusive ability; and at that moment, just as Geordie's eyes drifted across and away from him, the saxophone, hanging limp against one thigh, stirred and came up, and there was for just that second a corresponding stir of vigor in his sound; and then he fell back into the vapid, thin tone, his horn descending, as if to say—and Walden heard —that he would be a slave to nothing, not even the genius inside him. His obsession was his last secret, the note he carefully never blew.

To Walden, he seemed a mask over a mask, all encrusted in an armored soul. Some said that Geordie had once stripped the masks away, one by one, with no intent but desire, had had a hint of the inside, and had been driven wanton out of helplessness. The secret must have been (as it most always is) that his need was formless, general—a need which persists only because no satisfaction can ever be fashioned for it; an inconceivable thing in a woman, a thing forever mysterious and infuriating to her; something peculiarly male, the final emblem of imperfection, impotence, but with a terrifying power to wound or create, the Jeremiah-like power of a fury at powerlessness.

So they were alone in all that room, absolutely locked together and alone, and yet steadfastly refusing to notice each other, and Walden knew that Edgar would blow all night if necessary, burst a lung, dredge himself to obliterate her—and not because he cared; not for her, but because of himself. Already somebody was thinking about how he could possibly describe it to the cats in his group the next night. "Man, it was positively the end!" would prove far too thin, and by the time word of it reached L.A., K.C., Chicago, it would be a kind of underground history, one of those nights that, passed from mouth to mouth, year upon year, become, in the alchemy of gossip, fabulous and Homeric.

Cleo, alone of everyone, refused to be drawn into the drama of their wills, but looked from Edgar to Geordie, not casually or with suspense as the others did, but with an expression of trembling, clear-eyed sorrow, his little hands automatically making the sad chords on which Edgar was shaping his humiliation of sadness, his lips saying softly over and over again: "Oh, man, what for? Oh, man, why? Oh, man, no!" Edgar only wiped a phrase across the words and wiggled his hips.

Walden, too, was struck dumb, all eyes, somehow horrified, for now Geordie's mouth was capped with straining avidity around the neck of the flask, the spaniel staring up at her with baffled dark eyes. Even Edgar watched this over his horn with a half-hidden, secretive sneer. And Walden, at that instant, suddenly thought of him as a Black Angel—something out of the scared, rainy nights of his childhood when his mother had tried to remember the Bible her mother had once, long ago in a bayou town, read to her, and had gotten it all mixed and filled it in herself in a droning, righteous whisper, till Satan carried a razor and Babylon was a place in midnight Georgia, and the fallen angels were black bucks run wild through the county like the city boys in the Cadillac, and even Jehovah wore a Kluxer's sheet, and everyone was forever lost. Edgar was a Black Angel all right, and Walden suddenly knew. For like many people brought up on the Bible like a severe laxative, he often thought, without whimsy, about angels and suchlike. Not that he believed, that wasn't necessary; but sometimes when he played and stared up into a rose spotlight so as to concentrate, he thought about some possible heaven, some decent kind of life—and groped blindly like any man.

If he had better understood himself and the inconsolable ambiguity of men's aspirations, the unforgivable thing he did then might not have stunned him so. But he did not understand, and knew little of the concepts upon which men struggle to define their existence (although down in his heart waited a single note of music that he felt would shatter all discord into harmony), and so when he found himself suddenly beside Edgar, his horn clipped to its swing around his neck, and heard himself break into the pedestrian chorus of "Out of Nowhere" that Edgar was blowing, he was filled with the same sense of terror that had swept over him ten years before, the first time he had stood up before live, ominous drums and cut out a piece for himself. Only it was worse, because there was a complex protocol to "after hours," unwritten, inarticulate, but accepted by even the most beardless tyro with the second-hand horn for which he did not even own a case. There was a protocol, and it did not countenance an uninvited intrusion from the watchers, no matter who. On top of that, Walden (thought of among musicians as a "good, cool tenor," reliable, with sweet ideas and a feel for riffs, but one who had not yet found his way) was presuming upon Edgar Pool, revered from a distance by everyone who came later and blew more, whose eccentricities were accorded the tolerance due to anyone embittered by neglect, and whose lonely eminence as "the Horn" was beyond challenge, a matter of sentimental history. What Walden did, then, was unheard of.

But he started the next twelve bars nevertheless, keeping a simple tasty line. Edgar, reed still between loose lips, gave him a startled, then slyly amused glance, telling Walden, all in a flash, that for the audacity and the stupidity of the move he would do him the honor of "cutting" him to pieces, bar to bar, horn to horn. But the affront had shocked everyone else; the room was frozen, speechless; and Walden knew he was, in effect, saying to them: "I secede from the protocol, the law," and further (and this he did not know, though it was the truth of what he felt): "What I know must be done cannot be done within all that." But thereby he was placing himself outside their mercy and their judgment, in a no man's land where he must go alone. Only Geordie was not transfixed; a slow, quivering smile had curled her lips, and her fingers had left the spaniel's ears.

Edgar leaped back easily, satirizing Walden's last idea, playing it three different ways, getting a laugh, horn hung casually out of one side of his mouth. The drums slammed in perfectly on top of Cleo's remonstrative chord, and

Walden started to swing one shoulder, playing sweet when it was his turn, knowing they would take only six-bar breaks from then on, to tighten the time, and finally only three, when a man had to make himself clear and be concise; the last gauntlet when a misfingered note could be the end.

Edgar slouched there beside him, as if playing with one hand, yawping, honking, aping him; and only his beady eyes were alive, and they were sharp, black points of irony and rage. Walden looked into those eyes, and blew a moving phrase that once another Edgar might have blown, and was, at last, victim of the naïve core of his heart, the unthought-out belief that it mustn't be Edgar's way. He looked at Edgar, loving him even in all his savage, smearing mockery, battling not him but the dark side of that Black-angel soul; bringing light.

It got hotter, tighter, and Cleo, staring at Walden as at a barefoot man exulting on a street corner, laid down solid, uncritical chords for both of them, that it might be fair and just—all the time his innocent, dewy eyes on the side of sweetness, whoever would speak up for it.

Walden looked at Edgar, sweating now and gloomily intent, and blew four bars of ringing melody, so compelling that Edgar stumbled taking off, unable to recall himself (for "cutting" was, after all, only the Indian wrestling of lost boyhood summers, and the trick was getting your man off balance). And then Walden came back clear, and knew (now so beyond doubt, he almost faltered) that his was the warmer tone, that this was what he had always *meant;* and so experienced a moment of incredible, hairbreadth joy.

The silence in the room came apart, because music was fair contest. The crowd unwillingly shifted the center of their prejudices, and between phrases Walden could hear Geordie crying sharply, "Blow! Blow!" but, looking out, found her rocking back and forth, her eyes narrowed now to bright wicks, and could not tell at whom she cried, and did not, he realized, consider himself her champion; but was only bringing light.

Edgar was shuffling forward, and blew four bars of a demented cackle, and for an instant they were almost shoulder to shoulder, horn to horn, in the terrible equality of art, pouring into each wild break (it felt) the substance of their separated lives—crazy, profound Americans, both! For America, as only they knew it who had wandered like furtive minnesingers across its billboard wastes to the screaming distances, turned half a man sour, hard-bitten, barren, but awakened a grieving hunger in his heart thereby.

America had laid its hand on both of them. In Edgar's furious, scornful bleat sounded the moronic horn of every merciless Cadillac shrieking down the highway with a wet-mouthed, giggling boy at the wheel, turning the American prairie into a graveyard of rusting chrome junk; the idiot-snarl that filled the jails and madhouses and legislatures; some final dead-wall impact. And in Walden, no sky-assaulter but open-eyed, there was the equally crazy naïveté that can create a new, staggering notion of human life and drive some faulty man before it through the cities, to plant an evangelist on every atheist Times Square, a visionary in any godless roadhouse; the impulse that makes cranks and poets and bargain-drivers; that put up a town at the end of every unlikely road, and then sent someone with foolish curiosity to see what was there.

This time Walden had the last chorus to himself, having earned it. By that same unspoken protocol, it was understood by everyone that he had "cut," and so Edgar stepped back—for though the victor might venture outside the law, the victim, having nothing left, must abide by it. And Edgar accepted. The crowd was on its feet when the drums signified by a final, ecstatic slam that it was over, Geordie standing too, but in all the shouting and heated laughter there, she alone was motionless, grave.

Walden's moment of joy had gone off somewhere, and he felt a chill of apprehension, and swung on Edgar, one hand extended vaguely as if to right himself. But Edgar, unsnapping his horn, only glanced at him once—a withering, haunted look, a look he had probably never shown anyone before, leveled now at Walden, without malice, only as a sort of grisly tribute to his prowess and his belief. It was to be Walden's spoils: that bewildered stare in the eyes of another man, whose effort, even to punish himself out of pride, had been thwarted. It was a look which had a future, from which heavy, fatal consequences must proceed; and with it went a weak, lemonade grin, meant only to cover the wince of nausea; for Walden knew then that Edgar had horrified himself, like a drunk who sees, in the single, focused moment of hangover, the twitching, blotchy ruin of his own face, the shadow across his eyes— knowing all along that the horror will not fight down the thirst.

At that, Edgar turned, taking his horn and case, and limped away, pausing only at Geordie, not to touch her, but merely to peer at her for an instant, mutter something almost without moving those stony lips, and disappear into the crowd, making for the exit. Walden's hand still lay, half-spread, on the air.

Then Cleo was at his elbow, staring past him after Edgar, eyes moist with alarm, voice choked with shock as he exclaimed in an undertone, "Catch him before he dies! Catch him!" And he, too, ran away, still on the side of sweetness, knowing where it lay, looking neither to right nor left.

So Walden stood there alone in the light, isolated in his achievement, and by it, breathless and transformed, the way a man feels who has, on an impulse coming up from far down in his soul, totally altered his life all in a moment, and then looks up, stunned, to discover himself in a new moral position to everything around him. And in that dazzling isolation, only Geordie approached him, coming so close her fragrance swirled thickly through his head, and he saw that she was exhausted, sobered, and somehow resigned.

For just a second they were caught in an odd, impersonal affinity, and in that second, she whispered, "Don't worry. Don't you worry now. You know what he said to me? He only said, 'He sounded good.' Just that. Don't you worry now, honey."

She gave him a last wan, forgiving half-smile just as her escorts hurried up, one of them snuggling the sleepy spaniel, and Walden knew, for all the smile and for all the words, that *she* was worried nevertheless. But she turned and glided away then, leaving him standing there by himself, while people he had known for years clustered and exclaimed around him as though he was a notorious stranger, and he held his head up manfully under their praises. . . .

Sitting on his bed, now, it all came back with blinding clarity between gulps of coffee; all of a piece, all in an instant, undamaged by sleep. He got up, shivering with the memory, to pour himself the second cup, and to realize, with dumb acceptance, that this was to be the first afternoon of his life.

He had brought the light all right, but the conflicts in a man's nature were not to be resolved by light alone. Edgar had fled in disgust and despair at what it had revealed, fled from the light because it was not for him any more. Walden was frozen, even now, hours later, by the power one man had over another; it sickened something trusting in him, even though he could not disbelieve the clear impulse that had prodded him to stand up. But the consequences of an action were endless, and he could not see the end of this particular one. He had taken a stand for once, and as he had discovered about his tone, so he had, for once and all, damned himself to going his way.

Then he knew that at some time, perhaps in the cramped second-sax chair of one of those tireless, all-but-forgotten road bands of the mythical past, this awful moment of human commitment must have been pushed up to Edgar too, and without thought or hesitation, Edgar had leapt in, cutting his road alone, and had blown, as himself, for the first time, and started, by finally tapping his sources and letting his sound out, toward that morning and Walden. That was the only secret, and Walden wondered, with all the astonishment of a new idea, what his end would be.

From now on, he realized as he stood before the bed, suddenly amazed by his nakedness, there would be dreams through the mornings when he alone slept in the busy world, and all the irritations and responsibilities of age and work when he awoke. The armistice with sleep and discord had been forever broken. From now on he had to fight for his life and his vision, like every man.

At that, the quiet loneliness of self-knowledge descended over him like a prophetic hint of the shroud toward which all lives irrevocably progress. And pulling on his shorts, he remembered what Cleo had said just that morning.

"Catch him before he dies!"

And wondered if that was to be part of it, too. But putting the wondering aside for then, he set himself to dressing methodically. This was his first day in a strange, lonesome country, and one part of that, anyway, was knowing it could not be postponed any longer.

RIFF

But coming down Riverside Drive, having reached the
Seventies by then, was a man with a horn case for whom
this day had begun the afternoon before. He had not slept
since then, and he came heedlessly along the walks amid
the faint rustle of curled leaves, mumbling now and then
to his young doe-faced companion from under the streak
of sneering mustache, something about his swollen lids
and uncaring mouth inexplicably suggestive of the night.

The young mothers, in their great twilight exodus of baby
carriages and knitting bags, and the ruminative old men
in the autumn's first scarves and rubbers, instinctively gave
him room, for like great poets and great sinners and all
men who live by an ideal or an illusion, that same something about him disowned their part of life, as if he had
been spoiled for it by a vision they could not understand.

According to their fears and prejudices, they probably judged him drunk or dope fiend or hood, and secretly grew apprehensive for their modesty or money.

But though he had opened a Harlem bar that morning —drumming an impatient forefinger while the bartender worked up the pressure in the taps, and drowned in beer the gloom that dawn bequeaths to those who will not go to bed, and had begun to talk, querulous and loosened by Benzedrine, and finally started downtown joyously, mockingly drunk amid the sober bustle of that Monday noon, only to refuse to eat, and to lose the joy in other barrooms, and so drink on to recapture it, almost forgetting the horn case at every move, and turning first silent and then sullen and finally talkative again in his thoughts —nevertheless there was nothing more threatening in him to the world of day than a lot of old songs, and the men who had played them, and the places they had gone.

He moved on in a shambling, thoughtless walk, staring over the imperturbable haze of the river, and smoking with the steady unconcern of a man who can no longer taste the cigarettes, talking all the while in disconnected spurts of Benzedrine-monologue to the young man beside him, whose alert gaze had the patient, wild delicacy of a small animal or an unjudging disciple.

Cleo (for it was he) had stuck by Edgar all day, with a blind, almost fatalistic tenacity that had in it more of reverence than respect, tagging along, dutifully emptying his share of the glasses, automatically replacing the cigarettes in Edgar's wrinkled fingers as they burned down and were dropped, and every once in a while suggesting, in a soft, urgent voice, food or rest or a destination when the monologue thinned to a ramble or broke off at a thought, only to be rebuffed or mocked or merely ignored; to wait his chance again.

"Man," Edgar was saying, as if imagining what the

young mothers and the old men were thinking. "Who's that carrying a piece of luggage through the streets? Who's that, that whenever you see him, 's got a goddamn suitcase in his hand, like he's always running late for a bus, coming from no place and going somewheres else? Man, who *is* that?" His eyes stared at the world remotely. "Like, lady, that's a musician, and that's a horn, and he probably got a change of socks, and his razor, and a coupla rubbers, and two sticks of tea, and maybe even a extra shirt in there with his reeds. So you watch out, oh, yes! . . . I mean, that man is a musician, and he's just transporting his horn from one place to another like usual, and probably don't own nothing else in the goddamn world but that goddamn piece of goddamn luggage. I mean, that man don't *live* anywhere, he only *sleep*. I mean, that man is God's own fool, now ain't he?" He sniffed, in a grimacing, evil parody of every hipster who had ever floated down a sidewalk in a dream of life that everything around him shattered. "He been toting it, and checking it, and packing and unpacking it, all the way since Fate was on the river—that's how long—the Big River"—Fate Marable and his riverboat caliope (Cleo seemed to recall), who had astonished the landings between New Orleans and St. Louis with the wild, harsh, skirling Gypsy music that wanderers have always brought to settled places, and left there, echoing in the young and restless even as it dies off round the bend; to linger with them thereafter, in the pelting roar of November midnights and the clickety-clack of lonesome valley freights, until they up one night and go after it in a battered bus, following the telephone wires that make a zigzag music staff against the evening sky—some variation of that basic beginning could be told for everyone whom jazz has touched and altered.

For Cleo, listening and yet barely listening, it was like watching a myth become incarnate in a man, a man grown garrulous and silly in his cups, aging implacably, but still somehow larger than life for all of that; a living connection to the whole tribe of jazzmen (a mere sixty years wandering now) who had shaped and protected the music which was all there was in life to him, through the dim fabulous decades that were only history as far as he knew; an actual, palpable link to all those who had ever followed his chosen trade and gotten through life with only a horn to show the way, traveling the bad buses, eating the indifferent food, sleeping behind the blind windows on the wrong side of town, to get up late and wake hard, and night after night bootleg a ragtime, upbeat make-believe to all the bleak main streets.

So he tagged along, awed and inattentive, the dead names (which were only names to him), and the living faces (which he had seen only through smoke and crowds) running through his head without sequence: the second cornets and plunking banjoists; the comb-blowers and tuba-umpers . . . Names like Woody, Jelly, Junius . . . The thick-fingered bassists with a bad beat; the whorehouse professors in celluloid collars; the dance-hall elegiasts too drunk to see . . . Wing, Tram, Pee Wee, and Tricky Sam . . . The nervous tenors who rushed the drums, and frowned, and blew short choruses; the coked-up clarinets and u-h-h-h groaning piano men and Juilliard theorists . . . Bunny, Benny, Bubber, Bud; Fats (Pichon, Waller, Navarro, or Domino, depending on your kick) . . . The show-off guitarists in flashy sports shirts, the wind-breaking drummers addicted to Juicy Fruit, the cool flutists taking tootling six-bar breaks on "Fine and Dandy," and the severely flanneled trumpeters who were too hip to blow . . . Names like Bean, Bags, Rabbit; Dizzy, Curny, and Little Jazz . . . The girl intermission pianists, resolutely ingénue in chokers and not much décolletage, who invariably played a three-minute version of the "Rhapsody in Blue," and tippled brandy between sets; the belters with a belly, the sexy wenches with whiskey in the voice, the pert silky torchers . . . All the chicks: Bessie, Peggy, Sarah; Neets and Mary Lou; Mildred and Geordie and Lady Day; Ella . . . And everyone who worked Schnee's Lounge in East Dubuque; and all tenor wildmen, who never tapped their feet but merely trod where they stood, walking the long road toward joy; and everyone who ever played "Body and Soul" anywhere, any time, any way, yes . . . All who comped with funk . . . Tristano, Christian, Blanton; Tatum, Metro, Monk . . . and blew the truth . . . King, Duke, Count, and Pres . . . and doubled in life . . . Bix, Satch, Bird. Yes.

"Man, I got one arm longer than the other," Edgar was saying as he leaned on the parapet over the river, "just carrying it! Not *blowing* on it, just *carrying* . . . And then they say, 'Horn, how come your horn come down? How come you don't hold it *up* no more?'" His lips curled back in a distasteful smile as he arched the cigarette away. "Man, *it* won't carry *me!* . . . And what do they know anyway? . . . I mean, you young cats think you study counterpoint, and live nice at home, and do a local gig some nights, and you can blow. I mean, *he* think he earned it last night, blowing in a session after hours, feeling good, when I'm off my tone anyway . . . But, man, it used to take years in my day, it used to take *time* to earn it. You didn't have no school where you could learn . . . Why, man, I learned *my* horn, reading arrangements no one listened to, in nine-piece hustling bands that didn't have no proper name"—ratty, smudged arrangements of "Dardanella" and "Roll'em" and "I'm Gonna Stomp Mr. Henry Lee" that had more mileage on them than most men, and had been opened on a thousand cramped stands, and read by two generations of section men, and stacked and unstacked by succeeding platoons of band boys, and spilled and scribbled and sweat on through aggregate years of one-night stands, and finally abandoned in a booker's warehouse in Columbus, waiting there still for the requiem of rats and mold: all part of that now legendary American enterprise—half-commerce, half-crusade—the saga of the swing band in the late thirties and early forties, that took jazz to the old horse towns jammed with Cadillacs, and to the spanking new cities without edges, their boulevards smack up against unscarred prairie, and to the gyms, dance halls, auditoriums and saloons that were there; all part of the straggling four o'clock departures, the john stops, the bottomless binges, the bright crushed faces of the kids of those years, and the bus, with all manner of crazy gear stowed on the roof under a tarpaulin, in which the journeyman-musician lived his life.

"He think he earned it cause he come all the way uptown, and caught me when my tone was bad, and I wasn't feeling like it anyway . . . Huh! Uptown!" he sneered, the hot passionless eyes devoid of self-pity, even though the mouth writhed there in the last light—small black eyes, still quick, that would not be degraded, and grew narrow with pique. "You kids today think you get around if you play Chicago, L.A., Boston, Philly and New York, and play maybe three sets a night in a club, but would rather play some concert where there ain't no ice cubes to distract you . . . Huh! You don't know towns. You never been to Billings, Crawfish, Grand Forks, Stockyards, Sioux City, Puckey Huddle, Big Chimney, Gnawbone—now, have you! . . . Yah! Gnawbone, Indiana! . . . You never played the Horseshoe in McKeesport, or Christy's Four-a-day in Minneapolis where the ofay strippers threw their meat right over your head, and you played 'Tiger Rag' landing on them bump-beats loud, and no foolin' no matter how you felt . . . You never learned to *save* your ideas for later, next week, next year; or play straight on some Sigmund Romberg that ain't got but one good chord in it . . . And then he think he earned it, because—" But he broke off with a wracking cough that seemed to require, not only all his body and the breath within it, to endure and outlast, but the rags of mind and will as well.

"But it don't matter— Oh, it matter to *him*, Walden, sure. He blew—though, man, in my time, you didn't just break in that way, and cut someone. You didn't do it, you never would have done it . . . But, all right, he sounded good. It don't matter to me to say it," and he lapsed for a moment, a hunched disquieting figure against the sundown river, like a ghost come out early to wait for dark. "And, anyway, there's a hundred horns can blow like him," he muttered abstractedly, "but there didn't used to be but one. There was only me," and he spit with a precise, somehow repudiating curve into the dusk below. "So I might as well go on home. I just think I will. Why not!"

He looked around with a sudden, curious horror in his eyes. "Man, it don't get dark *fast* enough these days! It stay light right up to seven o'clock. And it must be almost November now, ain't it? . . . And I don't want to be here in November. You can't never get your feet dry in November in this town." He swallowed something thick and dangerous in his throat. "No, no, I'll go back the way I come. I better do it. Cause, you know"—and he swallowed again —"something's gone weird in me, something's off. I'll tell you a secret. It's just umpa-umpa-umpa to me now—"

But then he broke off again, leaning farther over the parapet in a graceless stretch, for what Cleo was certain was only the beginning of the wracking cough again, but which, to his amazement, turned into raw, convulsive heaves, one after the other, as from some deep quease, that brought up nothing but a thin, pinkish bile. Cleo stood, appalled but not disgusted, one helpless hand on

Edgar's back, as Edgar shuddered, and waited, and shuddered again, and then straightened up, to say only, "I been doing that lately, just all of a sudden, even when there ain't nothing to come up . . . I got to stop something, I guess. It won't wait no longer."

He wiped his unshamed mouth, catching breath, a thin faint sweat visible over his forehead in clammy distribution. "So I'll just go on home. I won't tell nobody, just whoosh and gone on that morning bus, and let 'em wonder," and he snickered with tipsy immodesty. "I can make it, if I don't come down, or go to sleep. If I just keep going."

"You mean back to Kansas City?" Cleo said, rousing for a moment. "And all the time I thought you meant uptown—"

"And all I *need,* you see, is loot," Edgar added, eyes cagey and unscrupulous, but also dimly lit by those last, indomitable embers of fool hope that make it thankfully impossible for a man to believe his magic has left him for good. "I just need to con somebody for the fare is all, cause I figure it cost me fifty, sixty bucks altogether, and all I got is ten." He measured Cleo with a calculating eye. "You got any money, kid? . . . No, I don't guess you have. You just a colored-boy piano player like a *thousand* others, and your ma pays the rent, eh, eh?" he goaded with cruel indifference, already thinking of something else, and failing to notice the hurt that widened Cleo's eyes, or failing to care, if he did. "So what I need is a phone, and a drink to start me with," he concluded, standing back from the parapet all at once, swaying slightly, gaze level and remote as he peered into the gloom. "I just wanted to get a look at the river, but, man, it ain't much of a river after all, now is it?" and he turned away with a secretive smile. "Man, I feel like I'm hung up in Baltimore or someplace. Ain't there no bars in this part of town?"

CHORUS:WING

*"Let me look into a human eye . . .
this is the magic glass, man."*

MELVILLE

Wing Redburn was not alarmed when Walden caught up
with him and told him that Edgar had probably had
enough at last. He had just wedged himself into a slot in
the revolving door that interceded between the uncer-
tainties of Forty-sixth Street and the hushed cream-white
lobby of the W E L L Studios, when he heard somebody
call out, "Hey, there, man." He turned around right inside,
where the neutral odor of air-conditioning was always
the strongest, just as the door ejected Walden and continued to revolve with an autonomous whish-whah, whish-
whah. They stood by an ash stand whose bowl of fine
white sand had yet to know a butt, and drew together,
coat collars confidentially up, and Walden said earnestly,
"Yes, he cut out last night from Blanton's, where we were

playing, with a look— Oh, man, you know! *That* look! I thought maybe you heard, or had some notion—"

Wing was not alarmed, for nothing alarmed him much any more, but he knew the look all right, for Edgar's face struck everyone who saw it as laboring to produce that look—the face itself contending with the man to shape the expression (ironical, staring, doomed) for which it seemed fated. And so to Wing it was like hearing of the death of a man who had been mortally sick but who continued to abuse himself. For an instant, despite his annoyance at the figure of the young tenor man, hunched down with the furtiveness of musicians cupping cigarettes on Sixth Avenue outside the Union Hall, he felt like smiling sadly and nodding his head.

"I got to find him though, because he took it wrong. I mean, *I* cut him. You know?" with a wince of pained, earnest modesty. "But you *used* to know him, and I can't even remember where his pad is at. Where could he have gone, you think?"

"Man, I wish I knew," Wing sighed, throwing out his hands, for he had been overcome, not by everything contained in the word "used" (the years, the astonishing inconstancy of time, spent idealism), but only by the fact that Edgar's face had finally produced out of the man the look that everyone knew it would fashion once the man let go. For with that fact had come back to him not only the life he had abandoned when he gave up irregular employment in small jazz groups and took the job in the studio band, but also the puzzling realization that it had gone on without him. He would never think of that world, to which he no longer really belonged, without seeing Edgar's midnight face.

"Man, I wish I knew!" he repeated, this time somewhat defensively, for Walden stood as a reproach to him.

32

"Well, I got to find him. I mean, I blew just like him for years. I mean, he was the end to me. You know."

"Well, whyn't you try Geordie? Or Junius— Hell, I don't know where the son of a bitch could have got to. I don't *know* him."

"Geordie was there. She saw it. She got one look at him afterwards and— Well, you know, she pretends not to care, but I could see—"

"I can't help you, man. I got to go to work."

And he expected to see the pout that, three years before, had deformed his own lips at the obstacle-raising, the "well-buts," and the mechanical objections of the square: the man who was captive in a world of regular hours, transportation difficulties and lean thoughts. But it did not come.

There was only a crestfallen stare of disappointed awe that reminded him that he was not just another musician to Walden, but Eddie Win(g)field Redburn, the prima alto in modern jazz music, so startling and original that amid the changing fashions and new sounds he already occupied that peculiar obscurity into which only an unassailable fame can wall a man. He knew they said of him on Broadway street corners at three o'clock in the morning, "What ever happened to Wing? Where is he? What is he thinking?" and shook their heads, because where Wing went and what he did could not alter that part of him which already belonged to them; not even his absence from their night, his non-jazz job, his steady hundred-and-five a week.

"Oh, okay, Wing, I dig you. I'll try Junius then. But if you hear— Maybe I'll call you later. I mean, he may get run down by a car or picked up, and I feel responsible." Walden's face had already withdrawn from him with odd respect, and his glance was black and large and maddeningly without resentment. "Well, I'll cut out then . . . Later, pops," and he stepped sideways into the revolving door as it turned, and the words were sucked away.

Upstairs, amid the tangle of cables, music stands and folding chairs in Studio Three, the drummer for the house band good-naturedly chased Wing's warm-up runs with precise rim-shots, while the others smoked their cigarettes down to the end and tried to wake up. Wing stood, facing pointedly into a corner, his horn sitting on his belly, held vertical in a kind of present arms, and blew a little rondo on "How High the Moon." The others always listened, for (even when warming up) he blew more reed than horn—a strange parakeet of an alto, with a pure, savage, vibratoless tone. He never smiled or suffered or strained when he played; he just set his horn on his belly, widened his stance a little, took the mouthpiece between workmanlike jaws, and blew clear.

The other musicians in the nine-piece group (white realists who knew their trade, and had kept their eyes out for a safe berth from the beginning) admired him because, though he had stood up ten years before and, with those darting, bravura phrases that wheeled and flashed like the wings of a frenetic hummingbird (hence his name), had played things then that few other men could rightly under*stand,* and though they knew he sometimes listened to Bartók, Hindemith, and "those cats," and had accomplished (without self-consciousness or pretension) the feat of hearing all music with the same ear—though all of this hung about him invisibly, yet palpably, nevertheless he was there on time every day, and was a good, disciplined sideman, with years of band work already behind him by the time he began to be talked about in L.A. in 1944, when, in Junius Priest's shuttered apartment, he sat with his hat down over alert, emotionless eyes and blew strange through the afternoons. They knew that he had once heard the big, plumed Bird who sings somewhere in the center of America—a wild, harsh eagle song—and still sometimes heard it, even in the modest jump of their little band of lazy cynics; and soloing on some copybook riff, played clear, original things, and sometimes experienced a thin pleasure in it.

For, though his reasons for being there were much like theirs, Wing was not one of them, and when he blew with them on "I Cover The Waterfront" (the theme of the show), one eye on the engineer's forefinger that magically faded them away for the announcer, he was thinking of Edgar with baffled annoyance.

Something about Edgar had always annoyed Wing. The very name conjured up the specter of a hipness he had renounced: the soft collars and loose suits and wide ties that made the rashest movement languid and tentative; the weary, vaguely insolent language of the jazznight, growing ever more involuted as more and more aspects of reality became square; until what had started as an attitude changed to a neurosis, and what had been an individuality disappeared behind the uniform eccentricity of the dark glasses and berets, the rabbinical beards and arabic names; until a man's very inability to live in the world was a mark of his evolvement, and everyone repeated with awe Edgar's famous remark, delivered with a Promethean sigh: "Man, I got to get high before I can have a *hair*cut. I got to get *lifted* before I can *face* it!"

"He was everybody's evil father," Wing thought, remembering the young musicians during the war who were in ferment all over the country, to whom Edgar's horn and Edgar's pitiless standards had been an omen and a challenge and a promise, and out of whose obsession with his sound the irreverent furor of bop had come. He was everybody's evil, worldly father: the father never seen enough to evoke love, the father you envy and cannot impress, (the father who sees through your accomplishments and does not even *need* your admiration.) Wing thought of Junius Priest and Curny Finnley and himself and the few others who had taken everything that was latent in Edgar's horn, and brooded upon it through the wartime nights, and finally found a way to blow it out—and all Edgar had ever said to them was:/"All right, all right, I'm hip, you all can sure twiddle your fingers . . . But, man, now do me some *blues!*" /

Coming from anyone else, they would have sneered at this, because they knew that what they were doing would change everything, and that the grimmest resistance would probably come from the older musicians who could not hear it as they did. But coming from Edgar, from the Horn—whose tone and dress and attack and attitudes and even vices they had studiously or unconsciously aped —it worried them.

For the foundation of their admiration for him above any other jazzman of his time had always been that Edgar, years before most others, had been a skilled, devoted servant of his horn; an adept in the complexities of harmony and rhythm of which it was capable; able to comprehend, and even transcribe its magic in an abstruse notation that preserved it; willing to risk himself in the tenuous, hairbreadth rapport of improvisation so that the unnamable truth of music (which all can hear and no one can explain) might happen; as faithful to the horn as if it was, itself, the holy vessel of American song—and yet living at a time when most of these things were derided by the traditional, scoreless two-beat bands, and ignored by those who danced to them, and unimportant to the operators who paid the fee, and nonexistent to everybody else. He knew the secrets coveted and striven after and lusted for by Wing's generation, and knew them the only way a man can know such things: having coveted and striven after and lusted for them himself, and what is more, having done all this almost alone, for the most part unaided by the music or musicians of his time, and getting little from them but the scorn and obloquy which seem to be the one reward of those who are the first in any art to see what must come next. And so it seemed inconceivable to them that he would mock what they were doing.

But, still, when he bumped into Wing in the uproar of clubs thereafter, his mouth deceptively ingratiating under the drooping mustache, and the small watery eyes pale with irony, Edgar would always say, "Man, was that 'Night and Day' you just blew, or 'Begin the Beguine,' or what *was* that? . . . Like I was just saying to some stud at the bar, 'Now, man, don't put that boy down. He could blow "St. Louie," or "West End," or "Beale Street," if he *wanted* to,'" the laugh as soft and sly and impenetrable as the most careful innuendo. "You know, that's just what I said."

And this worried Wing, because sometimes when he was alone, running his scales, trying new changes, practicing, he blew nothing, blew just an easy, natural flow of notes around three simple chords, blew blues—and felt each time the inexhaustible welling of song potential in them, a strand of melody that might unfold endlessly in an ever perfecting symmetry toward the final, faultless music that a man could blow. And yet, intent just then upon his newfangled complexities, he had dismissed the feeling. Nevertheless, his annoyance with the hipness Edgar represented had grown in exact proportion to his suspicion that there was truth in what Edgar said, and the collision had eventually occurred.

It had happened just three years before, during a disastrous concert week end in St. Louis, for which the dickerings of an affluent entrepreneur had regrouped the nucleus of the original bop fraternity, now gone their separate ways—Curny temporarily between bands, Junius lured from home in Harlem, Wing from dreary two-weeks gigs around New York and Boston—with, as an added draw, Edgar Pool.

From the moment they boarded the seven o'clock out of Penn Station, it had all gone wrong, and whatever had once bound them together, no longer held. Separately, they had grown too eminent to be close. Junius was uncommunicative, as if he had finally gotten out of the habit of talk, his dark glasses lowered blindly over a volume on abnormal psychology. Curny rushed up and down the aisles, his face a mask of shrewd glee, deciphering time-tables with the help of weary conductors, checking his watch at every stop, renting more and more pillows as the dark came down outside on Pennsylvania. Wing mused out the window on the raw immensity of the American night, disheartened by the stir of old affections that were now somehow inexpressible, unable to revive the excitements of five years before, and unhappily aware that for months now he had been blowing as if he had blown everything before. And in the midst of them all, Edgar slouched with a flask and a cigarette interchangeably lifted to his sullen mouth, studying them with the gloomy exasperation of an old sinner biding his time among seminarians. All night he watched them with his cold eyes and destructive lips and closed heart—an atheist old man maddened by the certainties of youth.

Just two days later Wing was on a bus heading for New Orleans, fleeing forever from the nightmare which had grown out of that look of Edgar's, fleeing from the whining, haughty voice complaining about the rooms in the hotel and the food in the restaurant and the acoustics of the theatre, arguing about the rhythm section with which he was expected to work, and the amount of money he was to receive; fleeing from the carping voice which announced loftily to no one in particular that *he*, the Horn, didn't share a room with anybody "who got between his legs what I got," but, all right, if that was the kind of cheap gig it was going to be, Junius could take the other bed, because "he's the most like no one of any of you cats"—the voice explaining in an insulting drawl that he didn't like his chicken fried in batter but in grease, and when he said a *double* bourbon he didn't mean "no one-and-a-half-ounce shot of pig-water bar whiskey either"; the steady, echoing drone of that voice in the darkened theatre in the afternoon, rejecting one drummer because he was given to press-rolls, and lecturing another on "them bombs you always dropping on the bridge—oh, I heard you do it before"; the stubborn tactlessness of that voice as it said to the promoter who was staging the concert (a brash, eccentric young white man who affected high-button fire-house shoes, box-back suits, double-breasted waistcoats, and who drove a huge burnished 1929 Reo touring car): "Man, you a first-class fool! How can you ever make the nut to pay all these cats? You can't even afford yourself a *car!*"

Two days later Wing was trying to forget that he, too, had laughed unwillingly at this, and other things (because all ironies have truth, and Edgar was their ironical father after all); he was also trying to forget the argument with the white cab driver, and the incident in the elevator with the woman's hat, and what had happened at high noon at the Milles fountain outside the railroad station. He was systematically not thinking about Edgar's sudden two-hour disappearance before show time, and the frantic young promoter, sweating onto the phone dial, trying to locate him and regretting that he had ever gotten into this; and Edgar's equally sudden reappearance at the last minute, openly smoking the thin acrid cigarette (clearly not his first), which the surly young punk in the beard and the camel's hair coat, whom he had found somewhere, kept taking from him for a quick, hissing drag. Wing was trying to forget the image of Edgar peeking through the curtains, counting the house on his fingers and snapping out, "I coulda tol' you you didn't do enough advertising. Man, you got to spend to make. Don't you even know that, with your trashy shoes?"; and the sight of Edgar drifting up to the microphone, beyond which the huge thronged cavern of the theatre opened out, to introduce his first number; and the memory of what he had said into that microphone, while the promoter, standing nearby in the wings, unconsciously tore up a five dollar bill with shocked disbelief.

But he was not trying to forget the contemptuous, hungry glint in Edgar's eyes as the spots caught them while he played, the glint that said that anything but his own paralyzing boredom was absolutely square, the glint that too clearly stated: "There. That's good enough for you. *I'm* blowing it, ain't I? . . . Well, then, what more do you want?"

Indeed, he was attempting to remember forever his own thoughts as Edgar tweetled on in an indifferent parody of something he had played a thousand times before, never trying to blow as well as he could, and even refusing to solo at all on one number, so that the pianist went on hopelessly spinning out his chorus, waiting for the relief that never came. He was trying to remember what he had said to himself that had seemed then such a revelation, not only about Edgar, but about them all, and particularly about his own recent feeling of having blown everything there was to blow: "But he ain't good enough any more to justify this kind of hype. He ain't been good enough for a year to make up for the way he comes on. And only the work can justify what a man does . . . But nobody realizes it yet, *he* don't even realize it— But, man, all I know is, *this* ain't it. *This* may be good enough for them"—because respectful waves of applause were, at that moment, rolling across the footlights for the man, if not the horn, even though the man had turned away from them as if he would not even deign to notice what was only his obvious due—"it may be good enough for them to*night,* and next *week,* and maybe even next *year,* but it ain't good enough for me any more . . . Man, there must be something else!"

And sitting on that bus, with only the overnight bag he had brought from New York, and his horn case, he was trying to remember most of all the bitter look of emptiness in Edgar's eyes as he came off the stage, refusing even to consider the encore that the applause so humbly asked for—a look in which there did not seem to be even an inkling any longer that there could be something else, something else; a look that did not flicker or deepen or change at all, as he said, "Man, I don't have to work like this no more. No, no. Not for this cheap kind of money, I don't! Not *me!* . . . And where's that goddamn creep with the pot!" Wing sat on the bus, fleeing from that look, a look which (he felt with a shiver) all the concerts, gigs and jazz clubs of his own life would inexorably fashion on his own face unless he broke away—fleeing toward a girl and a truth, one of which he would have to lose to gain the other.

He fled down the immemorial Big River of his music, wanting to follow moving water because it went somewhere, and all complexities and attitudes and wraths were swept away before it. And so he fled down the Great Brown Snake that made the entire continent one vast watershed to it, and that from deepest, woodsy north at its trickling beginnings over smooth Canadian pebbles, to its final, timeless spending in the Gulf, drained out of the heart of America, melling Pittsburgh slag from the Monongahela with dust that blew across the faceless Badlands to the Milk, gathering as the rivers, tributary to it, met (the Platte, the Kansas, the Missouri; the Minnesota, the Chippewa, the Illinois; the Little Sandy, the Cumberland, and the Ohio) to flow, terrific, widening and assuageless, ever south, where still others emptied into it (the White, the Big Black, and the Red), until in huge, instinctive death beyond the last bayous, it joined the other waters of the world. Wing went down the river as jazz, just forty years before, had beaten its way back up after the Great Dispersal, going down it as if to listen to the source again, to hear the secrets of the river's mouth that in cane field, board church, sod levee or cheap crib had aroused some inexpungeable longing once that only jazz could ease.

He never got to New Orleans (perhaps it was fortunate), because one night in Louisiana, drifting down a shanty street on the edge of Algiers, he heard the crude guttural of a cornet, poked his head through a paintless door, and found a Saturdaynightfull of dock workers, drinking sour mash and whooping as they danced. Through the wild candor of all those hot faces, the faded print dresses snatched above the pumping knees of the girls, and the outlandish gusto that rocked the worn floor boards, his eye fell on one girl across the room.

Her dark face shone with that lip-parted, calm-eyed expression of anticipated tenderness, that tensionless acceptance of the world and its dealings which is a rebuke to all who look upon it. Her dewy gaze, eager for an object on which to lavish itself, was so utterly simple, so without sin, that had she suddenly impelled herself forward right into the throng of bent-kneed, flung-footed dancers, into the thresh of peg pants and French stockings, shaking her wide shoulders until her small hard breasts lifted, and raising her skirt, the action would have seemed too natural to the onlooker to be unchaste. For the whole reality of that night (so wild and rich and powerful-with-life after what he had just left)—the dusty pavements, the sweet odor of parched oleanders, the proximity of giddy flesh—seemed poised around her seventeen-year-old face, to which time had yet to add that something that denoted she must perish. She had more life ahead than death beyond, and she was as slender, fresh and inwardly shy as young girls have always been who make aging men stop dead and gasp with loss.

Her name was Fay Lee, and Wing never got to New Orleans, but found himself a room in a crumbling house by the river, and saw her whenever he could. He had no reason, and that was why.

He never even unpacked his horn, and the afternoon she first came there, noting the dirty shirts and trays of butts with a grave eye of respect for such masculine disorder, and let him touch her young untouched body, she stood, after it was over, looking at his sax (which he got out to show her) that was the color of new pennies in the shaft of blind sunlight falling through the arras, and suddenly exclaimed, "Oh, isn't it blessed! Isn't it just holy golden!" But he only seized her hand and drew her down again and lay, shifting and perplexed, through the heavy afternoon, robbed (as grown men sometimes feel robbed) of those furious male obsessions that always prove too brittle and unreal for mating with the simple nakedness of a girl. He wanted to lie upon the rugless floor with her and catch her moan in his mouth, and afterward feel the coolness of her fingers, fond, dear, and comforting. But she only blushed with an incomprehensible joy that somehow infuriated him.

He was near the river, and they loitered there in the long, opaque shadows of the motionless evenings, when silence seemed to swim out of the bayous upriver, huge, ominous and profound. And then night, which wakes a half-savage possibility in the American heart, brought the tart slice of whiskey, the shuttered laments of conflicting radios, and the lights swinging in the river like submerged lanterns. He sweated in his shirts till the backs were rotted through, and drank his whiskey neat, and the uncrushed, calm oval of her face always aroused him, as if it was a strange face, fleetingly glimpsed in a crowd, on which such inner recognition glowed that the intimacy of that one glimpse choked him with an unsuspected loneliness. She was simple, pellucid, and she learned his complex city ways with quiet joy in the learning itself; but still she undressed as if he were not there, folding her slip carefully in a square and placing her shoes side by side. Afterward, bathing his face from the chipped crockery bowl on the washstand, not daring to look back to the bed lest the very languor he had sought to create in her fine, agile limbs should infuriate him with a last desire now that it was achieved, he took to talking aloud, speaking as if he were alone, unconnected, unfinished sentences, a jumble of images from a hip, disordered world that she had never known. He ranted, he mused, he boasted and complained, he talked of Edgar almost obsessively. She listened with a steady, patient gaze, and did not hear or care about the words, and could not be impressed by fame or art; and then he watched her dress again, always with the same annoyed pinch of regret, and they went out and had a drink; and then he took her home to the kitchen that maddened him because, even with the new refrigerator set proudly so that it could be seen from the front room, there was an air of earnest humility about it; home to her waddling, bandannaed mother who treated him like a white man because he had come downriver, and her brothers who lounged around, splay-legged, listening to the radio.

His money started to run out, and he thought furiously, destructively, of marrying her, and forcing that simple, living look out of her eyes with awareness of him, *him*.

He bought her fancy underwear, all white-girl-silk, all scalloped edges, all hip and jaded and indecent; and talked aloud while she tried it on in the heat of his room, cursing, mocking her, wheedling. But she only giggled to catch sight of herself in his shard of mirror, and said, "Ain't I cute though! Look at that!" He stopped seeing her for a week and got out his horn for the first time and sat in his drawers on the bed edge and played absently, hoping for accident to seize him, but playing nothing that he had not played before. He slept in long, sweating binges in which he did not even dream. He wanted her blackly, and prolonged the wanting of her, until he realized that it was not her he wanted, but something else, that something else: the calm of her eyes at which he imagined Edgar drawling sarcastically, "She just a little Topsy, now isn't she? She's a rag doll!"

Then one twilight he wandered down to the river and saw her sitting on the pier, dangling her legs, a small, rapt silhouette watching the lights come on in perfect solitude. He drew nearer, thinking to reach around her unawares, cup her breasts, and frighten her into his life. But then, as he crept closer, he heard her singing an absent line of blues without words, a line too simple, too isolated from all other music by its spontaneity to be remembered, so that the moment it dried on her moist lips he could not recall it. He stood not four feet behind her, paralyzed by the perishability and the keenness of that moment, as by an immense truth. And everything there became real to him, at last.

The dusk, the small outline of the girl, beyond which the river swept wide and murky, moving heedlessly, deeply, gathering last speed before it gave itself up in broad, doomed immolation in the Gulf: its tragic swiftness in the huge hush, and the small awkward silhouette against all that impermanence, and the heavy delta smells, and, at the last, the inconsolable reality of that reality came up into his heart like a sob; and his illusions and his rages left him in an instant, and he was alone there in the way of human beings one with the other, with only a song between. He sat down and held her hand and used her no more. . . .

Now, in the studio, he stared at the crooner who was reading his ad libs from a cue sheet—that hard, unblinking stare that is so unnerving because there is no attention behind it—and he was wondering distractedly where she had gotten to. Moved to another street, married someone's brother, had gleeful children, given in to fat. Loss! He could not even remember her face, just the huddled outline against the evening river. And for a moment life amazed him again, because human routine, the flawless achievement of ambitions, and even the neatest of men were all part of its great, disordered confluence with time; and the truths and certainties a man shored against that fact changed it not at all. Loss—he had lost it all! He had squandered the calm he might have had with her; he had thrown away the simplicities of contact in his discovery of that song; he *would* have his music at any cost. Yes, yes.

He had used her no more after that, and felt the hungry, Edgar-like ironies in him die, and had known then that everything was simpler than irony, and even thought for a minute that he might show her that he knew, but then had seen in her eyes that utter innocence to which no river could ever be tragic, no dead irony real. So he had taken a bus for New York three days later, with his meager truth, while she wept on a bench in the bus station, weeping easily as women do, and then walked away, her sources of renewal undamaged. He had been unaccountably separated from the men he worked with ever since, playing a pure line; and finally he had separated himself from them by taking the studio job. And just then he realized in a flash that men have only this sad knowledge with which to heal themselves: when you lose life, you grow wise. But that is better than maiming life to hold it.

" 'Blue moon,' " the crooner was warbling, " 'you saw me standing alone' "—rubbing his neck—" 'without a dream in my heart.' " Wing stared at him fixedly over the curve of his horn—the high-waisted trousers, the $25 shoes, the handsome empty face: a nice enough fellow, quick, sharp, friendly, in his own broil. But everything that Wing knew counted for nothing to that boy, the years, the losses, what he had *seen* with his eyes. So what was it worth? he thought, just as they came to the release where sixteen bars had been left open for him. What was the moment on the river worth when he had realized that he had had that dark, sour look of Edgar's in his own heart all the time, and in the exact instant of the realizing felt it thaw and disappear? "All right, man, but now blow me some *blues!*" Edgar had said with an oily sneer, mocking not Wing but the truth; mocking it *because* it was the truth, and mockery was all the tribute he had left. What was learning that sad fact worth?

He started to blow, taking up the particular chords into his horn and forgetting them, his mind clear (as it was when he played) except for the feeling (that he had had since coming North again) that at the bottom somewhere there was song, the same song, the one song—to know which, suddenly, was worth to him whatever life might take away. He blew a long line, a tumbling zigzag in which he barely toed the chords as he passed, like an ecstatic base runner so fleet that he veers off the infield lines and cuts back to touch second, and then sprints, whooping, toward the farther stands, but wheels and comes home at the last, leaving everyone gaping and dumbstruck. He could not play any other way now, or forget what he knew, even though Edgar Pool had blown his poor head against his ingrown life for which that dark look was only a twisted image to repel the world.

He finished his chorus, and the crooner raised his small, pleasant voice again, in which there was no shred of knowledge that Edgar had been a doomed hero for a whole generation of rebellious musicians, a hero who had persisted beyond his drama to become absurd. But one thing does not change the other, and all men fall from drama into melodrama; and as Wing took his horn back into his mouth for the ensemble, he realized that Edgar was still out in the world while that night moved off the Atlantic over them all; and though he knew things as dark as Edgar now, and knew beyond them too, still a man's work, his blind pursuit of the single truth, cannot be destroyed, even by himself. And Edgar, no matter what had happened since, had chased it selflessly once. For the first time in three years, Wing thought of another man as a man should: "What's happened to him? Where is he now? What is he thinking?"

And knew that after this number, which was the last, he would get a taxi and head uptown, and find Walden somehow, somewhere in that night. And, free of Edgar now, look for him, able to care.

RIFF

". . . And, man, I don't care as long as I get together
that fifty bucks," Edgar was saying to Cleo for the fifth
time, still making no move to go back to the phone booth,
which, so far, had brought no results. "I mean, I don't
care, I really don't— You think I mind conning for it, beg-
ging? . . . Huh! I'll come on square, I'll hustle strangers,
I'll hit everybody I can think of. I don't mind. I'll hold
out my hat on Forty-second Street! Why not, why not . . .
And I got all night to do it in, I got time—"

One hand lay, large and motionless and almost disembodied, on the horn case that occupied the stool between
them, and the other (his cigarette hand) gestured rashly
as he talked, and only interrupted the gestures long enough
to lift the glass of beer, and return it, and then the shot of

whiskey, and return that too, only empty, calling it to the bartender's attention with a quick, disinterested snap of the fingers and a nod of the head in its direction. And yet, though his eyes were fixed, undeviating, glazed, and though his speech seemed more and more to emanate from some growing turmoil of thought to which he never directly referred, nevertheless (and somehow ominously as far as Cleo was concerned) he was not really drunk.

They sat at the almost empty bar of Parker's Tavern, a drab, ill-lit, absolutely featureless saloon that seemed to have wandered out of quieter, more ingrown neighborhoods farther west, and right into the huge, impersonal boil of Times Square, to accidentally locate itself just down Broadway from the Go Hole, and around the corner from Paradise Alley, and within a few blocks of most of the other haunts where jazz turned the midnights loud and long, becoming, as a result, a sort of unofficial, non-musical meeting place for musicians in New York, but stubbornly refusing to acknowledge this by any change—other than the hipness of the records in the juke box.

"And all I got to remember is my horn," Edgar reminded himself, tapping the case with a hollow drum of mute fingers, and then looking at it fixedly. "Goddamn piece of luggage, don't give a damn *who* blows on it. But, man, *it* can't get me to KayCee, and don't you forget it! . . . No, sir! Never got me nothing, but just enough to live and go on blowing it, that's all, that's all . . . But I'll tell you something—it ain't *real,* it ain't *me.* I could hock it, or break it, or just leave it somewhere's if I *wanted* to do it . . . I could . . . I got my *own* name."

He talked on and on like that, interrupting himself only when cigarette or drink demanded it, and beginning again, not where the words had left off, but where the mind had gone on, so that there was a final quality, almost incantatory, about his liquored ramble. Cleo sat there, fighting weariness with the single idiotic thought, "It won't happen as long as I can keep awake," whatever *it* might be, staring, not at Edgar, but at the horn case, content merely to catch (as if muffled through water or through music) snatches of the endlessly digressive monologue.

"And it don't matter anyway. I got *other* cats I can phone. It's just too early, that's all," Edgar said harshly. "And listen, kid, you listen to me— I've *had* all the kicks, and I don't need it now, I don't . . . But I can *still* cut all these cats two choruses to one," he spat out, "and play more tenor than them without even getting down to work," waving at the empty stools with sneering, tragic self-belief. "I can blow anything I want to on it, and— well, I can't blow nothing any more," he finished with a sniffing little giggle, and downed a shot at a gulp, and immediately broke into a choking cough.

Cleo stared at the scarred and veteran horn case with the strange hallucination that it held bottled, and temporarily quiescent, all the rash, intoxicating music of his life, needing a man only to supply the wind; and if he listened patiently, respectfully, it was because Edgar was the man who had.

For a moment Edgar's unmoving eyes stared back into the murk of years when there had been no one to talk to, much less blow for. "Well," he said, rousing, "all I need is fifty, sixty bucks, right, kid?" shaking his head as if from dizziness. "I got to get *going* here . . ."

"But, Horn, like I say," Cleo put in again without much hope that it would accomplish any more this time than it had before, and puzzled by Edgar's reaction to what seemed the simplest solution. "Why not come on over to the Hole with me later and sit in? It's Monday, man,

51

everyone's sitting in, and you can make twenty-five or even thirty for just an easy coupla sets. And, man, they'll flip just to get the chance to let you play."

But, as before, Edgar's face hardened all in a moment, and his fingers paused on the horn case and then came away from it entirely. "*No*, I keep telling you. I don't want to blow . . . I mean, I won't *have* to, I'll have my fare long before then— You think I run out of connections or something? Listen, kid, let me hip you—" But the haughty pout died on his lips as his gaze fell on the horn case again. "No," he repeated finally. "And, man, I just remembered," he said, winking with a lewd sagacity meant to divert. "*I* know. I'll call that blond Helen chick. Man, *she's* such a drag you wouldn't believe it, but she'll give you anything she got as long as you darker than she is," and all at once he slid backward off the stool, almost falling over, and ambled back to the phone booth in his lazy, flat-footed slouch.

He sat, closeted and on display under the lights, in a fume of smoke, trying to dial, making a mistake, sniffing and then beginning again, slumped down, chin drooping toward his chest as he waited with the receiver, face shadowed and indrawn as if he was asleep; and just as Cleo was about to go over, wondering how he would ever get the folding door open against the large ungainly body, much less get the body itself out, Edgar roused, blinking, and came out on his own, with a dim and baffled smirk.

"She's out meeting her connection, that's what," he explained with momentary absolute conviction. "She's one of them rich, *evil* junkies, you know, and she always used to get her fix about this time. Once in Detroit— What time *is* it anyway?" Craning around, blear-eyed, to look at the wall clock, and then, at a further thought, murmuring, "But, that's right, she been off her habit five years . . . But don't you know old fat-thighed Helen, kid?" mouth sug-

gesting all the age-old, cynical lasciviousness with which
men speak to one another about loose women, and then
twisting into a repudiating giggle. "No, I guess not. You
got so hip, so cool these days—you young colored-boy
piano players—you don't even get eyes for the white
chicks any more." He laughed fondly over old sins.

"Well, maybe that's all right too . . . I never could keep
my hands off though . . . I never got tired, I *took* everything, I *did* everything," one finger now picking out the
deep scars upon the horn case, as if he had let it lead him
into all the life a man might have, bad and good, turning
down nothing, moving aside for nothing—for more nights
than Cleo had even lived. "Man, I never even *thought* of
settling down, getting married, getting straight— Well,
some afternoons maybe . . . But not even with Baby, not
even with Geordie. *She* might have, maybe she did, but—"
The finger stopped for a moment to trace one particularly
ancient scratch up near the handle. "But, you know, I
never even *asked* her. No, now, I guess I never did," and
he sniffed to himself. "Maybe that was *one* mistake, eh?
. . . But, man, I'm gonna call Old Bitch Helen," he said
again, as at a new thought, "that's what I'm gonna do,
cause she was always good for eighteen, twenty dollars
any time," with the confidential, somehow ascetic wink of
one whore to another, as he started the long, unsteady trip
to the booth again, to dial, and wait, and then come back;
to get down another shot, talking on and seeming to forget, only to get up suddenly and try again—until Cleo decided that there was no real Helen, or that if there were
she had gone out of his life years before.

And staring at the horn, he imagined the bright, untiring
eyes, the indefatigable young flesh, its pulse tuned for that
night, that year (whenever it might have been) to the insinuative, veering music still bottled there inside that case;
the lax mouth parted as she, too, stared at the horn, the

way women stare, lured and heady, at all things masculine, and indissuadable, and fecund. No real Helen at all, or only a girl glimpsed briefly through a crowd over the neck of the horn, or known briefly on the road while playing it, or lain with briefly when he put it down; all of it years before perhaps, so that the startling, particular face or the characteristic voice or even the mutual pleasure of isolate flesh fused in the dark by accident or design, was lost, forgotten, wiped away; and only the name remained (and the generous thighs), forever connected in Edgar's mind with the old power of the horn itself, to come up out of nowhere, by-passing all the other more plausible names, to become a last-seized chance now that the power was gone. /Or perhaps, Cleo decided, just an excuse for forty winks in the booth. /

"Well," Edgar said at last when he came back, "I'll have to hit Baby then, I'll have to wake her up . . . And I'd better do it now while I still can."

"But, Horn, like I say, you can make twenty-five or even thirty."

"No. Now listen, I tell you I won't *have* to," Edgar insisted almost angrily. "I mean, I won't *need* to do it, man, really now . . . And I'll just cut over there in a cab."

But when Cleo started to get up, Edgar laid a surprisingly firm hand on his arm. "No, kid, you stay here and watch my horn. I only be twenty minutes—because she either give it to me, or she won't." He downed a last, stiffening shot, suddenly looking old and weary as he chased it with the rest of the beer, eyes small and trapped and yet refusing to relent.

"I stay any longer," he said with peculiar, hoarse candor, "I never come back," and then, all in a moment, he was gone.

CHORUS:JUNIUS

*"The deep, warm secret—the
life within the life."*

HAWTHORNE

Junius listened, unwittingly purse-lipped, to the interminable ramble—now ingratiating, now incoherent—on the other end of the line. Once he had gotten over the surprise of picking up the telephone and hearing Edgar's giggling "Guess who?" whispered in his ear, he had not paused to wonder what strange urge had produced his number from the murk of Edgar's head after having been more than two years lost there, for Junius distrusted telephones and could never quite believe in the reality of the voices that came out of them.

"—So then this square cab driver hung me up for a buck getting over here to Geordie's. A real white ugh, you know . . . And, man, oh, man," he clucked suddenly, "am I lushed. I'm goony . /. I lost my coat, and my 802 card,

55

and two sticks of pot, and—oh, man, you know, everything! . . . But I want to cut out, and make KayCee for a
while, and—"

"I heard you were booked next week with a quartet,"
Junius said, cautiously conversational.

"Oh, no-o-o," came back a suddenly weary, suddenly
impatient sigh. "I got no eyes for that now . . . I got to
go, man, I got to rest . . . But look now, you see, I'm out
of loot, and I thought maybe you'd slip the old man ten or
so to make the bus—"

"Is Geordie there?"

There was a scornful and suggestive sniff, so startlingly
personal to Edgar that for the first time Junius summoned
up his face—the drooping lips parted in a smile of wheedling insolence, the hard small eyes black with shrewd
raillery that always belied the drawling words. "Oh, yes,
man, Baby's here . . . I woke her up to make a touch, ol'
shameless me! . . . But she don't get paid till next week,
so even when I cleaned her out I'm way short. And then I
thought, 'Well, yes now, I'll just call up little Juny. He
lives straight, he goes slow, he don't lose his union card, and
get so juiced. Little Juny'll get the old man home.' "

"I'm clean. I haven't worked for three weeks," Junius
said, jollying him along without a second thought. "Whyn't
you go home and sleep it off?"

"No, man, *no*. I ain't going to sleep. You all just wait and
see if I sleep. *I* won't sleep . . . But, look, how about
your ma? She's got something stashed. Did you ever get
into the preserve jars on the back shelf?"

"Pops, I'm clean, I say. I got no lush money."

There was an abrupt silence on the other end. "Man,
I'm *not* going to lush, I'm telling you. I said I got to go, I
got to woodshed for a while, I *got* to . . . You mean I got
to hock my horn or something?" and he laughed with
baffled self-derision. "Well, well, the old man's really

bugged the world all right . . . But you sure about your ma? Even five, you know, even *part* of five, man . . . And look," he said with another suppressed and gloating sniff, "suppose I fix you up with Baby here. You always had a nose for her . . . And, *m-a-a-n*, let old Edgar hip you, Baby's mellow, Baby's cool, Baby just don't *care—*"

Junius heard the voice—confidential, sniggering, repetitive—shrivel from a throaty whisper to an unintelligible squeak as he lowered the receiver in a measured, unhurried, somehow final arc from his ear to the cradle from which he had lifted it. He heard that unhesitating squeak, which would have gone on and on in the prideless chattering hope that irritation might prevail where all else failed, broken abruptly by a click as the connection severed. Knowing clearly what he was doing, but unable to alter it despite the gasps the story would bring forth from those who knew them both, he hung up on the doom in Edgar's voice.

But then Junius Priest's oddities were as well known to everyone as his piano, which had backed Edgar's tenor sax for years in those apocryphal and wholly imaginary bands that the jazz fan is constantly assembling from his records and his nights, though (with one exception) they had never played together. But the finality of song to which Junius' sly chords might have driven Edgar remained a possibility that was enough to torment everyone with anticipated delight. For the young Junius had been among the very first to catch in Edgar's limpid, veering note the incalculably new sound that would echo, thereafter, beneath every cool piano and bebop horn. Like some few others, it set Junius doodling in the afternoons, and for him, even more than for the rest, Edgar had been the idolized source.

Those afternoons had led to nights in smoky clubs when Junius' fleet right-hand runs and sternly dissonant chords had seemed, in themselves, so emblematic of the new kind of jazz that pale young contrapuntalists in hip suits announced glibly, "Imagine him backing Edgar. Like, man, does that swing? . . . But who are all *these* cats!" with a glance of smirking disapproval at the musicians grouped around Junius on the stand.

For when he worked at all, it was never with men of Edgar's stature, but always maddeningly at the head of some gang of raw, wordless, wild-eyed tenors right off the bus from Carolina. With rigged union cards, crammed thigh to thigh with their beat-up horns, they were forever jumping up and down, sweating pop-eyed over the intricate arrangements, listening with feverish reverence to Junius' disjointed rambles over the black keys, and then leaping to their feet, often several at a time, to blow some crude, honking reply. They always attempted too much in these solos, staggering along over the chord changes like slippery stones in a brook, teetering perilously back and forth as the drums lashed the rhythm, and finally losing the beat altogether, spatulate fingers groping blindly for stops that were not there, but plunging ahead, nevertheless, with frantic selflessness. They never talked, even to each other, and seemed unable to read music or even words, but knotted their foreheads furiously all night, and gaped and jumped about, to vanish down into the subway when the night was over.

Junius slumped in the middle of their contortions, shoulders hunched as if weighed down by the elbow-patched corduroy jacket he always wore. His eyes were shielded from the world by a huge thick-framed pair of dark glasses, his mandarin mustache drooped over an undeviating half-smile (somehow expressive of nothing) that was in curious contrast to the mad forearm-pumping scramble of his fingers, and he sat slightly turned from the keyboard, *en passant,* and took off on a long, punishing melodic line that seemed to unfold in endless, tumbling convolutions that transfixed the sweating tenors. He communed with the music, as if he were alone there, but gave no hint of what it cost him in either agony or joy. He played, but he would not perform. His face, as curiously rapt and self-concentrated as that of a blind man or a monk, reflected nothing that he saw, as if everything "out there" was just the night and, proper to the night, a dream. Something about his face proclaimed too clearly to those who watched that they had no reality to him, and this was somehow infuriating to all those who had no other life but jazz.

Junius was not homeless, as jazz musicians habitually are—despite the houses in Astoria which success sometimes bestows on them. He had not left New York in penniless disgust, certain the money would be better elsewhere, finally (after time and the lonesome discoveries with which a man becomes himself—that harrowing exile in the soul that jazzmen know as "woodshedding") to be talked about in Chicago or L.A., and then return with new austerity to club dates and recording contracts and the melting eyes of reckless girls. Junius, with a single exception, had lived a sedentary Harlem life, and those who stared at his communing face glimmering in the hazy lights and imagined that some higher, hipper reality separated him from them, would have been astounded had they tracked him down the unlikely uptown side street to the rambling, commonplace apartment over the grocery store with the ancient cartons of corn meal in the window. They would have thought that the four-piece living-room set with the flowered slip covers, and the seventeen-inch television on the swivel table and the clean cheery kitchen that gave out on perpetually loaded clotheslines were all just a disarming front meant to mislead the square. They certainly wouldn't have believed that the frail, lined woman with the startled eyes, who padded about in bedroom slippers with a dust cloth, was his mother, and that he lived in the large dim room beyond, and always had.

For Junius was one of those queer, crank Americans, grown men in everything but that final orphaning of the heart which makes us men, who nod to their neighbors and are still thought of by the old ladies downstairs as "nice, quiet boys," but who are, all the time, writing an immense, standard-toppling poem, or conducting outlandish chemical experiments in the transmutation of metals, in their stuffy back bedrooms—laboring contentedly, incomprehensibly, without the pricks of ambition, untempted by fame: the great American inner life that flowers here and there behind drawn shades on the most uneventful blocks, and never dares the merciless glare of afternoon's cruel streets.

To his mother, who ventured into his room to straighten up when he was not there, only the indescribably second-hand piano, the stacks of phonograph records and the glossy-paper photograph of the dusky full-lipped singer tacked to the ceiling directly over his bed gave visible evidence of any life he had beyond that room. When she woke him at two in the afternoon, she always left the coffee pot by his bed and closed the door, and though she heard him moving up and down across the carpet, she knew the shades would still be drawn in there, allowing in only a cautious wedge of day. Then after a while the records began: the skirl of a nasal alto sax, the sibilant, repetitive tremulo of a piano and a drum. Sometimes she hummed along with the records that innumerable hearings had made familiar—humming happily, quietly, as she shelled her peas.

When he came out for the fresh coffee she had made, already wearing the dark glasses that she had long ago decided had some medical justification she could not be expected to understand, she would always say, "How about some nice baking powder biscuits, Juny, maybe with cane syrup?" And every day he would mumble, "Not yet, Ma, I'm not alive enough to eat."

Though she always clucked darkly over this exchange, it was as eloquent and reassuring to her as an unbosoming confession would have been, and she put her hopes in the eventless life to keep him close.

But then the unsettling times would come again, when she would know that he was about to start a week or two at one of those clubs, dangerous and far away downtown, for the awed, stammering boys would begin turning up in the late afternoons, with their frightened drawls and outlandish suits and battered instrument cases. It always began with a meal he could not eat, during which she chattered hopelessly on about the neighbor ladies to the nerveless absorption of his face—already, it seemed, irretrievably lost to her protectiveness; already, she knew, out in the motherless world which she associated with the face upon his ceiling: the world of the yearning eye, the moist demanding mouth, the confessional raising of the voice before a multitude. And then, right in the middle of a word, he would get up, muttering, "I got to get started, Ma," to put on the corduroy jacket, and kiss her dutifully, and go away.

Though this other life alarmed her, it never lasted long, and she was too possessive of everything about him to object or question. Instead, she lay, inconsolably old and fearful, alone but for the widow's God of Baptist revivals in dingy upstairs halls. When he finally returned, spent and empty, as she began to rouse in the first souring light of dawn, they sat together over coffee and he told her everything that had happened—names she had never heard of, terms that meant nothing to her. But neither thought twice about that: they were mother and son, and he told her as he might have told himself, and she listened and did not have to understand. Then, back in bed again, she would take comfort from the muffled record that he always played just before sleep, the single female voice—throaty, passionate, bereaved—the voice of the singer in the picture, whose name she sometimes heard the awestruck tenors mumble reverently: "Lift yo' eyes, boy—Geordie!" and who, she guessed, lived for the dangerous dark, like them, instead of in a proper dishes-dusting-diapers way. Drowsing to the warm and distant voice, she offered to her God the abject bribery of thanks that at least it was not as it had been that empty, letterless year near the end of the war when he was off in California: a name that did not signify a place so much as a condition that made him unreachable to her—like "mad," or "jailed," or "dead."

For that one year, 1944, had seen a Junius as different from the current one as a hope is from a certainty. Something moved him that he did not know: the war, the times, too many choruses of "One O'Clock Jump"—that reckless innocence of the world that urges all boys on toward their disillusionment. All of a sudden he had simply gone off into America, as his kind seems damned to do, waiting in all-night bus stations off dusty main streets, eating in steamy lunch carts down along the river fronts of booming cities—all the way to L.A. and the ground floor apartment in North Hollywood, where the revolution known as bop would eventually be hatched.

Now, sitting with his hand holding down the telephone receiver, in which he imagined Edgar's insinuative drawl to be still bottled, Junius found himself remembering, with a feeling of poignant validity, that year forever connected with Edgar in his mind.

The breathless glare of that Los Angeles July had the clarity of a traumatic childhood landscape, and he could remember every detail of that rambling building of disreputable flats on the street that eventually ran up into a dreary canyon—from the pocked stucco walls to the grubby palms that looked like bunches of aged elephant's ears. He remembered the job at the Rancho Rio, gotten because Edgar was playing down the street, and the small band of disconsolate ex-sidemen, working other jazz clubs on the Strip just then, who finally took to meeting in the afternoons in his almost furnitureless three rooms. Junius, who had never felt lonely, now remembered (with something of loss) Wing Redburn, blowing all his mouth in some furious, crude jumble of alto sounds that a man either dug with his mind or it was all noise; and Curny Finnley sprawled, knee-wide, on a straight chair, eyes whimsical under the lowering maroon beret he wore then, as he took his trumpet into ranges it never should have attempted; and all the others who had gone on, and drifted apart as their shoulder-to-shoulder proselytizing on any stand bore fruit, and earnest youngsters, with attentive eyes and new horns, moved out of the audience one by one up onto the stands, to apprentice in intermission groups and make reputations and finally records, to become, themselves, the object of afternoon researches by tomorrow's horns.

But more than all this, Junius recalled the effect of Edgar's presence on the Strip just then, which had nothing to do with knowing him (few of them did), but was rather an intuition (which no one who felt it in those years paused to understand) that where he chose to be was somehow "the next place." For, like Junius, all their ideas were running on that way, Edgar's way, and they instantly recognized in each other that same rash and exhilarating discontent that was so like the sudden cool storm-smell that often hung, motionless, in the air those afternoons, and was somehow so prophetic of a new and imminent reality, because L.A. was a city of dreams on America's last dream-haunted coast.

Even more than the others (because the world had yet to tarnish his ideals), Junius had idolized Edgar then, making no attempt to approach him (the most worshipful of tributes after all) but only listening, listening; and then, in the afternoons, sitting at the piano with lax-jawed, intent self-trust, letting his fingers find the next chord in a strange, keyless progression, and muttering an involuntary "Um-m-m" of recognition at the logic of it. Their minds ran on together—half-fooling, half-seriously pushing at the limits they had always known—and Curny would suddenly grunt "Uh, uh" between phrases, chinning the staggered off-beats of the drums, to splatter a fusillade of copper-clear notes, like machine-gun fire, on the ceiling, curiously arbitrary and released. Wing swerved off the line in fleet answer until, for just a moment, they were all chasing one another in sudden disregard of everything, to come down together, amazed, on the same surprising beat, with the intoxicated glee of inquisitive boys discovering an abstract truth. When it was over they all laughed with goofy bewilderment because it was so strange, not knowing that later whole phrases and transpositions which they stumbled on during those storm-heavy afternoons would form the basic vocabulary of modern jazz.

"Man, what are we *doing!*" Curny would cry. "I wonder what in the *hell* we are doing here!"

"We're winking at the moon," Wing said into his mouthpiece.

"Come on," Junius would mumble. "Come on. Come on." And they would start again.

The others had some sort of life—binges, girls, troubles —but Junius had nothing but those afternoons, and lived (mad-faced and absorbed) in a kind of continual, controlled fever, fingers moving ceaselessly over nonexistent keys on stained counters from which he lifted midnight coffee, or along his thigh as he walked. During the evenings at work, he found himself playing entire passages from the afternoons, dutiful yet impatient, among low lights and Scotch-rocks and those attractive disenchanted people who search so tirelessly in the dark, cool lounges of American cities for a moment of minor, blue surcease; who listen to the lyrics of her eternal twilight love song, and have a bittersweet taste in things, and take sad cabs when finally they leave. But he did not know whether they heard or not, they were not real to him after all, and the evenings were just practice for the afternoons, just exercise, just scales; and between sets he always was off in wild, arm-flapping, obsessed flight to the club where Edgar was working with a quartet, as a man might go again and again to a beloved, though superseded, text, to be sure, to be sure. They were passing Edgar every afternoon, and no man had been where they were going now, but still Edgar's sure, indifferent swing was what had set them searching around the beat; and then, he might have caught sight of Geordie there (she was Edgar's Geordie after all), though he never did.

The afternoons broke up into sudden thundersqualls over which they blew their cackling, defiant riffs, and with them came the curious who had-heard-tell, the hangers-on who never got to bed, the dusky girls with firm, palpitating thighs. Some drank, some rolled acrid cigarettes that made them giggle, some wan few boiled their junk in the bathroom and came out with new eyes. On Monday night when no one worked, it got to be a crowd: a bandleader or two, white afficionados who brought bourbon and blondes, sometimes the police. Junius sweated on the piano, playing weird and true, and said, "Come on," oblivious of corruption in his absorbing innocence.

Then one night, as it was bound to happen, as people had said from the beginning that it would, Edgar came with lidded, sleepy eyes under the broad-brim felt he would not remove, shuffling through the crowd that fell away before him with gaping deference, as if his only interest was a chair in which to rest himself.

"Baby," he said to a girl he recognized, "that dress is such a drag! . . . Didn't I tell you once?" And he looked away, smirking blandly.

With him came a cohort of pale, scornful disciples and their girls, in whose midnight lives he was, just then, the central fact. Where he went they followed, vying crossly with each other to anticipate his moods, finding everything inadequate until he smiled, treating everybody else as vaguely nonprofessional, though aside from a wealthy, dissolute white boy who could keep a beat on drums, none of them could play an instrument, and all they talked about was money and connections. They hovered around the chair where Edgar slumped, lighting his cigarettes, bringing him drinks, whispering snidely in his unlistening ear. He ordered them about in limp, ironic tones, he drank their drinks, and then sat, nodding, in a snooze that set them yawning to the music, far too hip to comment, only to be interrupted when he began to tap his foot to one of Junius' angular, flatted arrangements, and said, "That swings, that's sorta cute . . . Maybe I'll cut that next time, do you think?" To which the bulge-eyed, chain-smoking white boy (rumored to be financing a small record label so he could play with real musicians) exclaimed, "Man, that would be a gas!"

"Maybe I will," Edgar sighed with languid self-indulgence. "But who knows?" . . .

Sitting now, still near the phone, hearing the shelled peas drop with hollow, regular klooks behind him where his mother sat with the pot between her knees, Junius dared the hardest part, remembering his own fool excitement to be playing where Edgar was, as if the world had suddenly halted in its fleet convertible beside his dusty lemonade stand on a country road. He had played proudly then, hoping in an honest sweat of humility to please, but Edgar only lit cigarettes, chattered with his cronies, and afterward pronounced, "That's shroud music, boy, that's goonybird music . . . Man, I'm too *lazy* to play that way."

Nevertheless, a week later, to his giddy disbelief Junius found himself in a rented studio (summoned by a dawntime phone call from a sleepless voice vying, at its end, with other sleepless voices), sitting at an unfamiliar piano among the mikes and music stands of a recording session, waiting for Edgar along with a bassist whose taped fingers drummed a weary little rhythm on his bass.

He finally came half an hour late, borne up (as it were) by a jostling, haggard bunch of hangers-on, among whom was the white boy for whose phantom company the records were to be cut. One look at Edgar's face, and Junius gawked unthinkingly, for he looked as if he had been gotten into the stained and rumpled suit by unfamiliar hands while he was lying down, although it was just as evident that he had not slept, perhaps for days. His face was swollen with exhaustion and alcohol; he blinked and coughed, and navigated, unseeing, among the cables and horn cases to the neck of the piano, to stand there, swaying just a little, eyes banked and thoughtless, a forgotten cigarette burned down close to bitten fingernails. Once he mumbled to no one in particular, "Who are all these cats, man? . . . Do we need all these cats?"

The white boy, whose sallow face was ravaged with the effects of nightlong kicks, took hold officiously (it was his money after all). "Now pull yourself together, pops. You know? . . . These sides've got to be pressed next week."

To which Edgar only blinked and nodded, groggily intent on merely standing up.

Suddenly Junius recalled the rumors about Edgar and Geordie (the *one* jazz singer and the *one* jazz horn who, by poetic truth, should have been in love, and somehow incredibly had, in reality, actually come together)—the rumors that their near-legendary affair was just then in the final stages of its collapsing end, amid violence and public scenes and dissipation; the rumors that were everywhere in the air that month, like the thunder's premonition of a squabble among gods. Even Junius had heard, though the accounts had scant reality to him, but one look at Edgar now revealed to him a rawness of the nerves which even stimulants could not disguise, and the giddy disequilibrium with which only a gluttony of emotions can surfeit the mind. He stared at it as if at something he had never imagined before but recognized instantly, as sinless children somehow recognize a sin.

"You bring that bottle?" he heard the white boy mutter to a tanned youth in a beachboy shirt, whose face betrayed a repulsive mixture of health and dissoluteness.

"This'll put him *out*, man, after all that pot. This'll *sink* him, you know."

"It'll lift him long enough to cut two sides. He's nowhere the way he is now . . . Give it here."

A petulant girl was adjusting a stocking on a folding chair, and Junius saw Edgar staring at her thigh passionlessly, with empty concentration on the simple fidgets of her fingers, but could not tell whether Edgar saw or not. "Let's go to the beach," she kept saying peevishly. "Let's get high and dig the squares burning."

The boy with the greenish-looking tan was on the phone in a corner, arguing with a connection. "Those mothergrabbin' *slacks* you sold me yesterday is what I'm talking about, man! Who you trying to hype or something? They were full of *seeds!*"

"What are we gonna do-do-do?" the fairyish drummer drawled, shifting his buttocks gingerly back and forth as he sat, and working his gum.

But Edgar did not seem to hear, and only choked out of the bottle obediently, his undeviating glance holding to consciousness by the few white inches of the girl's soft thigh.

"Couple of standards," the white boy put in peremptorially. "Maybe 'Comin' Virginia,'" and he snapped Edgar's horn into the sling around his neck.

"How about that, man?" the drummer said to Edgar's back.

"He'll fall in okay. Let's just get started . . . You all set up in there, Bernie?"

And before he knew it Junius found himself stroking out the opening chords against the light introductory brush of the drums, certain it was all a joke or some misunderstanding, for Edgar seemed incapable of work and stood like a ruin amid their readiness, upright only because of the brief flicker the whiskey had brought to his eyes, sweating steadily, coldly, and staring lifelessly before himself.

But the moment it was time for him to come in his hands stirred up to his horn, and he began to play, gasping and slow, always just in danger of falling behind the beat, eyes fluttering open and shut, but nevertheless working with a sort of painfully premeditated diligence, isolated from everything, even when a streak of saliva ran down his chin from the mouthpiece that kept threatening to get away from his shamed lips.

He blew three uninterrupted choruses—fragmented, arduous, spaced with poignant and terrible intervals, at the bottom of which Junius' soft chords lay, somehow breathless, waiting; and when it was over he choked again out of the bottle, wordless and lidded, about to reel, and they all pretended not to notice, but were astounded nevertheless (down to the most cynical) by the curiously undefeated, though unresisting, will to endure in the splashed and quivering figure.

"What'll we do for the flip side?" the drummer asked the silence.

"Hey, le's do the goony-bird's tune," Edgar mumbled all of a sudden, lurching around toward Junius with a bleary, secretive smirk lighting his damaged face for just a moment—shocking, because it had never occurred to Junius that Edgar even knew he was there, much less recalled a song heard once a week before.

"It doesn't matter," the white boy said impatiently. "They buy the standards anyway, but let's get done."

And so they made the record that would eventually be called "Junius Sees Her" (an odd, melancholy melody based on the chords of "I Only Have Eyes For You"), the possibilities of which numberless hornmen would explore toward dawn in the years to come.

Now Junius recalled with sorrowful clarity Edgar's dangerous sway against the piano, naked before them all in the indignity of his efforts, not to play well, but merely to remain standing; and remembered thinking over and over again, "Why does he play at all? What is it? Doesn't he *care?*" trying to concentrate on the chords that alone could sustain Edgar's precarious grip on the melodic line, but knowing, also, as he listened to Edgar's horn (hesitant yet strangely pure, crude but curiously unencumbered—a quality that would forever isolate this record from the others Edgar made), knowing for the first time that the sources in Edgar were deeper than he had imagined: the mindless, dumb, finally humble and unquestioning response just to the chords themselves, which was the result of years of simply trying to manipulate the stops, and further years of the impatient expending of this mastery on worthless tunes, and finally that first astonishing moment when the skill was adequate to the idea. He suddenly felt his naïve self-belief give way, as if the costs and consequences of his chosen life had just come home to him, and he stared at

Edgar's wincing, sodden face in the first disowning horror of repudiation and respect.

But as Junius gaped, Edgar came to the stumbling end of his chorus, relapsing against the piano; and before he knew it Junius took off on a panicked solo just to fill the silence, thick-fingered in his confusion and unable to think, but after a few bars hearing (to his shock) that he had fallen back on a literal extension of Edgar's last idea, as if he had suddenly lost the ability to improvise at all, even on his own song. For a moment he knew with sickening intensity the loss of faith, and so aped Edgar in a slavish, baffled sweat, unable to invent himself, and somehow managed until Edgar's horn came back at the end for a momentary reprise.

And then, looking up dazed, he heard the curious drawled words that weaned and sobered him at once, and also ended it for him; for Edgar, going into a lurch from which he would not recover, was staring at him with bleary, fixed detachment, as if he was thinking of a joke too complicated to communicate, of which he (Edgar) was the butt, giggling, "Hey, boy, Ah'm not me . . . *You're* me," just as he pitched forward, with a shameless, capitulant uproll of doused eyes, onto his face. . . .

That had ended it for him, Junius thought, turning slowly from the phone to watch his mother's unhurried splitting of the pods, unchanged for all the phone call had evoked in him. He knew she would not ask about it, as (ten years before) she had not once asked what finally brought him home when he turned up that day just two weeks later, but had only put another plate upon the evening table, and been grateful.

He had simply packed and bought his ticket and had gotten himself all the way back through the acrid fog of gathered exhausts at highway intersections; all the way back the way he had come, abjuring the world as he went.

He had locked his woodshed door, and was wearing the dark glasses without which he was never seen in public after that, when he returned.

For something had told him that if all *this* could lead to all *that*—the simple, feckless resonance of the right chord lead to the winced eye and the shrewdly supplied bottle to keep it open—it was not for him. He had listened too closely to Edgar (digging him as only like-souls dig each other) to end up different from Edgar if he went his way. It was too late to feign enough belief in conflicts, scale, bookings, temperament, to cope with them; it was too late for worldliness, and thereafter he never worked again with anyone for whom all that was real, but slumped among the rash tenors as long as their thirst for sheer nights, sheer jam, sheer truth was uncorrupted, and somewhere turned up fresh ones when it was. His woodshed was the world, and when a man has learned what he can or can't accept, one part of wisdom is accepting this acceptance. All this he knew, and so he came back to his mother's homely, parlor warmth, and back into himself.

"Ma," he began then, not knowing exactly what he wanted to say but having to say something, because her patient, agile fingers, that had so tirelessly sought to protect him through his life, were suddenly dear and lost to him in their unawareness of their failure. "Ma—" but then the phone rang again.

It wasn't Edgar, as he first suspected, but only Wing Redburn wondering where he was.

"—So I guess we ought to find him, June— Oh, I know, all the trouble, all the drag—but I heard from someone that he's really sick this time. I mean, out of his head, hasn't been to bed for days . . . and *sick,* you know?"

"Man, he's probably just drunk somewhere. And what can you *do* anyway?"

"I know, I know. But, after all, it's Edgar, June, the Horn . . . And I hear he's bad, I mean, *grave* . . ."

At which Junius heard again the wheedling voice in his inner ear, "I got to go, I *got* to"—prideless, he had thought, willing to go down: the smirker giggling as he fell. "You're me, you're me!" Who knew, he suddenly wondered hopelessly, what reality was for another man? Who could say? For him, the isolate chord, the long brood, the steaming rice and gravy on a plate. For Edgar, buried years, fame that came too late, whatever demons goaded him. Who could say? Or judge?

"He's down at Geordie's, man. At least he was."

"Great. I'll get a cab. Meet you there in ten minutes."

Junius considered it, staring at the chair from which his mother had just gotten up, and hearing the reassuring clanging of her supper pots upon the stove.

"No, man," he said slowly. "I can't make it. It's time to eat. You know?"

There was a hesitant silence. For Wing, too, perhaps the past was there again—the heavy afternoons, the naïve beginnings, the solemn boy before the piano. "Okay," he said, "I dig you. I'll call you later then."

"But look, man, have you got an extra ten?"

"Yah, sure. Why?"

"If you find him, give him ten for me," Junius said. "I owe him from a long ago."

RIFF

"'Just last night,'" the juke box sang, "'life was an old routine, life was an evergreen'"; words that so clearly articulated his own thoughts that Cleo (who had not been really listening) now discovered he was drunk—he, who could still count his binges on his fingers and separate them easily in his mind, one from another. He considered the discovery as he ordered another beer, dimly aware that he had to go to work in an hour or so, but nevertheless moved by the aptness of the lyrics, as American popular songs will sometimes move those who listen, with a brief glimpse of the way they do, or did, or want to feel.

He could hear Edgar's droning voice (somewhere in all the murk of talk, sometime during that long day) saying: "It's like the lyrics . . . None of you music-school cats today even listen to the lyrics, so how do you know what it's about? How do you know what to blow on it? Man, jazz is still songs, and songs is *words* too . . . And I bet I know the lyrics of every tune I ever played . . . Go on, test me, try and stump me . . . But you ain't *old* enough."

And so Cleo listened as he waited on, and finally took to getting off of his stool, going down the bar to feed quarters into the juke box, selecting almost at random before he returned to his glass; listening until the money was used up, and then getting off the stool again; buying the bright, depthless music; buying each tune's three minutes of pleasure or nostalgia or mere noise; buying songs.

. . . Songs that at three o'clock in the morning an all-night disk jockey on Vine Street in Hollywood played to put his faithful thousands to sleep, and with which at the same moment a brother oracle off Madison Avenue in New York (where it was six o'clock) woke his thousands; songs that during the dozen-odd hours before night came to the one and afternoon to the other, and the great concave slab of the continent had lurched away from the sun, would have spun their gay or doleful arch of notes in every corner of the land.

. . . Songs conceived in unvarnished hunger for money by a professional tunesmith in a smoky office on Thirty-fourth Street, or come full grown out of the head of a pianist with a hangover working a pit band in San Diego; songs that were sold, not so much like objects, but like ideas for which there must exist the proper emotional climate.

. . . Songs that Geordie sang—the sad, lone, throaty songs that women sing, and men write for their voices in a curious moment of comprehension; songs that concerned themselves with the splendors and miseries, the illusions and realities, of great Homeric clichés, like love, pride, honor, vengeance or deceit, but which, nevertheless, sometimes caused millions to think an original thought, or dream an extravagant dream, or be startled by the inexplicable poignance of a memory.

. . . Thousands of songs that were only variations of the one Great Twilight Love Song that has changed in forty years only as Americans (hungry, inquisitive, restless in their audacious cities) have themselves changed; songs that for a moment seem to crystallize the music, which churns inside us here, forever seeking adequate notes.

Cleo had a sudden hallucinated vision in his drunkenness of all the songs that had unrolled in unbroken thread since (perhaps) one which said, "Oh, didn't he ramble, he rambled till the butchers cut him down"; songs that were, themselves, born of jazz, or those secular spirituals, the blues, and which had given birth, in their turn, to jazz again. He realized that without "Easy Rider" there could have been no "Stardust"; but also that most truly superlative jazz solos (massive hawsers mooring American popular music to greatness) had been woven out of frail lengths of melody, cut from that selfsame thread in the first place. If Louie's "Sleepy Time Down South" and Bix's "Comin' Virginia" and Bird's "All the Things You Are" were greater than the songs out of which they were made, nevertheless it was primarily the curious give-and-take between genius and the raw material with which it worked that kept an art alive. Sitting there, he was struck by the apostolic succession, song to song, man to man, Edgar to himself, by means of which jazz had made the transition from a folk music to an art music in barely sixty years of life, and he blinked in tipsy awe, amazed by the propitious accidents of history, and feeling the meagerness of his paltry eighteen years.

What right had he ("a colored-boy piano player," as Edgar said) to think that he could save Edgar from the ironies which were a part of any history, no matter how propitious?/ What did he even *know* of them, except the angry echoes he had heard in Edgar's work? /

He felt baffled and dizzy and tired with his thoughts. Everything was much more complicated than he had imagined when he ran after Edgar "just last night"; and for the first time his own simplicity, his urge toward sweetness and toward harmony, seemed to him naïve. For a single sinking moment he thought hopelessly, "You can't do anything. Not even *really* understand . . . Get up, and go away, and let it happen"—whatever "it" might be. "Man, don't be a square."

But when he turned from the bar, pushing his half-filled glass away, the first thing he saw was Edgar's face, pale and weary and desperate, peering apprehensively through the window to see if he had waited—the face of a man so worn by the obvious evaporation, one by one, of all schemes, all hopes, that he could clutch, with tragic eagerness, at the companionship of a boy he hardly even knew; a face that instantly assumed an expression of gloomy nonchalance upon being seen, and even managed a bitter, crooked smile as it came through the open door; the face of a man besieged, who had forgotten how to capitulate, or never knew.

CHORUS:GEORDIE

*"Captivity is consciousness,
So's Liberty."*

EMILY DICKINSON

Against the just-closed door, exactly like the abandoned white ladies of a thousand afternoon movies, Geordie leaned for a moment, realizing that only Edgar in all her days took something of her with him when he went. This man, of all the men she knew, had stirred her life profoundly. She had not felt that for three years (not since the last room from which he abruptly took himself), and for a minute she was possessed by the sorrowful recognition that nothing had changed, and that she belonged to him still in that impersonal, unwanting way, though everything between them was shattered, and the broken pieces again shattered, and whatever was left, buried without a stone. One look at him in the bleak evening light in which she awoke to find him at her door (tapping and chuckling as if recalling all the other times he had awakened her) had told her that it was still the same, even though she was unable to pine any longer, unable to covet. It was the same, and for a moment she was relieved—at least to know. His tragic little laugh was everywhere in the room still.

She walked to the ponderous varnished and revarnished bureau to get a cigarette, and caught a curiously objective glimpse of herself in the mirror.

"Just look at you," she said aloud dispassionately. "You thirty-five if you a day."

What she saw was her own flesh (for she had on nothing but a slip); what she saw was the faint beginnings of wrinkles in her neck, and the skin's sheen across her wide shoulders imperceptibly duller, and the breasts softer and heavier than she remembered. This was what he had seen just now, and not the supple, firm-fleshed girl he had taken out of a Charleston ginmill years ago; and she was suddenly shocked to realize that she had not been that girl for a long time, but that no one had said anything, not even Edgar a moment ago, who might have been expected to scold or mock, having coveted the girl so long, having pined.

But looking closer she saw *it* for a moment too, as night after night the bright, secretive eyes beyond the warm spotlights saw *it* when she sang: the head thrown back, widening the candle-wick eyes that were always, it seemed, about to flare; the broad shoulders poised to assure some slurred and quavering note, then curving forward so that her breasts beneath the gold lamé dress seemed to shiver of their very weight. Those watching omnivorously saw the intake of breath wrinkle the sheer material across her belly, saw her thighs brace against the sway of her body, saw the wide, volatile lips part abruptly—moist, tremulous, the spotlight occasionally reaching right into her mouth where all was pink and dark and warm, the lips curved away from the note, the tongue lifting and flattening to perfect its shape. *It:* the simple impact of her stubborn, living flesh—no skinny, sleek symmetry, but soft, but warm; the sheer physicality of her weight that was too astonishing to arouse mere desire, but built instead that full head of passion that always suggests rape as the only assuaging pleasure, and made the sneering, pale-eyed hipsters elbowing at the bar (to see who'd made the scene, and who might have *what* secreted in an inner pocket) pause, paralyzed in their attitude's cocoon, *having* to have her, to experience her, to know, to *know*. Over the years the gathered want of men's eyes absorbing her as an object had become harmless to her, and in her heart Geordie, like many women, harbored this conviction: boys, bad boys, all boys, just boys. Anyway, at the end, alone in pink light through which smoke drifted gray, she stood amid the applause her confessions elicited, only slightly expended for the surprising thing she had just done, having sung very pure for those who knew no reward for purity but further loss.

Looking now, she saw that the slip was frayed across the top, and one strap had begun to ravel. Wouldn't all the eyes beyond the spots be shocked (she thought), imagining she had nothing but lace, nothing but sheer against her skin? After all, even lust desires perfection to dishevel. The stark, attentive light might dim, as it had dimmed in Edgar's eyes, who had seen her vomit, gasping and shameless, in a bowl; who had caught her staring in a mirror, lifting one breast to study the small brown mole beneath it; who knew the humble, lonely commonplace behind the mystery. But then the eyes beyond the lights were different (aroused white eyes), and though she was a good part white herself, you only had to have a little black for that thing to come up in white men's eyes, the thing too blunt for them to ever show a woman they thought of as a person, inviolate in an identity. But the faint honey-brown of Geordie's skin, like dark rum in a low light, brought it out, and she was a female creature to them (for all their adulation), and they wanted an old, a simple, a crude thing.

She looked at herself, seeing *it* as they saw *it*, but knowing also that now she was more complex than that, though her body had remained too strong for any emotion to crush or maim. Nevertheless, sometime or other, she had shriveled within it, and come to inhabit it, smaller in a way than it was, crouching there inside, animating the startling husk of flesh. Edgar knew this, Edgar only.

His tragic, bleary little laugh was everywhere in the room still.

"I need fifty, Baby, so I can get straight . . . I been lushed all day," though she knew he was sober now. "You alone here? You wouldn't hide no one in the john from ol' Eddie though . . . Where's your dog?— But, you know, I never seen where you live before." And so he looked around.

It was one of those old bleak-corridored hotels somewhere west of Times Square, in which the heavy carpets are worn thin, the rooms are dark, with large varnished wardrobes and standing lamps, and the ancient radiators bang and clank as the steam comes up, always too dry, too hot, and the lone bellboy is over forty. Edgar seemed amused by it.

"They think you white *enough*, I guess," he said, smirking as he slumped in the sagging armchair. "You got an extra forty or so?"

His eyes, red-rimmed and drawn as if abused by a harsh light, were nevertheless just as they had always been— lidded and attentive and dimly ironic no matter what he was saying. She watched the eyes, shocked because they were all that was left of the Edgar she had first seen years ago: the sullenly handsome, lean Edgar, in natty, loud suits and thick-soled expensive shoes; the Edgar at whose peevish mouth below the pencil-thin mustache she had openly gaped, because it was the first sophisticated thing she had ever seen.

What he had become was no surprise to her. She had seen photographs in music magazines, and even once or twice (like last night) sat beyond the lights herself and watched him lift his sax, aware the old stories stirred up again in the minds of everyone around, and half enjoying the breathless whispers, the suspenseful eyes; perhaps enjoying most of all the curious, impersonal intimacy (all that was left to them) of knowing that Edgar, like herself, would take no notice, and even turn away when she swept out. And raging at it, too.

But now he had grown flabby, jowled, soft; his hair stuck out, board-stiff, over his limp soiled collar; his flashy suit, rumpled and stained, had that sorrowful jauntiness that is only a step away from outright destitution; and she was secretly shocked, knowing well enough that everyone said he was through, because he should have been pitiful but somehow, damnably, was not. His eyes would not give up their gloating, shrewd, ironical involvement with life; and so she stared at them, remembering without remorse or pain that same face the first time she had seen it.

Memory had lost its sting in time, and she did not remember so much as become aware (in a simultaneous, returning flash) of tree-heavy summer Charleston, 1936, board-sidewalked in the colored section; aging, paintless, dusty buildings in the heat-haze shimmering the streets; and inside one of the buildings, the shimmered idiot-circling of the juke-box lights gliding across the unmoving shoulders of the sullen stranger at the bar, as she raised her voice for pennies to a record. Just past sixteen, with the ravished horror at midday on a country road already riveted into her young life forever—how had Edgar described her later to friends, or sometimes just to anyone who'd listen?

"You should have seen her—in her feed-sack dress, like scared and roll-eyed, pickaninny mud on her knees, crooning 'Trouble in Mind' all breathy . . . She was so cute, man, I almost bought her a sourball to suck, didn't I, Baby? Like, man, I *laughed!*"

He hadn't laughed though, he hadn't even listened as far as she could tell, but only sometimes raised the foamy glass of beer to pitiless lips and sipped in meager disinterest.

"'I'm gonna lay my head on some lonesome railroad i'on,'" she sang in the brave, unmodulated lament of all children fetched in among adults to do a risqué song they barely understand, "'an' let that 219 train satisfy my mind,'" all the time thinking (how strangely, how clearly she could remember this one thought out of all the later introspections!): "He ain't about to th'ow pennies, that man. He th'ow a dolla, or he th'ow you out."

He hadn't laughed, but finally he looked, and when she was done beckoned her with a short, impatient jerk of his head. "Come here, girl," he said, peremptory as a white man, looking her over like a piece of goods, and sniffing drily to himself. "How've you kept all that in one brown piece?" he said with a liquored narrowing of eye that was (she sensed) related to the widening she had come to know in other men's eyes when they got a close look at her, a look she had learned to parry with a flaunt of head. "I bet I *know*," he added.

And remembering it now, she realized that perhaps he *had* known, after all; and it was not just the sniggering dirty talk that precedes diddling, but that he actually knew that a young and motherless girl, bursting out of a calico dress not meant for a ripening body, could be already too well handled by importunate life to be afraid of bars and men, and yet be as innocent as calico in spite of it.

Calico dresses, dimity waists, muslin drawers (she thought all of a sudden), boiled in a big dented tub, and hung out in the sun to flutter; good red dirt worn deep into sticky palms; the hushed gabble of childish voices under a piney tree; the sourball passed from mouth to mouth. Her mind had not gone back that far (before Edgar, before the nightmare on the rutted road) for years. And abruptly, from the incredible distance of her New York room, she longed for her childhood, as we can only long for something not only lost to us forever, but unreal, unreal. Just for a moment, still standing before the mirror, she ached for the country South, of which she retained only fragmented images at best: great dark, fragrant barns, yellow school buses standing empty in the incinerator-backyards of poorly houses, cow-pies by a branch under the pines, muddy water standing in the prints of hooves, the cuddy soft mouths of cows in indolent Southern August— Oh! Had she *ever* been a girl, and talked in the slurred gush of innocence? Breastless, all scrawn? Wriggling while a warm-smelling mother did her hair in plaits? Had she? Ever?

"Just look at you," she said, sternly this time, staring at last night's traces on her lips. "You thirty-five, and Ma was only thirty when you saw her last."

Calico, dimity, muslin— Edgar had changed all that forever, coming into her life, smoking and distracted, suspicious and resentful even of awesome Charleston, hate-filled, tensed against it, sneering, watchful, alert; in his Northern suit that was too sharp, too striped, too long in the jacket and unoutlandish, too much like a white-man's suit for a Negro to wear down yonder without arousing bitter blood just by the sight of him. She had sensed the difference, even scared and just sixteen—the difference in him as he sipped his beer and talked: that she had never thought of herself as anything but a Negro, but that he was like a white man who had to keep recalling to himself, in bitterness and irony, that he was not. . . .

And now—what had he said just then, sprawled in the sagging armchair as she searched her purse, his eyes alone in the thickening face the same as they had been so long ago, but nevertheless looking at her naked shoulders without the old narrowing, for she was no mystery to him any longer, and *that* at least was over between them?

"I'm gonna cut this time, Baby . . . Like all I need is bus fare. I mean, when some goony sideman tenor can blow me off the stand like last night, well . . . Oh, he played good, I'm hip, but *he* never gigged a hundred towns, and worked a dozen bands, and been a bum, and he—" He passed a nail-bitten hand over his eyes, his swollen lips twisting into a frown that became a shameless little snicker almost immediately. "No, I mean this town's a drag this year anyway, a hype. Chicks, and strippers, and accordions. And, baby, I just *can't* flip my hips like you. I got nothin' to *shake,* you know—" He made a coy grimace, arching one shoulder like a weary, drunken queer. "Besides, I lost my card somewhere, lushing with a piano player, and my overcoat . . ."

She found fifteen, and felt his eyes on it as she pulled it out; prideless, hungry eyes, still calculating, despite the shabby nonchalance of a quivering cigarette.

"*You* know, I'll make KayCee, maybe just get me a room somewhere uptown, or even out in the county . . . Maybe later pick up gigs with a downhome band, or— Could you make it twenty, Baby? Just for beers to get me on the bus. Like I got to meet a cat, and— Well, no," he added with a smirking, crooked sniff as she turned up her hand empty. "I'm hip. Don't *bust* yourself. I got some other babies I can touch . . . Would you believe it, they still think the old man's cute!" he added with a sour smile. "And, man, I got connections in KayCee, lots of swinging cats, lots of oozy little chicks. I get me some real rest, just goof a while, you know, and get my tone back, and— Well, anyway, I *got* to do it, that's all," he said with sudden baffled-eyed intensity. "You never know, after all, you never do. You *never* really know."

There was something terrible in this to her, the desperate and shabby little dream, the shuddering necessity that must have manufactured it. Edgar? Edgar of the mean midnight streets, the thronging bars, the cigarettes cupped against the wind of cities, and the cops? Hip-suited, crepe-soled Edgar? . . . Working a country band, guitars and bandannas? A cheery-curtained, brass-bedsteaded room in someone's board-front house by a siding out of town? Doctor Pepper in the Main Street sun? Sunday chicken, rice and gravy, collard greens? . . . No, no, it was a sad and tragic dream, born of an awful inner urgency she could not imagine in the Edgar *she* had known.

The radiator wheezed like an old man who will never really catch his breath again, and she snapped out of her thoughts. Last night's red rose lay, waxen and brown-edged, upon the bureau where she had plucked it from her hair, and she dropped it into the wastebasket among the others: the six dead emblems of a week of work which had come to her each evening fresh and wet from the florist in their crinkly shrouds of green paper and their tiny cardboard coffins. Their elusive odor, as fleeting and perishable and lovely as the songs she sang, lingered in her hair, and for a moment she thought of the hundreds she had left in wastebaskets and gutters, on hotel bureaus and ginmill tables, flushed down johns and thrown down stairwells, in the hours before dawn. A chain of dead flowers stretched behind her back into her life, all the way back to the night when Edgar first had thrust one in her hair, large and red and still moist, and standing back, had said with a purse-lipped little giggle, "Get a new one when it dies, baby, get a wet one. You gonna be *Miss* Baby, you hear me?" And then with sudden, stern intensity, "But don't you ever think because your wig's got flowers, it ain't no wig!" /

She turned to the window, unpleasantly hot, and threw it open, and looked out on the dim clotheslines webbed against the square of lowering dusk between the blank brick of neighboring buildings. It would rain soon, silently, steadily—lonesome autumn rain filling emptied ash cans. The air, already freshened by the showers moving over Jersey, almost chill, came in in a cool wave over her breasts as she leaned on the sill, and she automatically thought of Edgar, coatless, somewhere in the streets, and frowned.

"I just keep going till I make the fare," he had said with a curious crooked look. "I *got* to . . . I can sleep when I get home."

Home? KayCee? Yes, once, sometime, he had been born there, as he said; and over the vagrant years, wheeling around the country with the one-night bands, he had gone back. But home? She shook her head in slow bewilderment, afraid down in her chest of that thing, terrible and unknown, that was alive in Edgar now, and could awaken such a desperate haven in his mind. Home?

She knew him better than anyone in the world; she had heard him goof, play sour, pretend; she had heard him moaning through his dreams, and felt him fitful in the heavy dark; she knew his heart to be too soured by a decade of neglect, when he had blown complex and minor in the midst of vulgar stomping swing bands, jitterbugs and ricky-ticky-too, to trust the tardy worship of the hip when bop came in; she knew they thought of him as if he was a sort of martyred symbol, copying his phrasing and his talk, the very flaws indifference had bred in him; she knew him much too well to ever live with him again—and yet this drowning clutch at the idea of home he'd never let her see.

Their life came back to her, the life that he had shown her in the world she always thought to be the only world he knew: the Northern world, the night world, the city world, the world without limits; and she passed it over in her mind, looking for the word she had ignored, the glance she hadn't understood.

He had taken her so easily out of that bar, out of the South, out of her urchin-like reliance on sharp eyes and wit to keep alive. "Here," he'd said morosely after only forty minutes, handing her two dollars, "you spilling out of that one. Get yourself a dress that's built the way you built, you hear." He never knew how soon she felt obedient and trusted him, not to be gentle, not to understand, but to direct and discipline and finally take care. He never knew that going to his room was easier for her than asking it had been for him, or that his lean adeptness, all his hollow gallantries, meant nothing to her.

He could have been an awkward field hand, schooled by the mare's fierce rutting in convulsive spring, for all she knew; for, awed and taut, she climbed his stairs toward the drawn-down shades, the rumpled bed, the inevitable abject uncovering of modest flesh, without a thought, as women go toward some capitulations, tensing stoically and shoring up inside.

He took her in the light, intent, annoyed, somehow on loan. There were no little words, no gasped avowals meant to be forgotten when the thing was done. Above her, watching, watching, his eyes were steady, wick'd, unblinking when hers fluttered open at a swallowed groan that grieved his throat; and that, more than anything that afternoon, had shocked her deeply.

Then he was only a sideman tenor in a band that swung continually around a circuit of the smaller cities, playing theatres, dance halls, roadhouses, senior proms; getting off a bus and setting up, later taking down and getting on the selfsame bus again. It was only one of many bands he worked those years, the tireless jumping colored bands that flourished like a backwash after the initial wave of swing. But already he was blowing strange long lines, rising out of the section, indrawn and resolute, to stand before the circling dancers, tilt the big horn roofward from his body, and play his weightless, sharply veering phrases over the chunking of unsubtle drums. In those days, no one heard.

When that band left Charleston, Geordie followed in the rear of local buses, changing in dusty county seats, eating Hersheys, working north. At first the great dreary cities under their canopies of smoke had terrified her with their limitless possibilities, she who knew only the carefully circumscribed necessities of the South. But eventually she learned to walk white neighborhoods and not look at the pavement, and even to order coffee from an ofay waitress in a voice that could be heard. In barely seven months she knew one-night, side-street, bus-stop America; had seen Jim Crow, Mail Pouch, Jax Beer America; and that billboard America of Clabber Girl and Andy Boy and Old Granddad. She'd washed her new silk pants in gas-pump restrooms and in the toilet bowls of rooming houses; she'd eaten standing up on ticket lines in morning Denver; she'd been awakened by the grieving wail of freights in Harrisburg. And slept again. And had been three hundred miles away that night. And learned the difference between South and North was just the difference between knowing *what*, and *who*, you are.

He had given her a sourball to suck all right, though she would not know it till later, when, having other men, this man seemed distinct. She was baffled all the time, merely content with keeping up with him, trying to learn his ways. They owned nothing, they had nothing, they took nothing more with them when they left a place than they had brought—two suitcases and a horn; and when she came to pack that last time out in California, too weary to be sad, too wrung out for sentiment, she found she did not even have the stubs of old bus tickets, baggage checks or room receipts to show for all those years: not even that which, even if she'd hoarded carefully, would have been all there was to save.

He sat and read the paper in his undershirt and drawers while she pressed his band jacket with a borrowed iron on a bureau top in St. Louis. He and a few sympathetic sidemen from the band were resting up for an extra job out in the county that week end. Down the hall the drummer snored off last night's liquor, and two trumpet men played cards. Downstairs the landlady loosened her girdle under the kimono, and poured a shot of hootch for the indefatigable bassist, who had yet to sleep, and didn't intend to, certain he could go forever, thinking the others were a drag to have deserted him at nine that morning.

Geordie crooned to herself unwittingly as she tried to get the iron in around the buttons: cabin-crooning that you did not have to think about, a soft laze of repetitive sounds, thoughtlessly content.

"Hush up," he said behind the paper. "Or if you gotta sing, sing words."

She stopped and looked at him. "They ain't no words go with it, though."

"Then sing something else, or hush."

She put down the iron with a disobedient thud. "No, I want to sing *it*. My mammy used to sing it for an hour without no—"

"Your *mammy!*" he snorted, dropping the paper, his eyes steady with mockery, the way they got whenever life unsettled the brooding surface of his face. "You mean Aunt Jemima!"

She began to cry at that for some reason, sniffling and

blubbering softly into her fist, astonished by the childish pang of lonesomeness in her heart.

"Your 'mammy' run off, didn't she?" he was saying. "When you got out of the can? Your 'mammy' just up and moved away, didn't she? Leaving you, and good riddance, didn't she now?"

"But I *think* sometimes, Eddie," she bawled. "Don't I got to *think?*"

"But you think *back,* baby! You always thinking *back!* And what're you thinking back to? . . . Colored diners, colored buses, even colored crappers . . . 'Yassah, nome' . . . Back o' town, tip yo hat, move along . . . Baby, I think back to *that,* and I go goofy . . . You brush their coat or pour their booze or play the music for 'em, but you don't think *back!* . . . Play *your* music, baby, make *your* money, and be no one's *'nigra'* any more. And when you sing, sing words . . . And, look it now, you've singed that coat—"

He moved the iron with a dry chuckle, and his lean-fingered hands were turning her around. He felt her by the shoulders, and his eyes were banked and penetrating, and she stood before him all soft and incredible in the warmth and tears of girlishness. "You funny," he murmured harshly. "Look at you."

His hands suddenly felt of her wonderingly, moving, moving in the old astonishment of men.

"No," she said, frowning away the last of tears.

"We got time," he breathed, his stern hands coming up from her waist to cup her breasts, "before we go and eat . . . I'll play you this time, baby, like my horn."

"No," she said again, pouting and pulling away.

"Yes. I say yes . . . And least *I* ask you first."

But her wince at this, and at the sudden memory of violence erupting on a noontime road back home, violence with liquored breath and impatient hands, was drowned in her involuntary arousal at his wish, and afterward she lay, tingling while he drowsed, singing again with idle self-involvement, till he suddenly mumbled, "Whyn't you play this week-end gig with us? This guy'll give us fifteen extra if we bring a chick. And you getting so you blow."

And, incredible to her, he prevailed over her terror at the very thought, and she went, and thereafter worked his extra jobs with him.

She remembered him so clearly back all those years, straight, embittered, but full of his peculiar, isolated truth. Then he had possessed himself, uncorrupted and unquestioning. His power to go his own way, blow the way he felt and move on if it cost him his chair, pursue the years in lean and tireless communion with himself, and dive always for the very bottom of a thing, had kept her with him, even when she changed. . . .

" 'I looked for every loveliness,' " she sang softly there in the gathering dark of her room. " 'It *all* came true,' " a line justly associated with her lone, brave quaver, a song Edgar had shown her how to do, her voice rising with sad, hopeful avowal at the end. Whenever she sang it (in hushed, worldly clubs, or over portable radios melodic in the night by pine-pent lakesides where, out of the fire's warm range, the lovers gasped together), it seemed a startling revelation of life's caged yearning to those who heard: a woman's truth, a hip chick's childlike wish. " 'It *all* came true,' " she repeated idly, staring out into the uncertain night out of which the annealing rain would certainly fall on baffled streets, and thinking, without shame or heat or even loss, of her simple coupling with Edgar years ago at the stir of simple need—the way a woman thinks of the fevers and obsessions of the past, without shock, because they have happened. It had happened to her, all of it, so many beds off dark halls, in old houses, in a hundred towns: an ever deepening privacy in their lives, in which her youth and innocence had gradually dropped away, and Edgar's mind, coiled, always worrying things, had patiently, assiduously, and out of a sort of blistered insatiety, taught her sin. His curious sniggers, the rude glut of words, the surprising bliss behind his eyes had all led her further and further, sometimes even to catch a glimpse of herself (stark and wanton) in them. She remembered her own arousal with a quiet acceptance that everything, everything was life.

She lit a cigarette, rubbing her chest and pulling the slip away to let the night in. She had never felt more alone. Marco, her little spaniel who slept away his days beside her in the bed and went with her, patient and fatalistic, wherever the night might lead, came out blinking from under the bureau, wriggling himself awake. He trotted over, silken-haired and instantly concerned, and when she looked down, sternly fond, he wagged his whole rear end.

"You ready to go out and do your stuff?" she asked him, bending down to touch his nose, and moved as always by the clear, uncomplicated affection in his eyes. "You didn't even wake up for the visitor, now did you? Did you? . . ." Her few quick caresses were enough to reassure, and he started poking sleepily around the radiator. She blew smoke out onto the new air, and sighed.

"Marky, he's a fool, now ain't he?" she breathed, visualizing Edgar a sort of trophy around KayCee, aging, eccentric, forgetful, playing to respectful but indifferent audiences who had heard the name somewhere but could not quite remember where—doing *his* stuff. No, no, she couldn't believe it. He only wanted lush money. He had been giving her the elaborate con. That was the Edgar she could understand, and for a moment she banked her hopes on his deceitfulness, knowing with stubborn bewilderment that it was not so.

"When I lost my card, like I knew that was a sign," he'd said. " 'Course, I decided before that. This town's nowhere right now, and I could use a rest"—this last pathetic because he was so patently near collapse. "But losing the card . . . that proves that I was right, you know?"

She remembered it now, helplessly aware as well that Edgar, very deep inside himself, had always believed in signs and omens, and like many scornful, eccentric men, selfishly intent upon themselves, believed that he was fated, too. "I heard all this in my mind ten years ago," he used to say archly when bop was new, to hornmen giddy with as-yet-unplayed ideas. "Like what do you think *that* means?" And it was not entirely arch.

"But lordy, lordy," she breathed again angrily, "he go *crazy* with the drag out there!"—he who had become, as years went on, further palled by more of life, until little by little the great morass of boredom had edged in all around him, covering the joys and pleasures of the past, till only more remote and weirder kicks could stimulate him.

But as she thought all this she knew as well the sudden, inexplicable desertions that can happen in a man, as if his talent or belief inhabited his mind, but was not of it, and sometimes left him abruptly without warning, so that though he heard the chords he simply could not think of anything to play on them; or had played so much, and so explored and mapped and mined his urge to play, that all at once the vein ran out. No man knew why it happened, but Geordie knew the terror and bewilderment of one day listening to oneself and hearing only noise; and (not yet alarmed) trying for the higher music once so easy to attain, only to find that nothing would come out. The once-agile fingers became thick with fear; a frustrate sweat hung, chilly, on the eyebrows; a man who'd blown a dozen swirling choruses and been hardly out of breath when he was done, took to worrying about his wind. Oh, yes, it happened, who knew why.

And if that was in him now (the ominous suspicion that he was emptying), his only thought would be to get away; and once again she saw him in some little town outside KayCee, where a granite soldier stared unblinking at the courthouse square which Negroes only crossed on Saturdays in humble watchfulness: a monument to those who'd either fought for honor or for justice once, depending how far north or south of Kansas City the soldier stood. She saw Edgar there, his horn still packed inside a smelly closet; she saw him glancing at the door sometimes and then away; she saw him putting off the time when he would have to get it out and try.

"He never make it all alone," she said aloud with a certainty, involuntary and immediate, that caused Marco to look up from the black suede pump he'd found beneath the bureau, his docile eyes alert for censure. "Not alone."

She got up from the window, smoking fitfully, as the first keen drops of that night's rain came down in quiet desultory spatters on her sill. She walked up and down, a distracted woman accustomed to lonely rooms, but no longer thinking of herself. Suddenly she stopped.

Why not? she thought, looking around. What did all this mean to her? The parched and curling flower, last evening's dress crumpled for the cleaners on the chair, tonight's still hanging in the closet in its paper sleeve, the stray match books on the bureau telling in clearer terms than memory where whim or the suggestion of an escort had taken her last night. What did it mean?

Next month she would be idling away the early evening in a room exactly similar to this in Boston; two months from now, the flowers and the dresses would be littering another bedroom in L.A., and only the match books would be different. What did it mean? Why not KayCee?

She could go out, take off as long as necessary, perhaps work a week or two if things got tight; in any case, be there, help him, occupy him. For he could never make it all alone; a man can fall too far. Who knew, she thought with a stirring of old hopes long ago known to be illusory, perhaps it was not too late for him, for them? Why not? Why not? In a small quiet room, in a careful life, with big uncomplicated meals and early nights, they could see the sun again, turn inward, mend. One night the mocking light would come up in his eyes, and he would grow expansive and ironical again, and take out his horn and, one-handed, blow a wheeling, glittering scale, and then—

"You dreaming, Geordie," she murmured, pressing out the cigarette, "just like him."

It was no good to believe she could go back, much as she wanted to believe she could. This, all this—fresh flowers and clean dresses, though each evening killed the one and soiled the other—was the life that she had chosen. A room, her dog, a window on the night: to the world, to half the men she knew, it would have seemed an empty, lonely life at best, and no one would believe her if she told them how it suited her. And yet she had come so far to get to this, she had been so zealous in keeping it untouched, and now, in just ten minutes, Edgar—

She sat down at the window once again, sighing heavily. It was no good to dream. She did not want what being with him meant, and in any case she could not worry anymore. She had forced sleep last night with pills so as not to think about him, for she had done all the thinking long ago, and what good had it been? Some men have to do what they have to do. It is a matter of blindness. Or perception.

But did she love him? Her heart had produced that question when there was nothing else to ask at every dead-end moment once their lives began to change, and often in the lonely mornings since. In the beginning she had never thought of love and had never heard the word upon his lips. For love was the province of songs that cried for a human voice to shape their simple pang, her voice's province: lost love, larky love, sad love; love compounded of the premonition of loss, the brave urgency of having little time. Somehow she never felt the irony of singing about stardust, Maytime, hands across the table, what a little moonlight could do—she, whose life had never been like that, and for whom love had mostly happened under a naked bulb in unadorned assent to human need, and from whom the city night had mostly kept the sentimental moon. For long ago she had discovered that all words are alike on their levels, and so she sang the papier-mâché, stagey, white-men's words, lending them the brief sincerity of her dark voice to express the truth beneath their cheap shimmer. But love, for Edgar? No, for a long time it had been something beyond love, beyond the crave. They were damned together by their knowledge of each other, and there is nothing you can do with knowledge, not even forget that you possess it.

For the firm, selfish hand upon her arm, moving her where it wanted, and taking from the steady heat of her assuaging female flesh renewed resistance to the world of men, had one day only lit another cigarette; and the clipped instructions about where to meet, and where to purchase tickets for, had vanished in ironical and harmless chatter. Nothing had come between them. They had simply grown too close to see each other.

In the first drizzly winter of the war, when everyone in Harlem seemed to be up all night waiting for the moon, they found themselves between bands, and took a small group into a bar on 125th Street for two weeks, Edgar blowing curious, melodic answers to her throaty songs, and criticizing her pettishly in the alley between sets.

"Baby, no! Baby, will you please! . . . Make them cats work to *you!* Do you hear me, what I'm saying? . . . Why not make them bend to *you?*" And tapping his foot, he would drawl a little of the song in his rather thin soft voice, slurring a phrase end over the beat and pulling back on it.

Later, after another try, he would exclaim, "Baby, you no shouter, you no sweating, big-lunched Memphis yeller! . . . Don't you let me catch you listening to them drums again or I'll goose you with my horn. I'm gonna prod you where you sit . . . Listen to the bass if you got to listen— You want me to move him up so you can hear him? Cock your head! Cock your head!"

But she listened to him instead, she cocked her head to him, knowing after a while (and somewhat alarmed at the discovery) that it was not mere obedience any longer, or the happy submission of the uncritical girl, but that the singing had become important in itself, and what he said made sense.

" 'I'm black, and I'm evil, and I did not make myself,' " she had sung then, seemingly impervious to the group behind her or to the noisy bar, expressing the rhythm only by the steady hunch of her shoulders, head thrown slightly back, shaping, shaping, calmly working at each phrase, stretching it, bending it, beautiful and intent. She had not done that one for years, she realized, she had not even thought of it. " 'I'm black, and I'm evil, and I did not make myself' "—flat, bare, minimum, the way the blues should be, for they were the source of everything after all, all song. There was so much to be done with them that still sometimes, when the grave, accomplished mood came on her, she would do a whole set; varying only the rhythm and the words, and how she chose to unfold the ancient, repetitive lament. Blues like "Black and Evil" were never done any more in the midtown cellars where she worked. They were Uncle Tom, and times had turned against the kinky-headed wailers, sweating earnestly for the white folks, who had sung them simply and without a second thought. But the blues themselves went on, even behind the bittersweet of show tunes that had their truths as well, and Geordie merely listened to the words, and sang the same.

But then she had done "Black and Evil" and "Back to Johnson City" and "Tell 'Em About Me When I'm Gone," until, feeling her control one night, she tried "Blue Moon" and "Mood Indigo," listening, listening, and singing well.

After a month of packed bars and word of mouth and curious parties disgorging from downtown cabs, they moved to Fifty-second Street (just then the axis around which jazz swung), and made their first recordings two weeks later.

Giddy months followed in which there was no time. Exhaustion and exhilaration spelled each other, leaving no room for slow emotions in between. They rushed meals, they slept hard and never long enough, they were always on their way somewhere in a frantic whirl through the wartime nights that pounded so loud, and there were always throngs of people when they got there: sidemen from the sections of a dozen bands still indefatigably on the road; the fresh and restless girls who picked up with them and were crowded, tipsy, into cabs, and never seen again; white purists who bought Geordie drinks and quoted matrix numbers, explaining the profundity of what she sang; young pimply servicemen who sweated, wept and cursed, the music moved them so. Something sweet and brief and unsettling was in the air.

"It never got like that again," she mused to herself, remembering, not so much specific nights in those years, but the feeling of continual unfoldment, the feeling that there were no limits, the hourly discoveries. Edgar had been supercharged with a strange, twisted power then, sensing (as involved, original men seem to sense it when it comes) that it was *his* time. He played night after night (behind her voice or all alone) with an astonishing, unfaltering fecundity that took the breath away. The buried years of band work had built in him a bitter discipline, and the sudden freedom of a bookless combo seemed to release the flood of ideas which that discipline had taught him how to hoard. He played all night, and afterward went on to sessions where he played some more.

The time was right for both of them. The war was starving out the bands; the draft boards took their toll among the sections; the auditoriums were emptying. The bands broke up and limped back off the road, and everywhere disgruntled sidemen got together into smaller combinations, and the nights began to echo with their rash, experimental sounds. A kind of underground celebrity attached itself to Edgar, for he alone seemed already to be playing something that everyone was working toward; and for a while the work itself sufficed.

But America does not give to a man commensurate to his talents. It despises or it idolizes him. He is a dog or he is a god, and no man is ever really either. Edgar experienced both positions in too short a time, and finding that what had lost him jobs two years before ("Don't play that nightmare music in *my* band!") attached disciples to him now, froze something in him that would never thaw again. The very fickleness that made him the *one* horn to everyone in those years seemed to shatter some idea of equity that even Geordie had not dreamed was crucial to him.

Irony overtook him, and drove him on to play well and at the same time scorn those who listened, to mock them, and then himself, and finally even what he played. Their life grew steadily less their own: sessions, parties, hipness; and with hipness, hip nights and hip kicks. She remembered waking to find Edgar rolling reefers for the night on an oilclothed table, in his shorts, humming to himself: " 'In a little Spanish town, 'twas on a night like this . . .' "; she remembered the dry taste of burnt grass in her throat as she came out of the ladies' room between sets to the glass of wine that kept the mouth sweet, and the lazy giggle that, unsuspecting, came up out of her when, later, standing in the warm light, feeling the warmness in her voice as if it were not hers, Edgar played a little burbling run, idiotically apt, though only (so it seemed) to her; she remembered later, still later, somewhere where Venetian blinds were down against the first of dawn, Edgar crooning, " 'Stars were peek-a-booing . . .' " as he tried to unsnap her stockings while she held his cigarette.

She remembered a wild, hot drive to Chicago in someone's car (whose was it?), during which Edgar slept in the back for almost twenty hours, one foot out the window, and she sat in the front in her slip, wearing dark glasses against the day she was unused to, while the driver (who *had* it been?) told her a story that seemed to have no beginning and no end about stealing cars in Arkansas, and she laughed and laughed. She remembered getting separated from him in Philly when they were squeezed into different raucous cabs, and somewhere eight hours later, among lights turned against the wall and perambulating people and muffled records, coming upon his face, smiling elusively, pink-gummed, as he drawled, "Baby, is it time already? . . . It ain't time yet, Baby. Is it really time?"

She remembered the money coming in, and going out, and the queer dreams through the unreal noons as night increasingly captured them, and the wild historic sessions, and the eyes drawn with weariness, and the surreptitious, confidential men pressing small white packets in the palm on credit, and the hesitation, and the what-the-hell, and eventually the hot load of junk spreading in the vein. She remembered, as well, the months going by without a trace.

"Baby, I'm gonna make the Coast for a while. This whole scene drags me now, you know."

"But I got two more weeks at the Deuces, honey, and then Cleveland—"

"Well, Baby," he said, concentrating on the radio, "you make it when you can . . ."

"What happened?" she allowed herself to ask after a pause. "What'd I do?"

He breathed heavily, eyes fluttering shut. "Well," he murmured, "I suppose you had to say that."

Cancellations; the anger of bookers, which, unwittingly, she turned on him; disputes and self-abuse; drunken reconciliations in a lower berth. . . .

But she pulled herself up short, for she did not want to think about the rest. It was nearly nine, the room was filled with dreary shadows, and the rain came down in a steady, droning hush: that most lonesome and most solemn of all city sounds. She got up, sighing, and snapped on her bedside light. The wan glow revealed Marco looking up at her guiltily, the suede pump between his paws, a piece of the innersole protruding from his mouth like a pale tongue.

She sighed peevishly and frowned, but all she said was, "You not much better than a man. Now, let that go . . ."

He backed away from the shoe, the piece of sole still sticking comically out of his mouth, and began sniffing with sheepish unconcern around the chair where, not an hour before, Edgar had slumped and smoked with much the same feigned casualness.

"You only hungry," she murmured oddly, "and you got no sense to know what for."

It was Monday night, and no one worked, though there were impromptu sessions everywhere. The night would be a long one (old friends, gossip, being pressed to sing), and who knew where the dawn would hear her last good-bye?"

"Who's bugged?" Edgar had said carelessly. "If I can't raise it, I could make the Go Hole, and pick up twenty-five or so sitting in. They're not hip I lost my card . . . This bus don't leave till six o'clock tomorrow morning. I just keep *going*." She shook her head, knowing with sudden hopeless clarity how long the night could be when it was not the first one you had gotten through since sleep.

Pushing away the thought, she took the pocket pad and stub of pencil with which she sometimes wrote out the lyrics of old songs to test her memory, and tried to concentrate. "Forget Me When I'm Gone," she spelled out in her quick, blurred hand, underlined it, and then proceeded to write down the verses, punctuating with impulsive dashes. "Speak bitterly of me—pretend I'm a pawn," she wrote halfway down the page, having to run the last words over onto the next line; and then she stopped, the melody continuing to unreel in her head. But no more words would come.

" 'Speak bitterly of me, pretend I'm a pawn, and knowing you love me,' " she crooned, trying to remember, but somehow unable to think of anything but the smell of eucalyptus: the strange, yellowed, shadeless odor of it wafted in open windows those last stunned months in L.A., when she would lie through whole afternoons, utterly motionless in the steady, unhurried perspiration of July, her mind a maze of random, disconnected wonderings, into which occasionally a clear and awful idea would force its way,

103

spoiling everything: "You alive . . . now . . . despite how it feels. If you take a pencil and jab it hard into your arm, you bleed—" Once she had even tried it, and watched the small dark welling on her flesh with curious absorption, and tasted it, tasting the lead and the drug and even, she fancied, eucalyptus . . . but no blood.

She worked somehow, dressing, making up, managing the rose. Leaving a cigarette burning on the piano when she went out into the light, she picked it up, burnt down and wet with melted varnish, as she came off, clammy down her back and thighs with tense sweat, so that she had to change three times a night. She met Edgar at the club where he was playing, or if she missed him there, tracked him down before the night was done, knowing with disquiet even then that their life was narrowing to the giggling and precautionary faces that furtively locked the door behind you when you came, narrowing toward the giddy equilibrium at the center of a maelstrom.

"Look at that," Edgar would say, his lidded eyes bright and cold, "just look! She goofed *again!*" and he would pluck the flower (forgotten in her haste to get to him) out of her hair, and turn away, pulling the petals one by one. Sometimes, later, when they got off alone, he would mumble, "Tonight I blew good. An' you know what I kept saying to myself, Baby? . . . I kept saying, 'Blow, you black bastard, blow.' He, he, he," he sniggered soundlessly.

Finally, she could not work any more (there did not seem time enough), but instead did crossword puzzles, and went out without stockings, and spent the interminable afternoons in movie houses, trying to space her next fix. Edgar went on and on, his will seemingly impervious to the habit, as if he were not flesh at all, as if time were not inexorably passing, and "that night" was not the furthest forward he could look. But time began to terrorize Geordie—just time, time that was nothing but a vague, shapeless blot to her, out of which came the occasional flicker of pain and craving when she missed a connection. And it was when she realized that only the pain had any reality, and that all the rest was drift, that she could admit she was hooked; and admitting it, decide secretly to throw the habit.

Edgar was gone most of the time just then, recklessly swirling in a sort of twilit unreality in which the only light was the sallow, detached faces (dire, odd children, they seemed to her), waiting wanly at the end of the bar each night to take him off somewhere. But never after in her life would she be able to forget him standing in the doorway of their room, noting her as she lay on week-old sheets, soggy with her own sweat, one wrist held back taut against the headboard by a pair of dime-store handcuffs (a trick she had learned in the Carolina reformatory years before, after the assault on the country road and its consequences had put her there), the key thrown across the room, a shallow glitter in a pool of sour sunlight on the floor.

"Baby," was all he said with drawled distaste, shaking his head back and forth slowly. "Baby, Baby. You are an impossible square . . ."

But, nevertheless, in the charade of his nights he brought her food, or sent someone; and sometimes sat through a morning with her, smoke from his motionless cigarette drifting across his frozen features, not listening to her pleading or her tears, on the nods, and mumbling now and again, "Yes, yes, Baby . . . yes, yes, yes . . ."

Only her mind could free her, she realized sometime during the third day (Edgar had taught her that long ago), and chained to the iron bed through two weeks of shameless horror, her flesh vanquished by its needs, her mind finally saw the dreadful captivity of the body, a poor dumb thing always gesturing outward toward food and sleep and pleasure; and seeing that, and clinging to it blindly through the worst, somehow she rested and gave her body time.

A strange solemnity enveloped her when it was over. She pulled her hair back straight from haunted cheeks, and did everything carefully for a long time. Her new mood did not mesh with Edgar's, and without dispute or agreement they saw less of one another. For a while she was curiously involved in a single thought that she found, unsullied and graphic, at the bottom of her mind every morning when she awoke: that dawn should always find us willing to arise and strive, always awaken us with despair alleviated, always mend the wounds of night, always give the body time—what strange equity in this incomprehensible life! For a while she was occupied by her amazement at this crazy truth, and hoarded it all day, and could not wonder too much where he slept or what he was doing.

But she could see his face (in her mind's eye) in the flat unhealthy glow of a street lamp—had she *ever* seen it in the sun?—at a crossing on a palm-lined boulevard where she waited for a bus. "Just back from Malibu, just this minute— We . . . I been digging the ocean, Baby, the *ocean*—or I'd been around to see you"—knowing by the surprise around his wide, weary eyes that coming upon her this way had reminded him of time, and that she had become *his* reality. "Baby, now, Baby," he mumbled, insistently. "I— How about Friday, you know? I got to see you, but now, well, I'm due, and—" So he drifted away, hurried and troubled, after the two white boys who waited, muttering to each other softly, under the next light.

There were good times, but still the change (curious and wintry and frightening as life's nameless changes always are) had come at last. Nevertheless, he came around, not realizing (because he was out of step with the day) that it had happened.

"Baby, Baby, these weird cats are blowing weird at this crazy apartment, and *every*one, I mean everyone's a head—you know, just *everyone!*" And when she said nothing: "Baby, why is it? You don't listen to me any more! It's goofy . . . You used to *listen* to me—" And he tried the old half-sneering laugh.

There was the time in the restaurant when he suddenly went to sleep in the middle of a long harangue, his forehead docile in a dish of olives; there was the syrupy all-words-run-together Georgia drawl that he took to affecting, shuffling and pop-eyed, on streets and buses; there was the first of many nights when he walked off the stand in the middle of a number, and didn't turn up again for two days. There was also the time he tried, in desperation, to turn her on again, when, waking suddenly, she saw him preparing the needle, a confused secretive giggle in his throat as he stared at her bare arm lying motionless along the blanket. Finally, she took to avoiding him altogether, having still too uncertain a grip on herself to take a chance.

But one way or another he plagued her anyway. He was at the bar with a couple of his coterie the first night she felt sure enough to work again; he turned up, pale and scornful as a ruined prince intent on doom, at private parties, inevitably making scenes. The stories of his exploits hung, thrilling, on hip lips everywhere—how he had just missed arrest in Laguna, how a rising starlet from Metro was destroying her career over him, how he had collapsed at a record session.

Geordie tried to have a life despite him. She worked hard and lived carefully and tried not to think. She even took up with a trumpeter, but the very first night, when (bewilderedly deciding it was the thing to do) she took him home with her, there was a soft, steady tapping at her door toward dawn, and opening it, she saw Edgar there in a dirty sports shirt, standing stock-still and curiously rigid, an unlit cigarette hanging from his stained lips. For a moment he looked dead at her, and then vaguely past her into the room, a peculiarly pitiful glow in his large dark eyes. But all he said was, "You got a light?" and when she produced one in dumb astonishment, he turned on his heel and went away.

Three days after that he was found wandering, half-naked, in a canyon in North Hollywood, and kept saying in the squad car: "Talk to me, mister. Tell me what's the matter now . . . Talk to me. What's the matter *now!*" Or so the story went.

But the day she heard that he had allowed himself to be committed to a state sanatorium, she packed what little she possessed and went back to New York. . . .

Eucalyptus, she thought, the pencil still poised over the paper, eucalyptus and unreality; and suddenly she experienced that flush of relief and blessed safety that overcomes someone who has just recognized a danger that is past. No . . . no, she was well out of it. God.

She looked around the room—the litter, the great dark unloved furniture, Marco trying to forget his hunger with the shoe—suddenly glad of it, suddenly able to breathe there. "And knowing you love me, forget me when I'm gone." That was the end, she realized with surprise, putting down the pencil. There were no more words.

So she got up and went to the bureau for another cigarette.

"I just keep going," he had said from that very chair, "and you know how I go when I have to. There bound to be rhythm at the Go Hole I can work with . . . I'll do some of the old ones for 'em. You know. The old solos, the old records. Sure . . . And if I watch myself I'll be all right—" But then he laughed derisively, and she winced because his self-perceptions had always been the hardest to endure. "But you never know now, you never know . . . Playing for home, I might blow something good, real good . . . You never *really* know . . . If I get me something to eat, I might blow wild for 'em . . . Once I used to blow wild—"

"Eddie, Eddie, Eddie," she moaned there alone, all against her will, closing her eyes in the desperation of remembrance, "we *all* gonna die one day . . ." for she had been overwhelmed for a moment by a sort of deadly foresight: Edgar just dying, in no noble, worthy setting but in a furnished room, as he had lived, without tragedy, perhaps still raging, perhaps merely cantankerous; his body, of which he seemed so little part, merely giving up; a death unexpected and unprepared for, without the foreknowledge that makes a man assess, or the ceremony which is proper to his death.

"Oh-h-h-h-h," she groaned at the sorrow and the horror of the thought. "What for? What for?" And then, pulling herself up short and staring in the mirror again: "Look at you, girl, just look . . . You lived, ain't you? Ain't you lived! . . . And he's a man, ain't he? Marky, he's a man, you hear me, and a man does—" But she broke off hopelessly, unable to keep up her fine bitterness, and thinking only, Why? Why? Why could she do it, and not he? How was it she could last, and he could not? In her way she had more reason than he to give up to hate. What was the difference? She had loved him once, and she should know.

"They think you white *enough*, I guess . . ∕ But don't you ever think because your wig's got flowers, it ain't no wig∕" His words came back to her as audible as an old phonograph record which in an instant telescopes the years. "You always thinking *back*, Baby . . . Be no one's *nigra* any more . . ."

But somehow, somewhere, *she* had managed to escape, and *he* had not; despite the fact that she had nothing that a woman ought to have, but had renounced the chance of home forever when she left that Charleston bar, and been damned to these lonely, puttering twilights the moment she saw Edgar, and had lost (along with the child of violence born out of her fifteen-year-old body, thankfully dead) all hope of future children, so that the wide-hipped fecundity into which she had grown was the crowning irony of all; yet she had endured and could think back, and had been (despite the ignorance and humility that had always infuriated Edgar) her own "nigra" all along. Why?

And suddenly it occurred to her that perhaps it was the rape itself that had preserved her, for in a curious way she had been complete since then. And staring at herself intently, trying to see the calicoed girl (short braids stuck out, crazy, all over her head) in the overripened woman with the smartly lacquered hair, poised there in the glass, she thought of it again: the rutted country road, shadeless in the early summer heat, the spattered flivver screeching to a halt, the two red-faced, rumpled white men lurching out, reeking of the cheap sour-marsh bourbon they peddled town to town, sweating with goofy exhilaration in the very sweat, talking dirty with boyish glee while they asked directions of her as she stood, docile, under a sweaty hand, and not thinking of the rape (she knew for sure now, and had suspected even then) until she pulled away, scare-faced, and then only thinking of it because why not? why not? And so one of them (the older one with the near-empty pint, most of which had been spilled down his shirt front) said thickly, "Hey, Austin boy-ee-ee, let's jazz her. We not gonna make no Orangeburg tonight." So that the other one (the younger one with the light, passive blue eyes) hooted out, "Ed, you a cotton-pickin', nigga-lovin' son of a bitch! . . . Ah get divvies though."

She could think (without horror) of the older one holding her down right there in the ditch, while the other one giggled and fumbled in her muslin drawers, his liquored fume coming down into her mouth. She could stare at herself now, and hear again her faint, trembling plea: "No, mister. Please, mister. No," and remember that at this he had stopped for a minute, as if bewildered by drink and sun, looking down into her rolling, terrified eyes, and then seeming to have an idea that settled his mind, for he got up, puffing slightly, and went back to the flivver and returned with a fresh pint, tearing at the seal, to mumble, actually holding her head up, "Come on, lil' gal, come on . . . get that down . . . gulp it down," actually drawing back on it when she choked, and waiting, and then giving her more, and finally taking a snort himself, and beginning again.

She could think of it without a twinge, and even look impersonally at the body to which it had been done so long ago, reflected now in that New York mirror, because the whiskey had done more than dull the pain while she lay there (the act was nothing after all, the pain nothing). But the giving of it had somehow blurred her hatred ever since as well, and taken some of the outrage out of it; and it is only outrage that cannot be endured, not agony; it is only outrage that blights and shrivels life. And Edgar had that outrage in him still. The years had blunted everything else, but that went on, no matter what he learned, no matter what he lost.

Edgar could deride the outrage, even use it, but he could not weary of it, he could not see it as the biggest drag of all. "I got some other babies I can touch," he had said with a crooked smile, knowing she would know just what he meant—white babies, jazz babies, freaks (as musicians called them) who attached themselves to hornmen, like camp followers, asking to be hurt.

She imagined him (perhaps right that minute, perhaps later that night) in a strange downtown apartment among half a dozen lost white children with sunken eyes and involved psychologies, who said over and over again at his merest word or gesture, "Yes, man, dig you absolutely," and played records to which they did not listen, pressing him with pot, far too awed, for all their hipness, to notice he was conning them. And one girl—Geordie had seen her night on night, and knew the dead-white cheeks, the faint thin lips, the blond hair chopped off short as if in purposeful violation of what was soft and yielding and female in her—that girl would smoke steadily, waiting, waiting, and then follow him into a farther room (perhaps imagining that by some indifferent glance in her direction he had selected her), and lie without a word beside him, not even putting out her cigarette; to wait, expecting at any moment to feel his crude, angry hands demand penance from her body for her race. But when he simply lay breathing heavily but without passion, she might touch him obediently, whispering, "Sweetie, sweetie," only to hear the high flutter of a tiny sigh, and the weary drawling words: "Oh, baby, don't let's put me down . . . I mean, who do you think I am—King Kong? I got nothing to use." And then after a minute: "But, you know, if I could hit you for ten or so until next week—"

Oh, yes, Geordie knew it, knew that he could go and go and go beyond the point where something personal and even foolish stopped most other men. He had no limits; there was nothing which the outrage couldn't do. It could even take him home.

"Well, *I'm* still a woman," she said firmly, knowing that although intimacy dies slowly, although it had taken years before she (who didn't even want him any more) could bear the thought of the little white girls, it was, at last, dead in her now. "I'm still a woman," she repeated, "even though he's no man no more . . ." Oh, yes, there was nothing that the outrage couldn't do, except die and leave him whole again.

"Well," she repeated, rousing herself, "no good thinking about it all night, Marky . . . Is there now? . . . Is there?" roughing his ears for him and laughing, kneeling down beside the bureau and stroking the warm soft nose, and feeling tears running down her cheeks. "Maybe he'll be all right anyway," she murmured, sniffling. "He'll probably be all right anyway . . . He fooled me so much before . . . And I don't know what to *do* about it, I don't know what to *do*—"

So she got up and blew her nose and looked at her watch. It was late, and last night's escort (the white man who owned all her records, and was thoughtful and adoring) would be ringing from the lobby in twenty minutes; and something instinctive and obedient and, yes, perhaps even Southern always made her want to be on time, so she started dressing.

She would see this one again, and probably again, and soon she would lie underneath him too, because he wanted it, and endure his earnest, faltering attempt to express to her his joy, her beauty, the *truth* of this; and would be (she knew) still out of reach to him (as finally Negro people are forever out of reach to white people, no matter how the whites strive or how they yearn); and so watch it fade in his eyes, and die, knowing another man would come to touch her.

Why, she thought idly, taking her dress out of its paper envelope, did white people want to touch you all the time, want always to get inhuman close to you, and drink out of your glass, and share your cigarette, and hold your hand? She guessed she knew: guilt . . . a strange and sorrowful guilt that demanded that they show you, over and over again, that your being colored meant nothing to them, nothing, nothing, *nothing*. And there was no way to respond to that, not even for her to whom such intricacies had long ago become unreal; and so she knew another man would come, and just as certainly go, and she would be sorry but not broken.

And even though she would weep over them (though never the slow, almost emotionless tears that she had shed just now), and fight with them, and sleep alone in a horror of despair, and humiliate and be humiliated because of the complexities that always seem to thwart the simple yearning of humans for each other—even though she would go through it all again, and then again, and be amazed some other evening by the baffling length of life, she knew that in Edgar she had had enough to last her all her days, enough of wanting. And beyond that, she knew that Edgar would die, and she would die one day, but that until then they would care and rage and be helpless, and somehow go on.

Putting on her lipstick carefully, her large calm eyes still shining with those sweet involuntary tears, she felt that that was all the wisdom that a woman could amass.

"Yes, yes," she said aloud, "yes."

She stood for a moment, thinking about it, and then she sat down at the window once again—the vast night outside still murmurous with rain—to wait quietly for whatover that night might bring.

RIFF

Cleo waited too, wondering what was taking Edgar so long in the men's room, just beginning to keep a worried eye on the door, for Edgar had been in there over ten minutes, having gotten up in the middle of a word, having talked a long time, having finally said, "And I always thought *she* couldn't make it. Man, I used to worry about how she'd ever make her bookings and get her mikes set up just right. I used to give her quarters for her flowers every night, and all the time *this* was how it was fixing to come out, all the time it was working out so now I'd have to bum from *her.*" He swallowed the astonishment with a gulp of beer. "Well, I touched her every other way, I guess . . . And she only give me fifteen dollars anyway, so I ain't got near enough, I still got to *think,*" knotting his forehead, struggling for unscrupulousness again, as if Geordie had corrupted the one thing that could see him through, his own perversity. "But she was good, all right. You remember it. Baby was *good* . . . I mean, I may have thrown it away, but I threw away something goo—" and right there, in the middle of that muttered word, he had broken off, sliding backward off the stool again, to lurch toward the men's room to be sick.

And now Cleo, too, out of the kaleidoscope that day and evening had become in his addled brain, managed to get off his stool and head back for the door—expecting nothing, thinking nothing, trying only to miss tables and not stumble—to push it open and be somewhat sobered by the thick, abrasive reek of disinfectant, and the soap-sloppy washbowl, and the graying porcelain of the urinals full of butts, and the cheap peeling cubicles where a man could be alone with his weakness or his sin, or whatever was most secret in his life, and (horrible and unblinking over everything) the dim naked bulb hanging awry on the braided wire, shedding its baleful light unjudgingly.

To his muddled surprise, someone else stood in the dimmest corner near the paper-towel dispenser, sobering and embarrassing Cleo all the more, so that he went to the bowl and witlessly began to wash his hands, trying to snatch a glimpse of Edgar's feet below the skimpy doors of the cubicles. And then he turned, flushing and horrified, on that someone in the corner, realizing it was Edgar.

He was standing bolt upright, hands hung thoughtlessly at his sides, face averted, motionless and rigid and somehow shocking in that posture (because anyone, just anyone might have walked in and caught him there), and it flashed through Cleo's mind: "He's dead, he's stacked up dead against the wall, and it's gone and happened while I wasn't looking," but then he heard the labored, careful breath; and, eyes bulging, he realized that

Edgar, his nose pressed into the corner between the cubicle and the towel rack, close in enough to look as if he was standing by himself, was fast asleep!

Impulsively he touched the arm nearest him, just touched it carefully, for he had thought, "It can't even lift the horn any more, but once, once—"

"Man, man, *man,* you got to stop this, you got to eat! Man, man!—"

And then, to his further consternation, Edgar suddenly turned on him a small blood-shot eye, so questioning that for a moment Cleo wondered if he had been sleeping after all.

"What? What?"—the voice rasping and thick. "What's happened? . . . What time is it? I fell behind—"

"Man, it's after nine-thirty, but you got to eat, and—"

Edgar passed one mute hand over his eyes, able to stand there before the wide-eyed boy and do it, even able to catch a glimpse of all he had come down to in the grimy mirror, and not think twice. "Well, I still got time then. I just thought, why not, why not?" He hurrumphed to himself, rubbing his mouth. "I used to sleep in the sections years ago, my horn right in my mouth up in the back row. Heh, heh, heh, I fooled *every*one in them days. They all figured I was thinking."

Cleo ran some water, too embarrassed to speak, hating his embarrassment, as Edgar's eyes wavered shut again, and he murmured, "Man, it's crazy, but I don't feel so good . . . How about that for crazy? . . . But like there's something in my belly won't wait any longer, you know. I mean, that's how it feels. I even heard it while I was asleep, and I stood real straight and quiet, but it wouldn't stop." He breathed heavily, as if trying to reach the bottom of his lungs. "You think food, eh? Sure, that's it. Kid, you right for once. And a drink too, a big, long, settling drink. Cause I threw up all them others."

He put his hands down into the water and then put them on his face, uncaring that he splashed his shirt or that the rivulets ran down into his cuffs. He rubbed his face, letting the excess drip down his tallowy cheeks and hang in curious bright drops on his mustache.

"You sure you got no money, kid? You sure? Maybe you know someone you could borrow from," he said dumbly as he yanked out a paper towel. "Everyone knows someone" —the towel coming to sodden pieces as he wiped his face. "I mean, what am I gonna do? Cause I got to get out, I really do." He peered at Cleo with nothing between them now but the shame he did not feel or care about. "And you play pretty good piano, too. Don't you listen to me . . . Only, cut off your phrases, cut 'em off so they can say 'uh-uh' between, so they can hear everything you *don't* blow, you get it?" and incredibly he gave a large murky wink, and nodded, pursing his lips confidentially. "That's the secret, you know. You remember that . . . But, you sure? I mean, think, man, cause I'm good for it. You ask anyone." And then all of a sudden: "Say, where's my horn, anyway? D'you just *leave* it out there!" the eyes flaring up. "Jee-suss, you colored-boy piano players're every goddamn one of you alike! Just cause you can't *carry* it, you trust the whole square world . . . Man, I lose that horn," he said angrily as they went out the door, "and you *gotta* get up the loot, I don't care where!"

But the horn was there, just where Cleo had left it, and a bassist with whom he worked at the Go Hole was there too, having a Scotch.

"That's right," Cleo thought despairingly at the first sight of the New Haven suit, the tasseled loafers, the argyles, "that's right. It could have been no one, or it could have been anyone else, but I guess it figured to be *him* if it had to be someone." For Billy James Henry was one of those solemn, pretentious younger jazzmen who were everywhere now, who had all been to Juilliard for composition, talked intelligently to Milhaud, and used the Schillinger method in their labored, atonal scores that carefully never swung *too* much; who all felt that jazz could *be* an art (forgetting that it was), and frowned on those who liked a hard beat, and worked the clubs reluctantly; who wrote arrangements with names like "The Thinking Reed," and really felt more comfortable in Europe. They always confused and irritated Edgar, and instantly his face assumed an expression of languid hauteur.

"Say, I hear you're trying to get out of town," Billy James said immediately, without getting up, frowning at Edgar's wide, florid, stained tie as if that, right there, was everything about jazz that most irritated him, his own tie being narrow, knitted, dark. "I heard you're trying to get the morning *bus,* but that can't be right, eh? . . . Hi there, man," he added to Cleo, noting his weary face with an impenetrable purse of disapproval.

"Now, isn't that a drag!" Edgar drawled, looking down his nose. "Cause I just planned to slip out without nobody knowing . . . Man, I told you, and I told you," he fretted pettishly to Cleo, "but you probably been phoning everybody *any*way."

Billy James eyed him expressionlessly. "No, I had to call Junius about my record date next week . . . But he said you were hung up because of *money,* man," he emphasized the word casually. "Well, I know it *happens,* but—"

Edgar sipped his beer with a trembling hand that managed an absurd urbanity. "Now, man, ain't that just like Junius though? I want to tell you! . . . That cat never could get nothing straight. I mean, that's what comes from living with your mother that way when you full grown. I bet he don't even blow his own nose," replacing the near-empty glass and surveying everything haughtily. "Man, I was trying to get back ten he owes *me,* is all, and like usual he got it all mixed up." There was something ghastly in his smile. "But I can't stay bugged at piano players, no, sir! They all like that. Did you ever notice it, man? . . . Like this kid here been following me around all day, like some little old puppy dog. Ain't you, kid? Ain't you?" And when he turned a desperate, jesting eye on him, Cleo noticed, with sinking heart, that his mustache was glistening with an even crescent of beer foam.

"Oh, sure, I'm a little short," he drawled on, cruelly unaware of it. "Like you say, it sometimes *happens.* Isn't that the way you put it, man? . . . And I thought I'd take the bus because it take *longer,* you know. See something of the country . . . Them planes—I don't know," he argued with himself, "you just get yourself settled, and you got to move again. And I can't make them goofy *landings,*" at which point a single drop of beer ran into the corner of his mouth from the mustache, held there for a moment, and then went on to hang perilously on his chin. Billy James' eyes were aloof and disgusted, as if such a display might be expected from a man who still wore that kind of suit and still played that sort of jazz, content with both; but Edgar did not notice. "Oh, I got some checks comin' through, but I look up this morning, and here I am low on cash. What do you know— But say," he interrupted himself, "maybe you could slip me—"

"Oh, I'd gladly write you out a check," Billy James put in immediately, as if he had been expecting it, "but my account's all fouled up this month." He looked petulantly at Edgar's dripping chin and then looked away, constrained and even annoyed by the impropriety, and Cleo knew that the last thing Billy James could ever bring himself to do was mention it. "But come on over to the Hole in about an hour," he went on uneasily, attempting to be generous. "It's free-for-all night, you know. Nothing *serious,* nothing difficult . . . And I'll be glad to fix it up for you, man. There's nobody much there on Mondays . . . And I see you got your horn," looking down on the ancient, scuffed case. "You know, I used to be sort of sentimental about *my* old canvas cover, too," he said idly. "But you come on over, man. We can pick up on some of the old ones, can't we, Cleo? It might even be kicks—"

But Edgar too was staring at the horn, as if he had not heard, the drops on his chin glittering as his lips twitched slightly, and for the first time Cleo thought, "He can't make it. He's a drunk, sick old man, who spills, who's come too far already, but won't quit . . . Why won't he quit? Why won't he just *quit!* . . . He can't make it, no one could make it."

"No, man," Edgar murmured queerly, eyes fluttering shut for just a moment, "I ain't gonna blow," and he looked away abruptly, rubbing his chin. "I got too much I got to—"

But the words lapsed as he brought his hand away wet. He looked at it distractedly for an instant, and then understood and tried to wipe the beer away without their noticing, his fingers shaping down his chin as he stumbled on, and then gathering into a fist of shame when he realized that they knew.

"Now, how about that for crazy—" he began, but then looked at them sharply with something in his punished face that was worse than his humiliation.

"You shouldn't let a man sit here with his chin all sloppy," he said with dumb reproach. "You could have *laughed* so I'd catch on . . . Man, what kind of thing is that." He turned his eyes on Cleo. "You could have wiped my chin for me, kid. You could have taken me aside . . . Man, in my time—" But he crushed the thought with a short, hissing, obscene word that so shocked Cleo, despite years of hearing it used indifferently to express all kinds of moods, that he could not look at the eyes—the dumb, hurt, stubborn eyes. All he could do was say, "Man, man, you got to stop. Please. You got to eat. Then you come on over and make your fare, and that's that . . . Cause what else *is* there?"

But when he did look, Edgar was on his feet again, the lees of whatever it was that had kept him on them all day long, enabling him to do it one more time. "I *ain't* gonna blow," he repeated furiously. "I *ain't* . . . And it don't matter anyway, I got one last cat that I can try. Don't you think I don't . . . And it don't *matter*, you know. You'll find out . . . You put it beside some other things, and playing music don't really matter one damn bit!"

But it was not until after he had gone, and Billy James shook a frowning face and said, "Man, I didn't know he was drinking so much these days, but I sure hope he doesn't sit in with us tonight, because I can't stand carrying these older guys when they're all boozed up"—it was not till then that Cleo looked, and saw the empty stool where the horn had lain so long.

CHORUS:CURNY

"Goodness sakes! would a runaway nigger run south?"

TWAIN

To his band, gathered in random groups around the music stands of the Polly Rehearsal Studios, the fact that Curny Finnley had still not shown up by ten-thirty that night was not surprising. They did not grumble over their containers of cold coffee because of it, for most of them had worked for him before, and knew that he was never happier or more at ease with the world than when he was steadily ambling along—late. Some were even certain that he arranged his afternoons so that no matter where he was, he was always due somewhere else. They yawned and jawed and waited, knowing he would come.

His personal manager, Mr. Willy Owls, came first—a pinched, nervous white man, incomprehensibly dedicated to jazz, always gobbling pills and striking his forehead, his

123

drawn gay little eyes and nicotine-stained forefinger testi-
fying to the harassed fatalism of his craft.

"Okay, gentlemen," he announced in his high, snappish
voice. "Tonight let's don't forget that Young America
likes to dance," exactly like a comic scoutmaster repeating a homily to an obstreperous gang of boys, hoping
that eventually it might take hold.

"Not to this band they don't," someone cackled.

With sardonic little rim shots the drummer punctuated
Mr. Owls' ritual removal of his wide-lapelled double-
breasted overcoat. Off one shoulder—klook; off the other—
klook; fold across the middle—klook-klook; drape over a
chair back—klook-a-boom.

"All right, all right, gentlemen, have your yocks, but
then let's get down to work. You all gotta be on that bus
at seven-thirty in the morning no matter how many laughs
I get."

"How can us field hands hoe without the Colonel?"
someone called out.

"Yes, man, there's nobody here yet but roosters."

Somebody blew the loud chirrup of a barnyard dawn
on his tenor sax.

"Does anyone know where he is?" Mr. Owls said, lighting one cigarette from another with the forlorn yet resolute
awkwardness of a decent man trying to do too many things
at once. "I don't suppose anyone knows where he is . . ."

"Man, not even his old lady knows where he's at."

"But she knows he's talking. He may be all alone, but
that man's talking."

"Don't you know it."

"Man, I'm no square. I'm hip."

"All right now, gentlemen, all right," Mr. Owls broke
in with weary briskness, clapping his hands and hurrying
up and down before the music stands. "Let's run through

something till he gets here. What are we working on to-night?"

"Who knows?"

"The Colonel knows."

"And he ain't here."

"I'm hip."

"All *right*," Mr. Owls repeated darkly, leveling a finger at the horseplay. "You boys get your kicks, go ahead, yock it up—but come seven-thirty that bus leaves for Pittsburgh if there's nobody on it but me and the driver. This band's gonna open tomorrow night if I gotta hire *him* on drums while I whistle. So go ahead, go ahead."

He sighed under his burdens with theatrical resignation, conveying his unshakable conviction that the next day and the next months on the road and perhaps even the next years would hold nothing but lost sleep and hotel rooms and wrangling and all the other monumental headaches of the band business, and that he was made for saner things. "Well," he concluded heavily, cheering up at having found a fate to which he might surrender, "I'd better start phoning."

The band settled back among the instrument cases and folding chairs and unshaded lights, a few blowing scraps of old songs to limber up, some chatting, all knowing (as itinerant jazz musicians, who had spent their lives along the maindrags, downtowns, southsides and westends of America) that no amount of phoning would ever locate Curny Finnley, that he was just downstairs somewhere in the huge, unreal glow of Broadway's perpetual Saturday night, staring with fascination at an untended machine winding ropes of taffy, gleefully dodging cabs at cross streets like a broken field runner, or was in the middle of some Socratic dialogue that had begun with; "Man, now you take life—just any old fat-mouth, droop-eyed *life*—

some cat's *own* life! . . . Man, isn't that crazy, isn't that sick!"

As it happened (though he had probably done all these things that night), just at that moment he ambled in the door, all smiles, in a massive astrakhan beaded with rain.

"Hey, let's go, let's go," he drawled, his mouth dropping open into a happy gape as he surveyed the room with a wide and jesting eye. "I'm so full of ideas tonight, I'm gonna *spoil!*"

"Now, what kind of way is this to run a delicatessen," Mr. Owls began severely, but Curny fixed him with an especially ingratiating grin, and announced, "Man, don't scold now, don't scold. You'll get sick . . . And I tell you I'm a horn screamer tonight, I'm a *caution* . . ." He extricated himself from the immense coat exactly as a fatter man might struggle out of a phone booth. "Cool me down, somebody . . . Distract me, is what I'm saying . . . Pour water on me, or I'm gonna *rot!*"

Everyone guffawed, for this kind of verbal extravagance was as typical of Curny as the nut-brown, pencil-thin panatelas he smoked and flourished between beringed fingers, and the soft, rakish fedoras he wore with a vaguely unscrupulous flair, and the completely inimitable goatee on which he braced the mouthpiece of his trumpet while blowing, and (indeed) the whole indefinable air of the river gambler or the eccentric planter that seemed so illogical in a hefty, pleasant-featured Negro.

"But you watch out," he chided the band with a twinkle, "one of these days I'm gonna get *grave*. Man, I'm gonna take time *off* for it . . . Hey, where is he? Where'd he go?" he suddenly interrupted himself, looking everywhere with quick darts of his head, and removing his cigar to gesture with. "Man, he got eaten by the elevator—"

Just then the door opened and someone came in carrying a six-pack of beer like a satchel, whom everyone in the band instantly recognized (not without amazement) as Edgar Pool.

"Hey, it's the Horn," whispered a trumpet man to his neighbor, staring at Edgar as at a living legend who, despite latter-day lean years, still has the power to evoke awe in those who had grown up on his records. "Man, don't he look terrible."

"How'd you get *loose?*" Curny said, replacing the cigar at that ceiling-pointed angle dear to wise-cracking and imaginative men. "Owlie, look who I'm comin' down Sixth Avenue ten minutes ago and I meet! Old Horn, old Edgar . . . Man, what you got there, what you carrying, what *is* that?"

"I never could make the water in them coolers up here," Edgar said, holding the beer forward with a sour, tipsy little smile. "I had them put it on your tab, all right?"

He stood there, coatless, sodden with rain, an indomitable, murky light in his small quick eyes as he coughed —a cough like the struggle of a kitchen sink to unstop itself; a cough compounded of coffee and cigarettes and liquor and sleeplessness and general abuse; a cough suggesting some tearing loose of essential tissue, some deep damage where it could not be seen or even known for sure. He coughed into his hand as he looked about the room incuriously, as if nothing there was of any interest to him, as if he did not even notice the cough, though, so clearly, it was bigger now than he. He wiped his hand indifferently on his baggy trouser leg, saying, "About a dollar-forty was what it come to."

"Y-e-s," somebody whispered with hushed admiration, "that man don't *care.*"

"You can take it out of the twenty," Edgar was continuing in a hoarse unhurried drawl. "Or I can owe it to you on top of the rest. It's all the same to me, man."

"Yee-ow! I almost forgot about it," Curny exclaimed,

halfway out of his suit coat and already revealing two-inch-wide plaid suspenders, gaudy against the pearl-gray shirt. "Owlie, you got twenty cash on you? We negotiating a loan here, but I'm short on everything but eyes."

"I got five and I consider myself lucky. That's just about what I came into this business with."

Curny stared in mock amazement, then he snorted almost soundlessly and crooned, "Man, loot is just around the oob-la, don't you know about the oob-la? . . . Well—well—well." He shook open a chair with a sharp whack, and said to Edgar, "Here, dad, have a brew while I get these boys set up . . . The cat in the cigar store downstairs takes my checks if I play it cool."

Edgar studied the wall clock uncertainly, although everything about him seemed destinationless, and then sat down with great care. His smile involved only his lips. "Man, I got time," he said finally. "Go ahead, finish up what you got to do."

"Have a smoke. Guaranteed Havana, Meyer Gonzalez, 118th Street, six for a dollar . . . Here, have two," Curny added grandly, fishing in his jacket. "We just got this one new thing to run through, then we'll cut— Hey, what's this?" he exclaimed pulling out, along with the cigars, some dog-eared correspondence, a wad of trip-insurance forms and two of those metal-framed photographs that penny-arcade machines produce all wet and acrid and ugly from behind their sleazy curtains. "I got my picture taken . . . Look at that. Why is it I like to get my picture taken? You think maybe I'm sick? . . . Don't he look *goofy* though! . . . Well," he concluded, throwing the whole batch of stuff on a chair and handing Edgar the cigars, "I'm too *deep* tonight, I get dizzy just considering it— But hold on, man, then we'll cut. I don't want you hocking your horn for no hardtime twenty bucks . . . What would old Horn be without no horn to blow?" he added, innocently pleased with the joke.

But Edgar's empty smile disappeared down into his mouth at this remark, and for a moment his features were so devoid of expression that they seemed molded out of lacquered cardboard. But all he said was, "Them thin kind smoke down too fast unless they're rolled real tight," and he fingered the cigar, making audible crinkles to which he listened with cocked ear. Nevertheless, he bit off the end between discolored teeth, spit it out with a distasteful curl of his lips, shaped and reshaped the fresh end, and lit up with loud plops, to sit scowling and cross-legged, one splashed sock worked down off his heel into the shoe, revealing a thin, spavined ankle. He puffed with steady detachment, posing in a growing cloud of smoke, through which he stared, gloomy and unblinking, at Curny's magnificent suspenders, crisscrossed on his back.

"Dig," the drummer murmured to the bass, indicating Curny's head bent over the lectern. "He don't want to see Horn now. Like he feels too *good* to see him."

It was true enough. For though Curny was one of those garrulous, high-spirited clowns that America still occasionally produces, as if to balance out the gloomy poets (like Edgar) who walk her main-street midnights composing maledictions, he was no less perceptive of the dark side of things than the poet. Rhetoric (wild, wordy and inflated) was his natural medium; the distance between reality and the ideal, his ironic subject; and he could always find something to slap his thigh about, even in a certified disaster.

Thomas "Colonel" Finnley was this tireless, authentic windbag (heir of the extravagant Mississippi boaster with his epic oaths, and the grandiloquent county politician stumping the hustings with a barrel of "hard," and the loquacious frontier journalist to whom life was rich and violent and interesting), and when jazz buffs (heirs of no tradition) mentioned his name it was always with the fond head-shaking laugh of the schoolmarm over the incorrigible, impish prankster.

Curny was inexhaustible. He had stood at his ease, chin faintly pecking to the bass like an insouciant chicken, before the concentrated roar of half a dozen wild bands, in the last ten years alone; night after night, from Lexington Avenue to La Cienaga, he had raised his polished horn to just-licked lips and blown the effortless, eccentric, double-tempo bop glissandi that long ago had caused such older Dixie trumpet masters as Brahmin Lightcap to mutter prophecies of "busted chops" and "ruint embouchure."

Curny had had many joyful nights (kicks lay everywhere for him, after all—more, more than he could ever take advantage of), and they had left their marks on him: deep laugh lines etched about his mouth, and a fine spidering of wrinkles all around his eyes. He was always ready to holler and talk and go, and he reminded people that laughter (whatever it may or may not do for the soul) keeps a man looking young. "Curn, you getting fat," they said, but it was always for lack of any other noticeable change in him.

Though he was, in certain ways, the most iconoclastic musician that modern jazz had produced (one of that introverted group of rash experimentalists who had created, in bop, a music that few could play and to which only the equally rash would listen), nevertheless he was always forming a new band "to hip the public, and incidentally make loot"—a band jerry-built each time out of wild hopes, esoteric arrangements and bone-grinding schedules, which invariably came to no good end after a few months, a few records and a sobering look at the overhead, in some out-of-the-way city on the road.

For all his sartorial affectation of a genteel plantation past, Curny lived almost entirely in glittering future schemes. "This time we'll lay on the entertainment with an old steam drill," he would exult to his patient and skeptical wife, Libby. "Every time we get on the stand it'll be like an act, a camp, a hype. We'll make the people think we *like* what we're doing! Yes, sir!" And six months later in Duluth, in the rain, he would pay off the saxes, slip an extra twenty to the trombone (with a habit and two ulcers to support), pack his elegant suits and gaudy neckwear, and catch a sleeper back to New York, to arrive each time, undaunted and optimistic, already full of fresh plans.

He had made money. Certainly, of all the originators of modern jazz he was the most successful, but the notoriety, the network remotes, the astronomical record sales and the river of cash for which he so schemed always eluded him. His bands were invariably uneven, boisterous, advanced. Each time he would go into rehearsals with the firmest resolutions, and each time he got carried away. It was no matter that each time Mr. Owls opined, "Curn, it's wild, the greatest band you've ever had, but it'll bomb because it's too far out for the average ginmill owner." Curny simply loved big, complex, *funny* arrangements, dense with conflicting section work, buoyed by relentless, driving rhythm, but (above all) *loud*—straining the ears with the prodigious volume of sheer noise that only the huge lurch of a swinging band, almost out of control and blowing just a little beyond its limit, can produce. Each time this left the dancers shuffling from foot to foot.

On top of this, the rigorous estheticians of modern jazz, who deplored any attitude toward music other than one which produced the outward symptoms of a migraine headache, liked to describe Curny, with malicious relish, as a "comedian who doubled on trumpet." And yet his humor was curiously indicative of the outlook of the young postwar Negro, and hip musicians reveled in him. No one was positive when he had first been dubbed "Colonel," but everybody knew that it referred to the Kentucky, rather than the Army variety, and no doubt Curny had selected the title himself, already giggling at its possibilities. It was part of his whimsically inverse reaction to race prejudice. For where the older Dixieland musicians had been content to play the good-time, landsakes Uncle Tom for the white folks, Curny (with a twist of poker-faced satire) liked to affect the haberdashery and verbal style of a landed Southern gentleman—a caricature that was fiendishly detailed but for the single, disarming fact that he was a Negro.

The stories were already part of the folklore of jazz: how once Curny had asked a young Princeton boy near the stand if he would pass up an extra chair and, on receiving it, had said with his huge, canny grin, "That's mighty white of you"; how Curny cut through the proprieties of praise when speaking of other Negro musicians by saying, "Let's call a spade a spade, man. That cat outthinks everyone"; how Curny had once replied to a famous expatriate Negro writer who insisted on the ingrained prejudice of all whites: "You mean, that's why ofays are born? . . . But, daddio, while it's true I wouldn't let my sister marry one, that strikes me as a guaranteed *drag!*"

And yet, despite this, all men have their moody sides—clowns perhaps more than most—and those in his band who had known Curny longest, knew him as a perceptive, highly inventive musician, a "wig" as primarily cerebral jazzmen are dubbed, whose talent was continually at war with his desire to succeed in the eyes of the square world. They also knew that there are friends whom even clowns cannot bear to see, because they invariably trouble and upset everything, bringing up old, plaguing, unpleasant thoughts just by the way they frown and light their cigarettes, and so now they kept sharp eyes on Edgar Pool's gloomy countenance, knowing that Edgar was this friend to Curny; perhaps remembering also that Curny sometimes said, "Man, I agree, Edgar's the greatest. I mean, *no*body can play with him any more. So that must prove it."

"Okay, let's go, let's go," he was bubbling now, reaching into a huge brief case, and hurling copies of a new arrangement in all directions. "Hey, what's this you got here?" he said, pausing to study the sheet music that was already on the racks. "Man, this thing is from the *old* book, this thing is all used up! Who set up around this chicken coop anyway? . . . Here, pass up all them number ninety-fours, come on, come on—'Mississippi Blood'—we're taking that one out, cause I've got a real screamer here! Eeee-ooow!"

His arms by now were overflowing with music, which he kept taking in and passing out, as if for the sheer goofy fun of it, getting everything mixed, dropping and stooping, chattering all the while in a giggling drawl punctuated by sudden guffaws as he fell behind. "*Now*," he finally said, heaping the rejected score on the nearest chair. "Let's get going. We don't want old Horn to hock his sax because we're shufflin'."

"Man, what a lot of *paper!*" Edgar suddenly remarked in a hoarse and obstinate voice, unmistakably touched with the faint scorn of the small-group musician for everything connected with a big band. He opened a beer can with a loud report. "You gotta extra bus for all them arrangements?"

There were a few titters from the band, and Curny, fiddling with his trumpet case, pounded a chair back with a roar. "Man, you kill me, I'll die, I'll crump . . ."

"What *is* this thing anyway?" someone said, perusing the new lead sheet.

"Looks like corn-shucking music to me—"

"Yah, what's this 'Alabam' written up here? I ain't gonna play none of that hush-puppy jazz."

"Now, slow down," Curny shouted over the babble, hands argumentatively on hips. "This here's 'Stars Fell On,' that's what's written up there. Only we do it a little weird . . . Can't nobody read?"

"Read? They won't even let me go to school with 'em—"

"Now, saxes jump in at letter D, and, man, when I say jump, I mean come down, stomp on it, *gouge* . . . And, George, up here I want lots of compa-compa-comp, right there . . . And we do it crisp now, you dig? . . . *Bay*-do, bay*do*, bay*do*, *bah!* Lots a drums, lots a drums," he finished, standing stock-still, blank-faced, brows raised as a sort of comic announcement that something more was coming. "Only we call it '*Bombs* Fell On Alabama'!"

The drummer made a resounding klook-a-boom, and everything was in an uproar again.

"For pete's sake," Mr. Owls pleaded, holding forth his wrist, as if even the boys in the back could read the time.

"Man, quit laughing or you'll hurt yourself," Curny snickered, running over the stops of his trumpet with a dazzling twiddle of deft fingers. "But, come on," he shouted. "Libby says get home by two or pick up my notice— You guys trying to bug me with my old lady? Let's try it from the top . . ."

Holding his horn up and ready, Curny tapped off *one, two,* shoulders and back gathering toward *three,* on which the whole band came down with a great roar, the transition from silence into sound being simply obliterated in an instant—an effect dear to Curny's heart. They got along well enough, until the place that the saxes entered with a burbling little riff, and then a piercing two-fingered whistle brought them to an uneven halt.

"What're you doing?" Curny drawled in wonderment. "That sounds like day-old coffee, right there. What're you doing?"

"The drums too *heavy*, man," a querulous voice said all of a sudden. "You can't hear to think with all that rumpus—"

Curny turned around to find Edgar sipping from his beer can and looking at him with cold eyes.

"Man, I like a small, quiet drum; just a light, brushy drum—" Edgar said. "You don't want no whoom-whoom-whoom when you work . . . And a respectful piano, you know?" he added, puffing imperturbably.

Curny decided to laugh, and doubled over in a breathless snicker, at which Edgar stared, unmoved. There was some shifting around among the chairs, and a few coughs.

"All right then, let's try it again, and you hear the Horn, Billy? Go easy on that tub this time . . . Let's try it that way."

The band worked smoothly, shoulder to shoulder, eyes skipping over the score as they rocked back and forth in unison, and then Curny lifted his horn, leaned back against the sound as against an invisible wall, inflated his cheeks until it looked as though he had wedged two apples into them, and blew a rollicking, exuberant chorus that veered and lagged and then spurted ahead with good-humored cussedness—the solo of a man not so much inspired as simply infused with delight at his own skill. Every now and then, eyes bright, he would peek over the bell of his horn in Edgar's direction, only to find him restively trying to open another can. Curny finished in a wild upflare of notes that seemed to deny the worth of anything but joy, toward which, nevertheless, Edgar's puritanical face refused to even turn. Then he waved the band to a halt again.

There was a clearly audible klook as the beer opener finally worked, and an equally audible: "The kind they give out in groceries ain't even sharp enough to cut your wrists."

"You shoulda kept up with me," Curny complained. "You shoulda come right back when I finished . . . Now let's get it brisk. Like uh-uh-uh," pecking out a beat with his chin, sharp cracks of thumb and forefinger punctuating the downward stroke of a pumping arm. "What's the matter? Who ate back there and who didn't? . . . There's a coupla heavy bellies somewhere who don't *care!* You getting fat and sloppy. You *nodding!* . . . Now, come on, uh-uh-uh-uh!"

So they began again. Acquainted with the arrangement now, the band swung so cohesively into it that even Mr. Owls, his lap full of bus schedules that kept falling open to unmanageable length, began tapping his foot—albeit in a rhythm unrelated to the one they played. They got past the difficult entry of the saxes, they came back crisply after Curny's solo, and when the trombones took up the lead, plunging ahead into virgin territory, Curny followed their burring sweeps over the piano with an ecstatic grin and convulsive hunchings of his shoulders as he waved them down, leaving the piano man still wide-handing the chords for a moment after everyone else had quit.

"*Now* you're picking cotton," he exclaimed delightedly, executing a clumsy flat-footed twirl. "Only right there—"

"But, you know, man, I'd slow it down a little," the same hoarse and querulous voice piped up again. "Them trombones are tripping all over themselves. And you got that *loud* piano anyway . . ." Edgar flipped his cigar ash on the stack of rejected arrangements without so much as turning his head. "Whyn't you just cut the trombones? . . . Man, I'd cut them right out."

"But they're real cute right there, dad, they're real funny—"

"Well, if you trying to be *funny*—" Edgar replied contemptuously, lifting his can, and then adding, "I worked a band once where we had them lighted shoes, them phosphorous shoes . . . And the trombones worked the slide with their feet when the lights went out—" He snatched a mirthful, knowing glance at the bandmen, as though to exclude them from his ridicule.

Curny rubbed his neck, deliberating, and then turned on a large ingratiating smile. "Look, man, there's no reason to hang you up this way . . . Why didn't I think of it! That cat'll cash the check if I write you out a *note*. He don't need to *see* me—" Already he was searching for a pencil.

"But it's no trouble," Edgar replied evenly, lounging back exactly as if the spindly chair were comfortable. "I got time. You go ahead."

"I could go phone him from down the hall—"

"But, man, this is sort of kicks for me. I ain't heard a band work out for *years*, not since I got steady jobs with a quartet."

"Or have Owlie go down there with you—"

Edgar's grin was oily with insincerity. "But, man, I can wait . . . I really can. I'll just have another brew, and you go right ahead."

Curny heaved a tiny, despairing sigh, and then began laughing again with empty hilarity as he turned back to the lectern. "All right then," he exclaimed. "All right, we might as well get on . . ."

"Just keep them trombones *down*, man," Edgar offered pleasantly. "You know."

And so began a curious struggle to get through the

number. A mocking, almost spectral expression had come over Edgar's face, as if the bitter memory of a thousand dreary rehearsal halls and the veritable avalanche of music paper that had thwarted his horn for years had possessed him, like an imp of the perverse. He rose unsteadily and walked forward while the band worked (as if he had gotten it into his head that they were going to try it his way); he listened skeptically, the tipsy frown deepening with impatience, fingers drumming on his beer can; he shook his head in such short, conclusive, petulant negatives that Mr. Owls stared at him in alarm, only to see him actually start to snap his fingers for attention, lips pursed like a temperamental impresario who is in such a perfect swirl of self-delusion that he does not realize that his presence occasions only groans. When no one noticed this, Edgar began clapping his hands, until Curny turned in astonishment, unable to believe his ears. The band went right ahead anyway, in a stubborn effort to at least get to a new part of the arrangement before having to go back. But when this only brought forth vexed cries of "Wait a minute, now wait a minute," and an audible stamp of the foot, they quit all at once, everyone deciding at the same instant that rebellion was hopeless.

"I'll bet that bus'll wait *anyway*," someone muttered, wiping the words away with the back of his hand, for Edgar now stood swaying at the lectern, haughty and self-satisfied, holding his beer can like a cocktail glass, between delicate, crooked fingers, and actually tapping for order with a single blunt forefinger.

Curny appeared to have decided that only steadfast and unrelenting good humor could cope with Edgar, but all his grins and nods and jokes seemed only to make Edgar more critical. He smoked and drank and coughed. He began capering up and down before the band, imitating the sound of the music by a wriggle of his hips and hoarse-throated little squeals, an expression of irrepressible mockery contorting his mouth. Curny snapped his suspenders and scratched his neck, and guffawed with increasing discomfort.

"All right, all right," he said, waving his hands tirelessly. "Let's change that part then. Put in an extra bli-ah for the trumpets right there— I like them bli-ahs anyway . . . Bli-ah, bli-ah-ah," he crooned, trying it out. "Okay, put in another bli-ah at letter L . . . Coy-eyed, suck-thumb bli-ah, sure, sure . . ."

But there was no satisfying Edgar. His gestures had a rash exaggeration that made everyone wary; his face suggested that all kicks were transitory; he would not be swayed by any effort to please him. Somehow the hunger wanted no food; clearly the need was insatiate; baldly the stare refused to deviate.

"But, man," he explained with weary condescension, "them horns are just too *loud* . . . You can't hear that pretty little part right there—"

By now Mr. Owls was unscrewing the caps of pill bottles and looking for the water cooler, and even Curny seemed about to clutch his head.

"But, Horn, you know when you got fifteen men like this you can't just have 'em sit around grinning at the chicks. These cats'll get out a pinochle deck right on the stand unless I keep 'em busy. It ain't like no quartet, dad—"

But Edgar was implacably at ease. "Well, don't listen to *me*," he said, touched by his own generosity in ignoring the slur, "just ask the *band*," this with a little conspiratorial simper in their direction, which vanished as a thought occurred to him. ". . . And, man, while I think of it," he said in a tone of mad, helpful preoccupation, weaving over to the lead tenor, the cigar stub beginning to gesture vaguely. "You got your reed too loose. I meant to tell you. You getting a fuzzy tone . . . You got to screw *down* on it . . . Here," and he actually reached over and clumsily twisted the screw, taking his lower lip between his teeth to keep his balance. "Now, man, try that."

The tenor stared up in wide-eyed amazement at the intent face above him, pasty and smirking, sparse patches of beard around the chin.

"Go ahead, man, try it. You'll see," Edgar encouraged him, shaking his shoulders in an effeminate approximation of a beat, and raising his eyebrows.

The tenor put the horn into his mouth, dropping his eyes in confusion, and blew an embarrassed little run, naked as a whisper in a church, which seemed to please Edgar.

"There now," he said almost gently, as a voice began: "How long we got to sit here, and listen to—"

"Now, Julie, that's all right," Curny hastened to interrupt in desperation. "You sound good, man, *you* know . . . But look now, Horn, we gotta get through this thing, so you and me can get downstairs. We don't want that cat to close up on us, man! . . . And them bli-ahs right in there make that part sound real clean, don't they, now? Sure, sure, that fixes it—"

"Well," Edgar pondered, sucking a tooth and picking up the lead sheet between delicate thumb and forefinger to study it with a bleary, tolerant eye. "I don't know," he murmured reluctantly, and then put it down again, as if compelled by a rigorous sense of truth into voicing a pitiless opinion. "I just don't know if it's worth your time . . . I mean, it ain't really *commercial* either, man."

"Well, what do *you* suggest?" Curny snapped out, pulling at his goatee peevishly. "Man, really, you're—"

"I'd just drop the whole arrangement, if it was me," Edgar offered in a slow and thoughtful drawl. "I think I would."

He stood there, placid but for his eyes, which seemed

to flare with an unnatural, triumphant heat, and every now and then an immense cough gouged at his chest, making him almost stagger. But he took no notice, and only wiped his drawn lips indifferently.

"Man," Curny pronounced with careful astonishment, shaking his head, "you sick." And then, as if shocked by the finality of the thought now that it was words, he added quickly, "When d'you eat the last time?"

Edgar's slack-jawed half-smile stiffened and vanished. "I got the money," he stated hoarsely, "if I want to."

"Well, man, whyn't you let me finish this thing up, then we'll both go—"

"Everyone's always talking about *food*," Edgar said with scowling fury. "Maybe I got no *eyes* to eat—"

"You do what you like, man, only—"

"You think I haven't got the money?" Edgar continued in an ominous monotone.

Curny turned. "Man, I *know* you'll have it once I get through this number. Not polished, not ready, not even really rehearsed. Just played through *once* right to the end."

"I got the money," Edgar insisted, peering at Curny with a stony gaze. "I just ain't got the time."

Someone snickered.

"I don't need his twenty bucks," he went on a little louder, looking around for the origin of the snicker. "Not to eat. Is that what you been thinking?"

"Man, *look!*" Curny slapped his hand on the top of the lectern emphatically. "Will you *please* let me do my work here, so I can get downstairs before dawn to cash you your twenty, and if I got a little extra time before I leave for Pittsburgh maybe even make it uptown to at least say 'Hello, good-bye' to Libby! Will you *please!*"

His eyes were almost popping, not so much with anger as with the efforts to suppress it that were obviously making him so unhappy. The band had rarely seen him so worked up, and there was not a sound.

"I'm not asking you to *like* my arrangements," he seethed. "I'm not asking you to *join* my band. Or *dig* my horn. Or get *with* my life . . . Man, I'm not asking that you do it! I'm only asking that you let me *be!*"

"All right," Edgar said with a shrug, his voice measured, as if it had just occurred to him that Curny, like all men who give out so easily, zealously guarded the quick of himself and kept it hidden from the sight of other men, and never gave of that to anyone. "All right," he repeated, "you join *my* band then. You get with *my* life," and he let out a tiny superfluous giggle. "Man, be my guest."

There was an involuntary chuckle at this, which made Curny shoot a glance in the direction of the band, as if they had, for once, laughed at him unkindly; and when he looked back, the dim, half-drunken smirk on Edgar's face completed his irritation.

"Well," he announced harshly, glowering at everyone, "it don't matter. You going to rehearse this number if I got to keep *all* of you here all night. Just let me hip you to that . . . And we are gonna do it *loud* on the trombones like it's written, and we are gonna just throw in all them little bli-ahs we can fit . . . And also we are gonna have it *funny* as a Chinaman at Christmas, twenty bucks or no hardtime twenty bucks!"

Edgar had turned during this and gone back to his six-pack for another can, but on the last words he swung around so sharply that he knocked the pile of music off the chair, and stood for a moment amid a litter of unfolded paper.

"I keep *telling* you," he repeated thickly, furiously, "and telling you. I *got* the money. I don't need no goddamn twenty bucks, if I don't want it."

"All right, man," Curny said with ironic tact, his anger subsiding as Edgar's rose again, "so you don't need it. But twenty more ain't gonna exactly *hurt* you, now is it?"

The heat of rage seemed to dim in Edgar's eyes for a moment, a long moment during which Mr. Owls' wrist watch could be clearly heard ticking along unconcernedly. "I been hurt by less," he mumbled tonelessly, almost to himself; and then once again the light came up behind his small black pupils, as if he could not rid himself of the one thought.

"But I keep telling you," he ground out, "I *got* the money. I don't need your twenty bucks to get straight again . . . Just I thought I'd get some ahead . . ." He was stuffing both hands into his suit pockets with mad, fumbling haste. "See . . . Look here," he stumbled out defiantly, one hand waving above his head, holding a fistful of bills, the hungry, scornful gleam back in his eyes.

"What do I need your twenty bucks for?" he asked haughtily, looking down his nose. "I got almost enough already, right here. Look at that." The old sour smile twisted one corner of his mouth as he thrust the money back into his pocket, and he looked around briefly, drunkenly, as if he felt better just thinking about everything, as if he was cutting quite a figure. "I got enough," he repeated mechanically, and then, as if the result of a decision so instantaneous that no shadow of hesitation crossed his face, he was at the door, managed to get it open after a short decisive struggle, only to turn, blank-faced, unsteady on his feet, and explain crossly: "Like I may have hocked it, man, but I never tried to blow *funny* on it before I did—"

And then, to the amazement of everyone, he was gone, and the door whished slowly shut again.

Curny stood, still near the lectern, without a grin, but

without anger too, not as if he felt rebuked, but rather as if he understood, looking in the direction of the empty doorway, absently pulling on one wide suspender.

"Man," he breathed with thoughtful admiration, "you can't take it away from him, that man *goes.*"

The nervous relief was as plain in Mr. Owls' voice as the two packs of cigarettes he had smoked that day. "Well, maybe *now* we can get down to business! . . . Headaches, headaches! I tell you I'm getting too old for this." But he was already bustling up and down. "We still got to get everything packed up, and you bring in a new number . . . at the last minute! . . . And, Curn, I tell you and I tell you, you got to remember what I say about this: Young America wants to *dance!*"

"Man," Curny said, turning back to the band and shaking his head with the funny, puzzled cluck of a man whom life has not yet ceased to amaze. "Think of old Horn without no horn to blow. Is that strange?"

"Oh, he'll be all right," Mr. Owls hurried on, trying to gauge his mood. "And besides, who ever *listened* to him. He hasn't played any good for years."

Curny gave him a friendly and yet distantly reproving glance. "Man, *I* listened to him. Everyone did."

He picked up the lead sheet again and studied it for a moment, as if to collect himself, as if to reassess it in the light of some odd new thought that had come into his head. Then he snapped his suspenders with finality, and said with a deep breath, "Okay then, we might as well pick cotton if we're gonna do it . . . And, Billy, like go easy on the drums here in the first chorus. It's a better sound all right . . . Unless, man, you just got music in you, and it's gotta come out . . ."

RIFF

"... Like, kid, when you ain't got no more *in* you, you go find that little man around the corner," Edgar raved on and on as they made their unsteady way in the rain down Broadway's merciless, bright blocks with all their flowing, varied life, in which any one man's work or vision or trouble seemed insignificant. "There's always that little man around the corner waiting for a musician, right there, down the block, across that street there, *near* . . . He buy your goddamn piece of luggage any time you get tired. He give you a lousy twenty-five bucks for it, even though it cost a hundred, any time, any time. Cause in this damn country, man, there's always somebody pay you more *not* to blow— Don't you even know that? Don't you? . . . Whoever got their first horn new! Whoever went in, in daylight, and got one so new it didn't even have no music in it yet? . . . Man, that horn was always somebody else's horn before, who got tired, or beat, or quit, or dropped dead holding it. You so stupid you don't even know that, you so good-natured . . . And you think they *want* you to blow? Listen, they only lend you that horn, or you steal it outright and run, and keep going with it as long as you can, and when you can't make it any more, they get it back. Man, when you can't carry it any more, it ends up back where it was before. So, listen, the trick is to get hold of it, and keep going, and don't look around, and keep playing on it no matter what, and sell everything else first, sell your shoes, but don't never—"

And then at last he broke off, no longer winking and nodding, no longer raving in the passionate, surreptitious whisper as if the passers-by might hear, but staring at the shiny pavement and the hurrying feet; for he had heard himself, and what he had heard seemed to him a mockery in his mouth. "Well, that's what you think when you young and wide-eyed and stupid like *you*, that's what you figure when you got it *in* you, that's the way it *looks*." The last irony was mute behind the small and bitter eyes. "But, man, that's only another hype after all. Cause look at me, I'm still up, I'm still me— And *I* gave it back for twenty-five in cash, I gave the damn thing *back!*"

At which, Cleo (at last beyond words) suddenly glimpsed the dark reality that sat like a nightbird, large and taloned and beady-eyed, in Edgar's brain, and knew the way life's streets must have always looked to him, and even saw the cold eyes of the wet-palmed little men, shrewd behind the wire mesh in airless, jumbled shops beyond the back-street store fronts that one hurried past in winter, who were always there with the jeweler's glass and buttoned sweater if a man wished cash money for the last thing a man should ever sell; always ready for the mutually distasteful contest in the half-light, knowing as in all seductions honor must inevitably succumb to need; giving a ticket in return that promised (like some old Satanic parable) a vague redemption on the same terms by some carefully proscribed future date that both knew was only an illusion to palliate the bargain. He suddenly saw the three sterile, pendant balls of compromise and cynicism and capitulation as Edgar saw them, horrible and tempting and at the end of every street down which a man might flee with the crime of the imagination in his heart.

"And I could try to get my coat back, while I'm selling," he was going on vaguely. "That might get me another ten or so—if I could just remember what kind of goddamn cab it was! . . . But look," he suddenly exclaimed, "man, just take a look," a loose hand sweeping around at rainy neons, traffic-signs, window displays, novelty counters, pitchmen, movie palaces, dark bars: the whole thronging chaos of the American city night—for all the garish main streets from coast to coast led here if you but went down them far enough.

"Man, art? Like, man, tone poems? Here? . . . You all so silly, you are all so square . . . I mean—hey, fella, *you* want a tone poem? Hey, you, hey—yah, *you!*" he brusquely asked a pimply, leather-jacketed youth who brushed by them at that moment with a twist of insolence on his upper lip that was obviously the expression he perpetually gave the world. He glanced at Edgar quickly, startled and alert, but saw only another drunk, another soggy, rumpled bum, and Edgar's snicker did not even reach him as he hurried on. "Man, he didn't *want* no tone poem . . . What d'you know . . ."

They were at a cross street now, waiting for the green, and ahead Times Square's astounding clash of lights and noise and crowds, through which the chill rain fell unheeded, opened out before them, like an immense cavern come upon at the end of a tunnel. Somewhere a band contended in muffled shrieks against the huge continual roar, in which no single particular sound could really be distinguished, and Edgar listened for a moment, eyes prophetically raised.

"And half of them wouldn't know what it was if you asked them, and the other half would say it's like that band, or on the radio, or something, and wouldn't like it anyway . . . So what's the use? God*damn*, man, what's the sense? . . . There ain't no sense . . . Ask 'em, ask *that* guy! . . . You think they *want* you to blow? Or *listen* when you do? Or *dig* it if they just can't make you stop?" he muttered furiously. "You think that what you blow is *good* for them? . . . It's a wonder, it's a gas! . . . But *I* got over it, *I* got no more in me, *I* gave the damn thing back," and he looked, wild and bleary-eyed, at Cleo. "And anyway, you don't know what it's like when they hate you. You never heard 'em rumble when you playing something they don't dig, and makes 'em *mad* because it just don't bounce along, ricky-ticky, empty, nothing . . . You never saw 'em shift around, all starting to rumble at the same damn time, and *hating* you— and I mean 'Let's-rough-that-solemn-nigger-up' kind of hate . . . Cause it ain't like that no more, there's too many of you new cats, and enough words written now, and enough records out, so they just walk away. But in my day they walked *towards* you when they didn't dig, they walked *towards* you . . . Huh! You still a silly, good kid with a straight life," he murmured. "But, man, you *see*," he added almost immediately with a desperate and quite naked relief widening his eyes, "now I *can't* sit in, even if I got so drunk or hung up that I might agree . . . See, kid? See? Now I *can't*, no matter what—"

"Oh, Horn," Cleo let out involuntarily, searching for some new pallor in the face, a sudden tremble in the lips, to go with this revelation, and thinking numbly, "No. Not just money. Not just home. Not just that— Castration. The way they say those crazy saints might mutilate themselves rather than risk a woman. The way a man is uselessly brave for fear he is a coward . . . But why? What for?" Edgar's words had a simple, literal reality that echoed through the sodden intervening hours: *"Cause what am I gonna do . . . It's all just umpa-umpa to me now."*

"Is this the way that it could end?" Cleo thought, looking ahead, in the bafflement of drink, toward manhood, as if his notion of the equity of his art had been damaged. Not just neglect, indifference, poverty and time; not just the little men behind the wire mesh, or the yelling throngs beyond the lights, moved (he had always assumed) by something deep and terrible and important in jazz. Not just them, and what they could do to a man and to his truth. But what happened in a man himself, what could happen to anyone, if it could happen to Edgar.

Fear. Fear that even the most godlike truth might yet prove mortal and uncertain after all; fear that the skill to utter it might vanish; fear that the pride in knowing it might one day no longer triumph over its continual rejection; fear that the audacity and the devotion necessary to go on repeating it might come to seem like sickness or obsession.

Was this how it could end? On a rainy Monday night no different from a hundred others, except that Edgar now was so afraid to blow that he had hocked his horn to make it finally impossible? Was this the way? . . . There was something ghastly to Cleo's youth in a man turning on his life so completely, and there was something equally terrible in a man's life failing him so cruelly when he was least prepared, when he was off his tone.

149

"And, anyway, it's all arrangements now," Edgar sneered in a sudden vicious return of pride, as if it was too late now to worry or be temperate, as if he was fatally free. " 'Put them horns back in, take 'em out again, letter S, letter H, letter I, letter goddamn T'— Fools! You *all* goddamn fools! . . . And all over arrangements, charts, scores, paper, *paper!* And every goddamn fool thinks *that*'s what it is . . . Well, kid, let me tell you something, you silly fool—I can read them notes as good as anybody, but it's *still* what a man gets up, all alone with only his goddamn horn on some fool's tune, and blows out of his own head that makes the difference, that changes it from what it was before he got up *nerve* enough to do it. Yes! . . . I don't care how much music paper, or music school, or fancy suspenders, or funny Stravinsky you got, cause all them scores, all them significant tone poems, all that—man, it ain't no *fun* if you can't get free of it long enough to blow your own damn thing . . . I mean, if you trying to do something serious here, finally you got to stop reading, and start to *think*. You got to start it sometime . . ." and then he humphed so abruptly to himself that it was like seeing his mind work—that involuted, devious, strange mind. "Well, it ain't this fool's goddamn worry any more . . . But, hey, *look!*" he interrupted himself in a different voice, actually pointing. "Man alive, dig *them!*"

For there, in front of a record store that had an outside speaker through which a husky tenor sax poured its poignant wail out upon the deaf, thronged sidewalks, were two young white men, muffled to the chins in flapping raincoats, transfixed upon the curb by the very sound, heads bobbing, fingers snapping as they sang along all unaware that they were singing, catching hold of one another as they teetered toward the gutter, their laughing, exultant faces astream with rain and sweat, riffing and entranced, oblivious of everything but that wild, hot horn.

Edgar stopped dead in the middle of the sidewalk, a few feet from them, letting people jostle past him, staring at them, a curious, warm half-smile unconsciously starting to touch his lips, utterly outward for an instant, just as the dark-haired one seized the shoulder of his friend in the glasses, and exclaimed, "Listen to it, listen! *That's* that new tenor, Paul, that's the one, that's him! . . . Oh, man, this *crazy* country! . . . And I'll bet he's going to blow his first, vast, really *great* solo tonight, just *tonight*— I'll bet you, and everyone'll be destroyed by it, and amazed they could have gotten through their lives not knowing it, not realizing!" He shook his friend by the shoulder, his face full of goofy, excited laughter. "Where the hell *is* he, Paul! Where *is* he!— And just think of his old bedroom down in Fayetteville or someplace, and his yellow Saturday shoes, and his hair straightener before he came up North, copying records all these years, all alone— Man, *think* of it! And maybe just tonight he's going to blow something nobody ever *heard* before! . . . I told you about him! That's him, that's him—"

Edgar stared after them as they went jiggling and gesticulating off into the crowds, his ravaged face, for that moment, no longer taut with irony or pride, but warm with his amusement and absorption.

Cleo stood swaying beside him, and suddenly he touched Edgar's arm, shaking him a little, jogging him insistently, just as the dark-haired youth had done.

"Blow for them," he managed to get out through the dizziness and drink, not caring how it sounded, too possessed by the idea to care. "Man, blow for *them*," he repeated, wondering how it had ever begun, the dark flight, if this was the way that it could end.

CHORUS:METRO

"By God, you shall not go down!
Hang your whole weight on me."

WHITMAN

"There's a side of Edgar that *I* never knew," Wing finally said, "and when a man's *bad* in his heart that side comes out first."

Walden nodded, knowing that Edgar had more secrets about him than most, but when Wing added, "So I guess we'd better try uptown, we'd better go find Metro," he frowned, as if to say, "What? Metro? Yawper in wild Harlem bars? Metro, who never comes downtown, and blows a sax as crude as a climbing stud?"

"Man, do they even *know* each other?" he said aloud, amazed. "Edgar blows so sweet, so deep."

"Man, he knew Edgar *first* . . . If he don't know where he's at, at least he'll care—"

And so they went and found Metro, as always, down a

cheap street, under buzzing neons, through a door with barely room enough to open because of the crowds beyond it, in a milling, smoky uproar dense with the smell of pork and beer and dime-store perfume and good rank human sweat. Through the laughter and the jostling and the whoops in there, they heard his skirling horn begin, and pushed toward it—past hollering bartenders in arm garters, working a bar awash with drinks—making their way to the back where, over shoulders pressed to shoulders, thighs to thighs, they caught a glimpse of a little, crowded bandstand under stark light that was clearly the center of the swirl.

And there he was, in front of one of those yelling, indefatigable rhythm sections with which he always worked: dark, exultant youths who knew nothing but rudiments, and played everything in B-flat, and having once made something that was not quite noise, though not quite music either, began immediately to go, and had been jamming ever since, wanting nothing more—a thick-shouldered drummer punishing a high-hat cymbal with the relentless chu-chacha-chu of scarred and vicious sticks; a bassist whose rolling eyes and twitching arm and ceaselessly plucking fingers suggested he was about to jerk to pieces in dumb, stricken amaze; and a pianist, crouched and enduring over a chipped keyboard on which he banged out terrible and final chords.

And there, in front of them, the bandy-legged figure stood, with wild wig that no pomade could finally subdue, a long drape jacket reaching nearly to his knees as he leaned forward to begin, his loose shirt collar already wilted with anticipatory sweat, baggy pants pegged close around the tops of plaid-laced shoes as huge as coal scuttles, foot-long watch chain swinging on his thigh; there stood Metro Myland, feet a yard apart, knees starting to pump back and forth as he worked into a nameless,

riffing blues, his wide and mobile lips fastened to the thick
beak of a cumbrous tenor sax, warm eyes level above it,
as if watching for the truth, chin protruded so precipi-
tously that all of a sudden his recalcitrant wig sprang up
beneath the gunk in back to stick straight out as stiff as
wire, while the sweat splashed down his eager cheeks,
and his black fingers contorted on the stops, revealing pink
and gentle palms inside, and his knees began to buckle
in dangerous eddies as he riffed higher, wilder, searching
for a few crude notes to smear against the iron chords
that shuddered the piano, the few right notes that would
distill everything the music was to him, and so swinging
his hips and shaking taut shoulders, treading as he stood,
and pushing the horn forward into the light in his efforts to
find the notes, and then blowing "zonk, zonk, zonky, zonk!"
with all the joyful certainty of discovery, knowing that
was it, feeling the rightness of it in himself, and in the
rhythm that quickened behind him, and the throng that
yelled "Ah-h-h!" in front, and so roaring out "zonk! zonk!
zonky! zonk!" on top of the careening drums, like a chant
wrenched from a mouth out of which all the thwarted joy
of the body pours at once—crude as the flesh most naturally is when the mind lets go; loud, wanton and repetitive
the way a chant must be—so that the crowd stared,
hypnotized, fearful, aghast, lest he suddenly fall to his
knees, groin writhing forward against the thick bell of the
horn, back arched to fill the lungs, announcing with his
wild insistent "zonk!" that only beyond such breaking
loose would all things finally be reconciled, howling his
idiot-truths like the first prophet of joy who dared to say
there was no sin; and already a hundred pairs of feet
pounded in terrified unison that paralyzed the air, thighs
shivering, breasts shaking, eyes popping, and mouths
gasped open in wild continuous "Ah-h-h!" as if at any moment Eleusinian mysteries would erupt among them, pip-

ing them all to a savage dance that only the final spending
of the mindless juice could end; and then, of course, he
did go down, as someone shouted "Ohyes! Ohyes!" right
there in the dust, right down on separated knees, without losing one piercing "zonk!"—face all puckered in a
crazy fist around the gleaming mouthpiece, as if he
merely held it and it played itself, so that even Wing heard
himself crying "Yeee-ooow!" in unbroken assent, without
realizing he was doing it, just as something in Metro gave
up, something capable of pride or weariness or doubt,
his knees now flatdab upon the boards, eyes uprolled and
out of sight, in a torrent of sweat, wig stuck out stiff as a
pad of brillo, the horn erecting over his prone body now
like some ritual phallus bewitched upon a jungle altar into
levitation, his suppliant body motionless beneath it, but
still somehow the vortex of that murderous beat, beyond
having to show by gesture that he felt it any more, except
once when his shoulder lifted in such trusting arch to hit
the single sweet note in the shrieking "zonk-zonk-zonk!"
that a sympathetic, tranced response to what was in him
lifted every other shoulder that was there—the gesture
and the note so wedded that though everyone felt his
own shoulder lift, no one was conscious that it had, because there, right there, where all eyes fastened with that
total awareness with which men witness the materializa-
tion of the spirit or the exposure of the flesh, right there,
now, the horn was raised horizontal over them, huge,
triumphant, indissuadable, a gleaming miracle in the
shocked light, repeating (of itself, it seemed) "zonky!
zonky! zonky! zonky! zonk!" in thin, high-pitched squirts
of sound that said a clear and untranslatable "Yes!" to
everything that was not of the mind, and then were
drowned abruptly by the conclusive slamming of the
drums, which brought the house lights up.

"You know, man," Wing said, managing to sound dispassionate in the hubbub that ensued. "He's split a gut like that every night for years . . . And it's his *only* gut." He shook his head. "But, come on, we'll go out back and meet him—"

They waited for him in the alley where the band cooled out, smoking against the damp brick wall under an overhang just out of the rain, Wing half sitting on a stack of Coke cases for which there was no room inside, as the drummer came out, spat, lit up, and crouched down the wall a ways, sitting on his heels in the age-old attitude of resting athletes.

"Edgar?" Walden mused, solemnly amazed to find the vast, encompassing night over the Harlem roofs unchanged, no matter how a man pressed on towards light, "and Metro?" Two men less alike could never be imagined. Yet Wing had said that Metro knew him first. It seemed impossible.

In a moment he came out with his peculiar loping gait, still out of breath, still wet, his wide moist mouth (caught between grins) and large soft eyes that lit up at the sight of them—somehow unconnected with the abandoned figure on the stand, yet not disowning it.

"Well, yes. Well, man, now this is nice," he said with soft, hoarse-throated pleasure, nodding courteously to Walden, whom he did not know, then listening with little shakes of his head to Wing, holding on to his arm without a thought, as if compelled to touch him by something rich-hearted, easily moved and even sentimental in his nature.

"So I been phoning the Go Hole every fifteen minutes," Wing said, "thinking he might go by there to sit in, cause Geordie said that he was talking about going back to Kansas City, and that he was bad, you know . . . Out of money, hung up, *sick* . . . You know, man, the way Edgar could get *black* in his head . . ."

"Yes, I remember," Metro said, warm, immediately concerned. "I ain't seen him in a long time, a course," he added with curious tact, meant to remind them that he knew he was not considered part of the downtown music world; meant to assure them that, in spite of this, he was aware of the rivalries and antagonisms that sometimes erupted among those who played a more ambitious jazz than his—the bitter, fluctuating prejudices (grown out of prejudice to begin with) that often marked the scramble to make a living and a reputation; and meant to tell them he had heard the whining voices: "A white cat can't work this town; only spades get jobs, man," or just the opposite, "There's no work for colored in studio bands, *you* know that," or else, "When did you last see a *modern* musician getting asked to sit in *there*," or its reverse, "I tell you, everyone's playing arrangements today, they just don't want my kind of jazz"; meant to tell them too that this was why he kept to the Harlem dance halls, and the gaudy, roaring bars where joy was the only reason that you raised your horn.

"But I remember," he said after a moment, with the quick nostalgia of a man whose emotions rise easily and flow through him unimpeded, strong, pleasurable. "He wasn't even *hurt* like anybody else. Even way back, before he got his horn, he was different, so I guess he had to be different in his troubles too."

"We thought he might have fallen by tonight," Walden began, "to borrow money. Geordie said—"

"No. I'd of give it to him, what I've got, but he wouldn't think to come to me." He said it simply, reaching and opening a Coke, which he drank off in great thirsty swallows, licking his lips with a soft moist tongue. "Though if he did, he know I'd give him anything I had . . . You know, I only took up horn because of him, though I never played his way. But I copied everything he did for a while, cause he was older, like a brother, and had that look, that he was going somewhere, and *had* to go, so watch out . . . Man, I remember when he *got* his horn, the first one," he went on fondly, eyes wistfully pleased, as if he had lived a long, hard life, and loved it now, and peculiarly had loved it even then. . . .

Coldest, most futureless 1932 in East St. Louis—a smoke-bound glut of dreary streets, blighted by chemical plants and sidings and industrial slag, where Metro had grown up in a dilapidated, sooty house behind a vast billboard turned toward the railroad tracks (that were fastidiously lifted over the appalling streets for the long fling across the river) in hopes the passengers might see, ignoring those who lived beside it day by day, as if acknowledging their unimportance, even as consumers. He remembered his jobless father's trapped eyes, his harassed mother mending and remending, the gang of younger children growing wild, the bittersweet Depression songs muffled from the barrooms down the street, "Chicago, Chicago, that toddlin' town," the early November chill that year, the complaining voices he overheard one afternoon (eager, just fourteen): "Well, he *got* to quit. He can pick ash pits, can't he? He can load beer, can't he? He's *big* enough. Next week we'll be down to nothing, Lou, nothing," his father's voice.

He remembered the very dawn he went away, not hurt but merely stifled by the fog of desperation and defeat already stirring up anarchic flickers in his heart; leaving to escape rootlessness, leaving to escape the discontent, the street gangs, the eventual crime that staying would have meant; and how one day on the highway (a tiny speck in the great autumn emptiness of the Mississippi valley) was enough to get him farther from home than he had ever been before, foodless and shivering, beating vaguely toward Chicago, Chicago—the days and nights that followed it separated one from the other only by the wan hope of rides and the certain knowledge of none, and yet leading him eventually to a railhead (in gothic, darkest Indiana, having patiently bummed the whole time in the wrong direction) where another vagrant had said (missing three teeth from the front of a wily twelve-year-old face), "Listen, no kid makes it on the roads. You watch me, see, and we'll catch us an empty down this line a ways"; the boy with whom he had later crouched in cinders by a switch until a freight came screeching and banging down the rails, and then followed, awkward, copying the light-foot run, to see vault up through an open door, and dart a hand down for his collar, and pull him up, too; the white boy who watched him gasping on the shaking boards, while searching for a kitchen match to light the butt between his toothless gums.

He remembered the year that followed when, as one of thousands of kid tramps in the great upheaval of Depression, his world became a world of brakies, reefers, redballs, railroad dicks in hard-up midwest towns, of which he only saw the jails, the missions and the doorways, in which he lived on dehorn alcohol, mulligan, dayolds, misery; always on the move, another freight going somewhere, lone "whooo-eee" down midnight tracks, change in Gary, work the stem for meatless stew and sour bread, dream your dreams (if any) on the rods. The Big Trouble (as they called it) was on the land: work lines that never moved, chow lines that didn't serve, strike lines that did no good, jail lines in which a boy was only another bum, black or white. But to him it would never after mean despair (which he'd escaped by running), or rage (which only rose in those who had enough to be impoverished), or politics (only a word that filled the papers which, wrapped around the belly under clothes, would keep you warm of nights). For him it would always be the moving

159

on, the moving on: scroonched up in a coal gondola racketing into a blizzard in Dakota; the bitter winter cities, gray in their brief industrial afternoons, where you repeated your straight-sob to chilly walkers in the streets, hoping for a dime; railheads in back-county Kansas where once incomprehensible delaying actions had been fought by fugitive Osage on their doomed flight into oblivion; where, later, Confederate marauders, black-mustached and bone-weary, had burned two barns; where, later still, the lawless backwash of old wars had gleefully shot up the town in drunken ecstasy; and where you, the latest wanderer, the youngest, snitched a pair of levis from a backyard line. It would always be the first dewy awakening in sweet spring fields moist with new-turned loam; the great mist-choked bends of continental rivers, tidal, tremendous, with their half-sunk cargos of orange crates and contraceptives and wishful, stoppered bottles, containing matches for imagined castaways, that had been consigned to the muddy current somewhere up in mythic Minnesota by dreamy farm boys, safer than yourself. It would be the long laze of murmurous summer evenings by a hobo fire near the entrance to a culvert out of town, the prolonged golden hush dense with all manner of chirpings and stirrings and water sounds, and the childish voices round those fires, boy and girl, saying, "When it gets colder, we'll head for California," "Keep out of Cincy in the fall—mean cops," "That Evanston mission, no —you got to stand up for Jesus just to get a crummy day-old bun," "I was carrying the banner down yonder in Atlanta, but watch out, keep out, stay awake—they throw bummies in for thirty days." It would be tales of the Great Black-Bearded Brakie, near seven feet tall, with a denture made of solid brass, who turned up anywhere, always carrying a length of pipe that had been bent on the skulls of countless bums, and who "is friendly at the first, and even shares your stew, but then'll smash your head, laughing like the crazy hooter on a snow-bound freight, and then'll throw you down the embankment to make a lesson of you, after trying on your shoes." It would be stories of the mission, some said in Duluth, some Rock Island, some (with veteran eyes) insisted that they moved it place to place, Loosfer's Mission, where they made the stew of mangled kids who fell between the couplings, and kept you overnight in lightless cells until you hollered "Yes," and shipped you in a phantom red-ball to a bayou chain gang, to lay track they tore up every night.

The Big Trouble was on the land all right—harvested out in places, rich with old blood shed uselessly in forgotten autumns, tired with hopes and passions and wars and change; having known its winter doldrums, its inchoate springs, its languid Junes, and the Big Troubles of before, which came down like the killing frosts of bad years, and passed again. But it would always mean the easy friendships of hard times to Metro; the unjudging acceptance of whore or queer or nut or Negro on the part of kids who knew instinctively or learned at last that in the desolation of reality all creatures have a simple kinship. And, most important, it would mean the final, reconciling sweetness with which *one* dawn, of all those wandering dawns, had suffused his boyhood heart.

The noon before, just as he and ten others (none over seventeen) were settling in a boxcar that was gathering momentum from a water stop outside Sioux City, they heard the slap-slap-slap of shoes along the cinders, a head appeared running beside the open door, an arm took hold, and Edgar Pool heaved in among them.

In a preposterously natty ancient suit somehow kept scrupulously clean, a suit striped and jaunty and suggestive of race tracks, but a complete suit (jacket and trousers) nevertheless; with nothing under it for those March days but a raveling khaki sweater; with patent-leather shoes, run over at the heels and narrowing to flashy points in front; and no hat, but carrying what was unmistakably a shirt in a laundry wrapper—he sat there, carefully wiping the soot from face and neck, grave and self-absorbed with the pocket handkerchief. He might have been eighteen then.

"Look at *his* front, hey," marveled a thirteen-year-old boy without socks. "He could work lake-front Chicago in that suit."

"Hey, dude," an older voice called out. "Wanta stand a poorboy to a cup of misery?"

Edgar looked down his nose, beneath which the beginnings of mustache lent his coffee-colored face an air of adolescent introversion, and then, settling his parcel between his knees, he looked around at the circle of smudged and curious faces, wan in the empty dimness of the car, saying only, "Look, I got a shirt and a dollar, and I won't need shoes till late next month, but I jumped more empties than any three of you. And anyone who jumps an empty needs to . . . What time we due in Omaha?"

Metro, awed by the suit, the shirt, the whole tone of not having succumbed to anything, make no mistake, and so not daring speech (though as the only Negroes they sat close by each other), dozed through the afternoon, and woke cold at evening to find only Edgar there, glooming out the door and chewing on a sandwich.

"Them others jumped it two, three hours ago," he said to Metro's widened eyes. "They got worried at the snow."

Outside, swirled to wild, inhuman shapes before a malevolent Canadian wind, the snow fled across the stunned and houseless fields as the vast prairie night came down, stark and Siberian, over thousands of square miles of nothing—a hobo's nightmare.

"I shoulda kept awake," Metro murmured, peering out at the gathering storm with trembling lip.

"Nothin' to bawl about," Edgar said gruffly, turning a vexed eye away. "No damn snow'd bother me . . . Here, finish this. I ain't hungry anyway . . ."

"I ain't bawling," Metro protested with stubborn, moist-eyed anger. "I'm cold, that's all," wiping his cheeks and, after an uncertain pause, taking the proffered sandwich.

"You be colder yet before we're done. You be froze to ice if you *let* yourself. I saw a kid once in Montana, worse than this, froze solid in a load of coal—"

"*I* seen worse, too!" Metro whimpered, mouth full of sour bread. "I seen plenty, and I can get along without no—"

"Okay, kid, okay," Edgar interrupted with a curious, uncomfortable laugh that was little more than a sniff in his nose—a laugh that relinquished for a moment the impenetrable hauteur of late adolescence which sees anyone a few years younger as a bootless child; a laugh meant to reassure, yet making clear that reassurance was not easy for him; a laugh that Metro never afterward forgot, and which was followed by the offhand question: "Where you heading anyway?"

"Out West, I guess."

"I mean, *where?*"

Metro had to stop to ponder that, thinking, "Denver? Tucson? San Jose?" for only rail points counted in his mind as somewhere, and even they were only pauses on the way to somewhere else; but before he could pick one out, Edgar, clearly eager to talk, yet piqued by this very eagerness, went on: "I'm making for Kansas City, and then I'm getting off and I ain't getting on again for nothing."

"I never bummed that town, but I heard the rail-yard cops'll let you board one standing still, and—"

"I'm going *back* there. That's where I'm *from* . . . And

I ain't no bummy either," he added with complacent, purse-lipped severity. "I just been saving money . . ."

Unlike most young tramps, who rarely talked about the things that set them drifting, Edgar was hungry to justify himself, lonely just for talk—a need so strong he did not seem to notice it was inconsistent with his self-reliant image of himself.

And as he talked it soon came out that, in a curious way, he had run off to escape his father—the easy-spending railroad porter with the razored cheek and eyes that boredom had made vicious, who (in his turn) had run off two years before Edgar, to go back to the red-eye, big-stogie, Saturday-whore life which, in a moment of aggravated lust denied unsanctified satisfaction, he had given up by marrying. Edgar had run off to escape the consequences of his mother's plaint just one year later: "Eddie, honey, whyn't you go down and apply like your pa? He always made good money portering." He had run off to escape her very acquiescence to the abandonment, knowing the tubs of washing over which she leaned in steam would keep her eating, knowing his absence would grieve her heart, but ease the rest.

But mainly he had run off to escape (in advance) the long, clattering nights to Wichita, spent in the gents' room under the harsh, tireless lights, and which could only be consumed by idling through a cast-off, day-old paper, and were inevitably interrupted by the red-faced hardware salesman stumbling in when the bar car closed, to vomit out its bad liquor, during which you had to stand ready with a towel, vaguely black-face and subservient but not too attentive, helpful but not angling for a tip; the long nights of snores and water stops in chilly depots, during which you were careful to keep the white jacket extra immaculate because you were colored, grinning and even managing a laugh at the ancient convention-repartee these ceaseless travelers took with them over the country like their scarred suitcases of folders—the immemorial jokes and boasts and stories of a man's loveless world (attenuated, naïve, and obscene), at which you had to laugh, knowing the night would pass, knowing you would draw a basin of water for the dawntime shave, and would have to respond a dozen times that day to the perennial query (always preceded by the inevitable pulling out of the heavy watch weighting the end of a braided fob): "What kind of time we making, boy?" with the well-rehearsed assurance that Tulsa's magazine stands and steamy coffee shops would turn up on schedule; to escape all that —the heart-stifling routine of civility and grins and helpfulness, relieved only by the railmen's shabby bedroom at terminal points, and the long return over a roadbed whose every missurveyed grade you knew by heart; to escape, finally and worst of all, the knowledge (impossible to forget entirely during the idle nights by the heap of towels) that this was the best that you could hope for, better than redcap, bus boy, janitor or truckee, and better just because of the hateful white jacket, and because men are naturally more vulnerable when relieving themselves; to escape (and something suggested that this was what galled Edgar most of all) the inescapable knowledge that you were circumscribed, and had attained some giddy zenith for your race, and should be happy and complacent, even supercilious (numberless boys back home had envious dreams of you, remember); to escape into freedom, any kind of freedom—or as Edgar said, gesturing sharply toward the front of the train, "I'd rather ride cold and nothing back here, than warm and nigger up there."

He talked along, not really caring whether Metro listened, eyes lit with that strange, banked pierce of certainty which only youths can have.

"And listen," he said with solemn confidence at last, as

if fearful of being overheard there in the half-dark car clattering across the blind prairie in a howling storm, with only a shivering colored boy to share his bitter dream, "I was being cagey there before about that dollar, with them others . . . I got me almost *thirty* dollars right here, tied up in a piece of washrag in my shorts . . . I saved it, pennies, nickels, sometimes quarters . . . I begged for it, drawled for it, dove pearls in mission kitchens all last winter for it, and I figure it's almost enough now, so I'm going back."

Metro was awestruck to be in the presence of so much money, and for a moment forgot his runny nose. "But what're you gonna do?"

Edgar licked a few stray flakes from his ragged, proud mustache. "I'm gonna buy a horn," he said, "a tenor horn."

Metro kept silent, yet respectful, before the riddle he could not hope to understand.

"I'm gonna play in bands, I'm gonna play *jazz*," Edgar went on, no longer trying to suppress the splendid details. "I usta fool with tin-can drums in an alley band, hustling for pennies, back home . . . And last year I spent two months in a pool hall in Chicago where this guy had this horn. And I already got some rudiments. I picked out 'Comin' Virginia' without no help from anyone, just listening to a record. I can play it near perfect already . . . And, kid, you get *paid* for playing music in Kansas City."

"You mean, colored too?"

"Listen, more colored play jazz than white in that town. They got bars up and down *both* sides of Twelfth Street. Some of them guys must make twenty, thirty bucks a week! . . . And take no crap from anyone."

"I don't know," Metro breathed, shaking his head at the audacity of the dream.

"*I* know," Edgar corrected him sternly. "I'm gonna buy a horn . . ."

It had become colder as they talked, darker, and the tremendous arctic blizzard roared on everywhere, until it seemed that the struggling freight was heading, sightless and insanely stubborn, right into the exact, magnetic eye of that wild, uncaring night, into an absolute, shrieking dark.

"We better sing, I guess," Edgar said with a frown, noticing Metro's clenched and quivering hands. "When you get cold or hungry, kid, don't *let* yourself . . . Sing. Remember what I say. And pull your hands up into that jacket now," he added crossly, indicating the double-breasted suitcoat (made for a hefty grown-man's belly) that came almost to Metro's knees. "You got enough coat there to get to Winnipeg and back if you *want* to bad enough."

Then he began to riff, slapping his hands on his crossed legs, and his legs on the car floor, making up words as he went along. "I'm comin' Virginia—I'm cold and I'm slow—this redball is wailin'—can't see for the snow . . . I'm leavin' Nebraska—I'm sayin' it twice—I'm leavin' Nebraska—like a bucket of ice," and on and on, losing the rhyme but never the thumping beat, raising his voice louder and louder as the wild wind rose against it. "Come on, come on," he interrupted himself, grabbing Metro's arm. "Don't matter what you sing, only sing loud!"

Metro began, at first beating out a hesitant rhythm and copying what Edgar had sung, and then, when he forgot some, adding nonsense of his own, realizing with a pang that there was no one out there to hear—no town, no house, no lost dog—and so singing on to combat his fright, until, all crouched together there in the bitter dark and cold of the car, snow swirling cruelly into their faces through the half-open door, the two of them sat chanting their crazy, scared defiance of the great storm.

"I could freeze, or I could go to ice—snowman, you could slow my blood—but not for good, but not for *good!*" Edgar yelled furiously.

"That old snowman's mean—when'll St. Jo's yard lights come—one little red, one little green—all the long way home," Metro answered, praying for lights, even a few valiant and besieged switchlights by an isolated water tower; any place where men were up and tending signals, snow or fair; and somehow part of a frozen hour passed, and then, miraculously, as if in answer to their two lone voices shrieking to keep alive, Metro's lights appeared.

It was little more than a switch and a siding (incomprehensible in that vast emptiness), and some buildings straggling off beyond them: a few flickering lights, a few unclear shapes. But as they waited there, someone joined them, crawling with a cursing scramble up into the car; someone who lay panting on the cold boards in the dim wedge of light coming through the door from a building near the tracks; someone who wore an overcoat that had been cut off at the waist, all stiff with snow, and ragged jeans stuffed into the tops of rubber galoshes many sizes too big; someone who lay gasping and then, catching breath, sat up unsteadily, seeing them for the first time with a fearful and then almost immediately thankful flare in the small weary eyes; someone who got out in a hoarse, spent voice, "Jesus, I swear I thought it wasn't going to come . . . Ten minutes ago I decided it just wasn't, and I almost lay down in them bushes, and quit"; someone who pushed the frozen leather cap back from a bone-cold forehead with a wincing gesture that revealed the soft, hacked blond bangs of a girl, not over sixteen.

She had the grim cheeks and thin colorless mouth and quick eyes of all resourceful girl waifs, so alert that her very unawareness of the miseries of her life seemed brave and terrible. She must have had a hard, rumpless, gaunt-limbed little body too (just beginning to breast and hair), but in the shapeless, castoff clothes she looked more like a small starved animal poking its wily face out of a burrow than like a girl, a child.

"I never should have gotten off last night," she said matter-of-factly. "But I got bad hungry . . . That place there is Hopeville, but keep away, stay out, pass the word—I bummed back doors all day, and all I got me was a runty old turnip and a slice of lard bread . . ."

As the train began to move again, groaning and unwill-ing, she crawled automatically to the other side of the car, out of custom rather than alarm, because that was the rule for unattached girls on the road, a rule too old for her to challenge or even think about; and the three of them hud-dled there in complete darkness, isolated from each other, silent, each engaged for the moment with the tremendous problem of keeping the blood moving, and so shifting to find a good position, accumulating bearable moments, knowing they would somehow gather into hours.

Over the howl of the wind and the rattle of the car, Metro heard the girl coughing, heard the dry crinkling of newspaper, heard the impatient sniffling, and then heard Edgar say to him, "You go to sleep, kid"—already getting to his knees, already moving off.

Metro sat there for what seemed a long while, and then heard Edgar's murmur, muffled but just audible: "I got what's left of a Hershey, and I got a coat I can spread." And hunching his collar up to cover his ears so that he would hear no more, nevertheless heard the hushed reply: "All right, all right . . . only keep me covered up, cause I'm bad cold."

After that he tried to think of something so as not to listen, grave and embarrassed and alone there in the dark

—having heard it all before in other cars that shuddered on the roadbed, having heard it just beyond the firelights in leafy jungles, always preceded by the clatter of old stew cans, kicked away to make a place—but, nevertheless, could think of nothing, and so heard the scrape of runover heels along the cold boards, and heard the slow breath, and the quick breath, and the two breaths joining; and, most of all, heard the terrifying, brutal silence over there in the darkness, the very silence of the mating in which no word or cry or groan was passed between: a strange initiation for him, which he never quite forgot; and then, after a while, heard Edgar crawl away to another corner, breath slowing; and later (but not much later) heard the hoarse, spent voice, weary but not too weary to be fair, that said, "You wanna love me, blackie? You wanna do it too?" and heard, perhaps most terrible of all, his own shame-faced response: "No, I . . . I ain't old enough," that brought the drowsy, soft "All right."

What must have been almost an hour passed, during which he heard her fitful cough and sniffle; almost an hour of frightened hesitation and the uncontrollable chatter of his teeth, and then, as if impelled by something primitive and innocent, he crawled away from the door and toward her, knowing she would be near sleep, chapped little-girl hands buried, crisscross, in her armpits or her crotch (he had kept them warm himself that way enough to know), and found her by reaching forward blindly in the dark, smelled the weariness, the wet and unchanged clothes, the woman of her as he knelt there, and heedlessly lay down beside her then, opening his coat.

"Okay," she murmured in her drowse, moving in against him, trusting and submissive as a sleepy, cold-nosed puppy. "I'm okay, you bet," she murmured, burrowing into his shoulder automatically as he wrapped the flaps of coat around her, under and over, feeling the stubborn, meager heat of her body merging gradually with his (like a mystery, like a miracle), the soft wisp of her bangs tickling his chin, her hands coming up across her chest to clasp together in tiny cold fists, their two breaths (faint and hot) inside each other's mouths—so that, out of nowhere, he was suddenly full of something fearful and moving that only years later would he recognize as a kind of love; and planning not to, planning to lie carefully, motionlessly awake all night, grave and protective for all his fifteen years, nevertheless fell instantly asleep, and woke to a sweetness that would last him all life long.

There was the girl in the morning light, a child's dream (simple and absorbing) touching her child's mouth with an elusive, tranquil smile; and when she stirred once in his coat, there before his eyes a tear was frozen on her weather-roughened cheek; though even as he saw it, he knew, with a thrill of understanding, that her eyes had merely watered from the cold, and she had not cried.

And there, too, over the curve of her shoulder, and just beyond, Edgar lay, sharp knees gathered up almost to his chest, arms crossed upon it in the immemorial attitude of birth and death, face indrawn, intent, as if occupied with the sheer accumulation of sleep, his breath making a faint and delicate vapor before his mouth.

And there, finally, over the curve of Edgar's shoulder, and beyond, the open doorway was bright with chilly sun, and miraculously they had come through the storm, and south out of the snow itself—for sere, cropless fields and clumps of naked trees and lonely, grieving barns flowed steadily, headlong, backward past the doorway, as if on the surface of a great river flooded from horizon to horizon.

It was all proper and beautiful to Metro—the girl and Edgar and himself in that new morning. He loved and understood and accepted them completely, and would not have wakened them, even to tell them that something in

the clear air, in the scoured light, in the very color of
the earth out there was murmuring "Thaw, thaw" with such
indescribable clarity that he lay very quietly, transfixed
with simple wonder, feeling "Thank Old God for His
sweet morning, thank Old God for His winter fields loosen-
ing towards spring, thank Old God I'm here, and haven't
missed it!"

It was quicker than that, what he felt; it was simpler,
and it was not words. It was, rather, a knowledge (instantaneous with what he saw, inseparable from it) that
night and its emotions pass, and the girl's mystery becomes
the child's tranquility again, and the bitter boy lies intent,
accumulating sleep despite his bitterness, and innocence is
all—the soul's innocence which is nearest us at dawn, and
cannot be sullied no matter how we try; and, in truth, he
felt, the end of life is not mere hunger after all, and we
would be as natural and sweet as animals, if we but knew
we were.

"Yes," swelled in his young mouth, "yes"—all of wisdom
he would ever need—"yes, Old God, I see our three heart-
beats in vapor on your morning air! Oh, *yes!*"

The magic of that morning held even when, half an
hour later, the girl woke just as they pulled into another
baffling switchpoint in the middle of nowhere, and scram-
bling to her feet, her eyes immediately bright and excited,
she sat, legs hung out the door, craning eagerly and ex-
claiming, "Oh, smell them? . . . Buckwheats frying somewheres, and molasses still in the can! . . . And, oh, I'm
bad hungry too," so that, as they ground to a halt, and
she poised forward over the tracks, face lifted with foolish
and ecstatic hope to catch that rare, illusory fragrance,
she looked around at them with a good, quick smile (as at
an afterthought) to say, "My name's Helen, an' I'm from
Waco once," already inching her hips toward the drop off,
mended by the night, ready for day. "But they always call

me Little Old," she added with a soft, delighted giggle, and then, just as she pushed herself off, already scenting out breakfast and warm kitchens and something wonderful in that outlandish whistle stop, she murmured, "So long now."

The magic lasted even when Metro heard Edgar muttering to himself as he stared out the door, ". . . get ganged in a reefer, or trip and fall under, or just give up some night when the snow won't quit, or get given the redlights by wild boys somewhere where no one even *cares* when they find her . . . you wait, you wait and see," but saw instead Edgar's passionate eyes following her as she loped over the dreary tracks in the ungainly, comic galoshes, making for a sooty clump of sumacs. "Poor, dumb kid!" he ground out, furious for feeling it, "dumb, ofay broad!" But then looked away quickly, sniffing nervously under Metro's gaze, to add with unhappy cruelty, "Well, anyway, a man needs his nookie now and then." And it was the magic that made Metro realize, in a rush, that he would not trade what he had had of her with Edgar, who had had the other.

After that, it was Kansas City, Edgar readying his bundle, meticulously brushing off his suit and shoes, frowning and sour-lipped at something in his head, the frown only deepening when he said, "Look, you ain't *going* anywhere— Where you *going* anyway?"

"I don't know. Maybe south. I could go south until it's warmer . . ."

It was Edgar's mouth, puckered and ungiving, as he said, "Listen, *this* right here's as far south as any colored boy should go. Don't you know that! Hell, you too stupid to be traveling. You only heading for another mission, or another jail. If *you* have any say in it, you get yourself killed, or froze, or sick . . . Look at them shoes! Don't you know no better than to let 'em get that bad before you start hustling for a new?" He seemed full to bursting with a bottled rage. "No," he said decisively, as if more out of concern for himself than Metro. "No, you better come with me. We find *something* you can do. Only get yourself cleaned up now. This ain't no bummie's town, this here's KayCee. Remember what I say."

It seemed already settled in Edgar's mind, and, curiously, it settled itself in Metro's too, all in a moment, with the thought: "All right, I *ain't* going nowhere, but I *ain't* a kid no more like he always says neither . . . so maybe it's time, maybe it's time—"

Thereafter, Metro tagged along—back to the shabby rooms off the shabby street, the drawn paper shades rotting in the sun, the smell of laundry soap and steam, the old linoleum and the dripping tap, and the small, nervous, bird-eyed woman folding clothes, who looked up, alarmed to see her son (taller, graver, almost a man), and began crying at the sight with a sudden uprush of self-pity that seemed to have little to do with him.

"You already broke my heart once—you broke your mother's heart, Eddie, you know that?—and here you come back again!" her tears flowing easily, as if weeping was the one thing she felt natural doing.

She gave him a helpless, vaguely recriminating embrace, which he returned with an embarrassed frown (he who a moment before had run up the last steps, unable to be nonchalant any longer), and then she put out a saucepan of cold chickpeas for them to eat, to which he sat down with hardly a word. Later she listened to his plans about the horn inattentively, watching to see that he had enough milk, and saying carelessly, "That's real nice, Eddie, yes, that's nice."

"But I'll make good money," he kept saying, furious with disappointment, just as if she had offered opposition. "You wait and see—"

"Now, won't that be nice," she muttered again, and then her eyes brightened with suppressed emotion. "Your pa's back, you know," she said cagily, "livin' down on Eighteenth Street. And he been around here already, just as if I didn't have enough to trouble me . . . And I never know *when* he gonna turn up, Eddie, just like that, all of a sudden, with his liquor, pleading and hollering at me. My, my, I just don't know what I *done* to be tried so," but, for all of this, she seemed curiously pleased and excited by it too, as if in some queer way she was being courted again. Edgar was pale with wrath.

Still later, Metro tagged along to the bare back room, and the inevitable pile of old records that lies on a table or the floor in boys' rooms all over America (gray in those grooves where some solo or phrase or mere fleeting sound had been learned by heart); the scarred records which shaving fathers curse to hear first thing in the morning, and patient mothers tolerate; the all but label-less records, and the crank cardboard-and-leatherette victrola to play them on, which were, it was explained, the spoils of an ash-can raid following the death of a man upstairs; the records they listened to that first night, Metro winding awkwardly, Edgar tapping his thigh as he had done in the freight car, absorbing with new attentiveness the scratchy, squeezed sonorities of old river bands jamming recklessly into an acoustical horn. Later yet, they slept in the same slat bed under a lumpy quilt, and Edgar said just as he turned over, "They don't think I will. *She* don't, anyway. But I'm gonna do it. I am. I don't *care*."

So Metro tagged along two days later, down through the gaudy streets where the black big-wheeled gang cars rolled like dreadnoughts to the pawnshop where, among the strings of watches and cheap rings, among the dusty hip flasks and feathered hats, Edgar had seen the horn a day before. He waited while the lynx-eyed broker eased it out of the window begrudgingly, even though the soiled and hoarded bills were visible in Edgar's fist, to let him try it—the dented old Selmer with squeaky keys and a bad rust spot on the bell, veteran (perhaps) of a thousand dreary afternoons in pawnshop windows all the way from Elkhart to KayCee—narrowing one eye while Edgar blew a few wheezing cackles, gauging how much the frowning, wordless youth would pay, and then naming a price (twenty dollars) with such good-humored insincerity that it would have been obvious to anyone less obsessed that it sounded fantastic even to him, so that when Edgar promptly counted out the money, saying only, "I'll give you eighteen-fifty, and I want the neck sling goes with it," it was all he could do to swallow, snort into a handkerchief, and exclaim admiringly, "Boy, you got yourself a horn— You can play a hymn on it, or a rag on it, or just naturally make noise, but no matter what it is, all that's missing from *that* there horn is wind!"

"You wait," Edgar promised as they took it home. "I'm gonna *play*, Met, you'll see. Cause all my fingering came right back to me when I tried the tone back there . . . You just wait and see."

Metro waited, and never afterward forgot the weeks that followed, for they were *his* initiation into jazz as well, and led directly to the wild bars in which, years later, he would zonk his primal "Yes!" For Kansas City, just then, was having its moment as the magnet for jazzmen from everywhere, and though no one can say whether this results from the juxtaposition of the right men and the right conditions, or merely from the accidental association of an idea with a place, jazz history is primarily the history of such abrupt and baffling geographical centers of attraction, and Kansas City's time had come. The nights jumped on and on, there seemed to be a piano everywhere, and the sweating drummers backing them never tired or let up; all the bars overflowed onto the sidewalks, and people drank hootch in the alleys, cooling off, and even dawn brought sessions for the indestructible, who could never get enough; a tremendous burgeoning was everywhere, and every bus or train seemed to bring some new horn from St. Louis, Omaha, Minneapolis, Dallas, Tulsa, or Natchez-Under-The-Hill, rumor of whom had already reached two-o'clock Twelfth Street.

Metro never afterward forgot the long, preparatory afternoons either, when Edgar practiced in the wood-room down the hall, while he lifted and carried washing for his mother, calling her "ma'am" and nodding as she contentedly laid out before him (as you might before a servant) all the burdens, woes and miseries of her life—"Oh, yes, he gonna go just like his pa, winin' and whorin', no matter what I do. They like to kill me between them, and I was raised gentle too, you know"—the long narrative of complaint which was her one delight; neither of them, after a while, even noticing the muffled throating of the horn (beginning, breaking off, beginning once again), except when Metro went for wood to keep the kettles steaming, to find Edgar, forehead all knotted and seamed with the contortions of his fingers, eyes clenched shut, sweating and tireless over his scales. "You got to work every day," he would explain, resting on the chopping block. "This guy in Chicago told me to play them scales till I could do it twenty minutes, thinking of something else . . . You see? Something else *entirely!*" He went about it with an all-excluding ability to dedicate, and apply, and never weary, fretting over his blurry tone, scraping his reed, screwing down on it, compressing his lips, and then asking, "But how does it sound? I mean, it's still all *wet*. It ain't *clear* somehow . . ."

Metro listened to them both, hurrying up and down the hall, properly grave-eyed when the mother so moved herself with her own tales that she took to weeping sympathetically into her tubs; pausing long enough to beat out the time with an old hairbrush on a wad of newspaper while Edgar lumbered through "Comin' Virginia"; somehow getting through the meals when mother and son closed over, each constricted by the other, each content to be silent in a separate egoism, each certain of an ally in him.

He got through the unvarying red beans and rice, simply because of the oncoming night, because of the pulse of excitement that seemed to quicken in the very air like some freak of climate as the sun went down toward Kansas over the viaduct, because after they had eaten he knew he and Edgar would go out, walking off the heavy food down the roaring neon blocks of jazz bars, to pick out one, Sam's Academy Club, where a fat bartender, working his frothy taps, yelled out ecstatically over a piano, "Oh, yes, I'm gonna jump and shout—yes, yes, I'm gonna jump and shout—I'm gonna jump and holler till the lights go out!" to stand there in the crowd, transfixed, with one beer and (though Metro was big for his age) one Nehi orange soda too, pressed close to thirsty men and laughing girls, fanning their chests in the heat of the place: all eager just to be moved by the music, the drinks, the night itself—full of a passionate appetite for life that was a revelation to Metro.

"But, you know," he would hazard between sets, "they play *different* things all the time. How do they learn all them songs?"

Edgar scoffed at his naïveté. "You got to get on to it. It sound so hard to you because you don't play nothing, that's all . . . You can't really under*stand* it, 'less you blow yourself . . . Now, me, I'm studying all the time when they play, and working out the fingering on my leg like this, see . . . I guess just about anyone can learn horn if he works at it," he added, solemnly pleased with himself. "But you got to have your *ideas* too, you got to have that *in* you."

Then one evening they came home and found Edgar's father sitting over a bottle of beer in the kitchen, the overhead light picking up the ugly scar along his cheek as he leaned back in the middle of some long harangue, to which Edgar's mother listened, cowed and uneasy over her stove, though when she turned and said, "Say Hello to your pa, Eddie," there was an odd but unmistakable exhilaration in her voice as well.

"Well now, boy," he said expansively, genuinely pleased to see Edgar, but ruffled too, "just look at you! . . . You got too big to whip. You almost big enough to have yourself a job and a gal . . . Why, I guess I been a year on the railroad when I was your age . . . But that's all right, you got time."

"I been two years on it," Edgar said sternly.

His father coughed with drink and laughter. "You ain't too big to sass though, are you? . . . And I hear you got yourself a horn to fool with— Well, that's all right too. I was out hollerin' all night 'fore I was really grown, and still made my schedule, sleep or no . . ." He banged the table with a big fist. "Yes, sir, boy, you at the great age, right now— Oh, I ain't forgot it. You just naturally want to drink up all the booze, lay all the gals, go, go, go, now don't you? Oh, I remember . . . Only, listen, you want to put something by for when you get tired too. Now, look at me," he said, turning tipsily thoughtful. "I never put nothin' by—worked all my life, boozed, went on, and got nothin' to show for it now. But I never got no *notions* either, no, sir! . . . You follow me? . . . No, boy, get yourself a job, good colored-man's job where you know where you at Monday mornings, and don't have no trouble with—"

"I'm gonna play horn," Edgar said, "and that ain't white *or* colored."

His father peered at him, eyes slitted over the bottle that was poised at his mouth.

"You listen to your pa now, Eddie," his mother cautioned in a defeated yet reproving voice, as if she was relieved to surrender to someone else's will.

"I'll listen to him all right, but I'm still gonna play my horn."

His father's eyes flared briefly, and he muttered, "You gonna be one dicty nigger, now ain't you?" But then he laughed generously. "Just look at that boy, El. He got so many *notions* . . . Well, that's all right too. I seen his kind on freights alla way from here to Denver—sassy, snooty, *lazy,* every one—" He leaned further back, at his ease. "Well, boy, you find out. You still got *time* to find out . . . And I be *here* when you do."

"What d'you mean?"

His mother's eyes darted back and forth, refusing to look at him, but pleading with him nevertheless, as if this was the moment she had been dreading. "Now, Eddie, honey, you be a good boy now. I done everything I could for you, what with washin' all day and worryin' all night, but it ain't the same. I need somebody *by* me, Eddie, I do . . . So your pa's gonna be livin' here again. And it's gonna be just like it used to be . . ."

His father's scar wrinkled crookedly as he smiled with faint scorn and said, "That's right, boy. And I guess you big enough to have a beer with your old man, eh? Now he's come home? . . . Get him a beer, El."

"I can buy my own beer," Edgar said, and turned away.

Metro would never afterward remember what happened next without the feeling that something essential had escaped his attention, for (all in a moment, it seemed) Edgar was gone, leaving him standing there staring at the hurt in the father's angry eyes, and then he was back, the caseless horn carried under an armpit and over a forearm, like a shotgun, as he got the outside door open, not hesitating at the father's harsh "You come back here, boy," or at the mother's sudden blubbering either, so that Metro felt called upon to murmur " 'Scuse me" before he ran after him.

He tagged along down the dark blocks, alarmed by the stubborn expressionless lips, the cold passionate eyes, just as he had been alarmed by Edgar's silent coupling with the girl; and wanting to say something to him, something about the frozen tear on the sleeping cheek, something about the scoured morning air, but did not know what to say, and could not have put it into words even if he had, so only blurted out, "He was mad, you know, but then he was sorry too—when you ran out . . . Where—where we going?"

Edgar said nothing for a long moment, storming along in his fury's terrible containment, but just as Metro was about to ask again, he said with a bitter and ferocious calm, "I know something he *don't* know, I do . . . There's more than—than just all *this*," and his head gestured rashly. "And yesterday, you know, I got an idea on 'Virginia' that I thought, 'Jee-*suss*, I can't stand this one, no one can take this one,' and I felt—well—" and he spat with impotent rage. "I wasn't going to tell no one either . . . Besides, we only got a dollar twenty left. But there's more, goddamn, *more*. And I tell you, I know something he *don't*, Met, and all I got to do now is find out what it is, that's all I got to do . . . Well, anyhow," he added, lips setting to against any further explanation, "the money get us through tonight anyway," and at that he veered to the left and through the door of Sam's Academy Club.

Even years later Metro was never certain that he remembered it correctly, and all he could have sworn to was a series of hectic images, like single frames from a movie sequence—Edgar standing near the stand where piano, bass, drums and two funky horns worked in a random huddle under a smoky spot, looking suddenly raw and long-necked and very young in his shabby and preposterous suit; Edgar bending over the piano to murmur into the cocked ear of the man there, who drew back, noting the battered horn already snapped into its sling, and the solemn, unpleading face, and shook his head briefly; and then Edgar waiting during the next number, intent and unswervable right at the man's elbow, fingers moving on the stops as he picked out the music in utter seriousness, to bend once more when it was over and repeat the few stubborn words again, undoubtedly the very same words as before, no new arguments added, not even the arrangement of the words themselves altered; to stand when he had said them, gaze passionless and unflickering, as the trumpet man came over, leaned, and listened, and then looked where the single finger of the pianist gestured; to find Edgar staring off at nothing now, straight-backed, tensed, yet obviously certain he looked casual, every now and then shaping the absurd fringe of mustache between two careful fingers. Then a mass of heads and shoulders blocked Metro's view, and when they moved away Edgar was no longer at the piano, and Metro searched the crowd for him, thinking with a wave of relief, "No. See. He ain't going to do it. He ain't," only at that moment to discover Edgar among the musicians, horn held gingerly up and ready, face full of crazy, grave resolve, as the trumpet man tapped off a beat.

"And I never really believed him *either,*" Metro realized in a flash.

And so he was not surprised when they took up the first chorus and it turned out to be "I'm Comin' Virginia," for, once having gotten them to allow him to sit in, it seemed only natural that somehow Edgar should have succeeded in getting them to do his tune as well. There he was, face strained and diligent as they jammed together, and yet curiously self-absorbed as well—sweat running down into his winced eyes to hang glistening on his lids as he struggled to keep ahead of the beat that waited for no man, and subdue the horn that was still just a baffling contraption of metal and wire to him, and yet aware all the time (Metro saw) how crude and uncertain it sounded; so that it came home to Metro just how much Edgar *really* wanted to play (aside from any of the reasons he gave), how deeply he had longed for the moment he was actually having then, how blinded to reality he was by his desire.

For during the solos, Edgar stood, lean and nonchalant, waiting his turn, listening to the others' work, attentive, even analytical as he rested one hand on the neck of his horn the way you might upon a convenient chair back, not looking at the soloist, but not exactly looking away either, only occasionally studying someone out front distantly, and then relapsing into the patient, abstract stare. And then at a nod from the trumpeter he began to blow, stumbling over the naked rhythm on which (for the first time) he had to shape his song, but then righting himself with a remonstrative tapping of his foot, and plunging ahead, buckled down to it now, pulled forward (as it seemed) by the very weight of the big horn, knotted face all stricken and obsessed and oblivious of everything there—perhaps most of all of the fact that what he blew was not very good; uncaring that the trumpet man watched him with a tolerant half-smile, or that the bassist was talking over his shoulder to someone; feeling it *in* him for the first time (whatever it was), so that all Metro could think of was Edgar, alone among the cordwood, with his inchoate half-feelings, too strong, too crowding to be experienced to the full, with only the unmalleable horn on which to expend them: his truth, whatever it was, coming on him too suddenly for him to worry long enough about his fingers to do more than blow a faltering hint.

But it was not until they finished up, wiped their foreheads, discussed it for a moment, and began on "Changes Made" that Edgar's intention to play, no matter what, came home to Metro with sufficient force to make him wonder, for the first time, whether a music that could awaken such emotions might not be more than simply a way to keep the belly filled and still sleep late of mornings. For, from the start, it sounded wrong, as though someone was out of tune; but there was Edgar, face all gathered in frowning concentration around his mouthpiece, long young neck streaked with rivulets of sweat, blowing for all he was worth, and yet blowing wrong. And then it occurred to Metro, with a flush of mortification and amazement, that it wasn't that he was out of tune at all; it was that he was still playing "Comin' Virginia"—methodically fitting it on the new rhythm, playing it loud and sure (because it was the only song he knew), even playing it better than he had before, but still intending to play at any cost.

The trumpet man darted a sharp, quizzical glance over the bell of his horn, and hastened into a solo, as if to save whatever was left; a solo during which Edgar held on, expressionless, seemingly at his ease, bright alert eyes almost blasé while the others passed it back and forth, pointedly leaving no room for him (though at each break his fingers readied themselves on the stops, and he started forward), listening attentively, waiting patiently, and when they all went right into the final chorus without giving him his chance, accepting that too, and joining them, still playing his one sure tune, perhaps even playing it well (who could tell?), but working hard and carefully one way or the other, while the drummer guffawed at the bent and witless sound, and people buzzed over drinks, thinking it a joke.

When it was over, he still made no move to leave, his calm, mad, unwearying face registering a clear intention to play the one song all night if they would let him, so that the others drew away from him for a moment into a whispering group at the back of the stand. Edgar, left there alone to hide his eagerness behind the crazy nonchalance with which he rested on his dented horn, shot puzzled glances toward them every now and then, too shy to intervene, yet straining to overhear; and then the trumpet man detached himself, came up decisively, put a firm and wary hand upon his shoulder, muttered a few miffed words, and then rejoined the others.

Whatever it was he said, it brought an immediate change to Edgar's face, as if he had been rudely shaken out of sleep. He hesitated for a moment, eyes downcast in his abrupt confusion, all the casualness turning awkward, lips stiffening with pangs of pride whose first demand seemed to be subterfuge, looking adolescent and inept, and for the first time pitiable; and then, all at once, he turned and reeled away without a word.

Outside, pushing heedlessly through that night's throngs, Metro tried to help. "They played a song you didn't know, but on the other one—"

"No," Edgar said mercilessly, tonelessly. "You don't know—"

"But you sounded *good* on the other one—"

"*No!*" he repeated with fierce conclusiveness. "Everybody can blow *one* song, everybody got their *own* song they can blow . . . But what is that. That ain't it—"

"But I *heard*, didn't I?" Metro insisted. "I know *something*, don't I?"

But Edgar would not listen any more, closing over inside himself, offering no further explanations, making no more excuses, though his bitter lips said much he could not say.

There seemed to be a hurt in him now that was beyond words, and he lay on his back in the slat bed, holding it into him as if the pain itself could teach: the first hurt of his life he could not ease with rage. And Metro knew there was nothing to be done, there was no help, and so tried to sleep, and did at last, and never found out what the trumpet man had said to him. But woke alone to find only the horn beside him, and only a note stuck in the bell to tell him why.

"I get me another one somewheres," it said. "Maybe even Hopeville got a horn— But don't you ever hock it. Give it to someone first— Your friend, Edgar Pool.". . .

"And I never did," Metro said at last, draining his Coke with a single swallow, and looking (warm with memory) at Walden, who had taken Wing's seat on the case of empties when Wing went in to phone the Go Hole once more before they left. "I still got it home on a closet shelf . . . But that's why I never blew like him, see, cause by the time I *really* dug him, coupla years later, I already had my own way, and besides," he added, looking down, "by then he'd found himself, and *changed*. You know."

"But that's how bad he is now, man," Walden said. "That's why we got to find him, cause *he* hocked his sometime earlier tonight—"

Metro stared at him, large-eyed, full of thoughts.

"Curny told us. Edgar came by his rehearsal, wanting loot, but all the time—"

"Poor Eddie," Metro murmured, and then added sadly, "no one calls him that no more, I guess . . ."

For a moment, neither of them said anything, staring out into the soft autumn rain that filled the alley with its unabated rustle, and Metro's look said that, though he was thinking of Edgar and the freight (lost or cut up long ago) that had caused their lives to converge, like two dissecting lines, for one brief period twenty years before, to center for a moment around one horn on which both had learned their trade—each heading a different way when they met, each taking different truths from the few things they shared (the girl, the storm, the horn itself), and each having gone toward an unalterably different end since then— There was nothing more that he could do for Edgar now—just as there had been nothing then.

But at that moment Wing came back, and answered Walden's questioning glance with only: "Yes. He's down there. He come in five minutes ago—and they say he's *bad*."

"We'd better cut then," Walden said, getting up.

"I got to get back myself," Metro began, grasping an arm of each. "But—well, if he needs cash, or—just anything at all, you phone me now," perhaps remembering that once a half-chewed sandwich and an impatient laugh and a scrap of angry song had saved him from despair. "You call now, man. I'm here all night."

And so he went back to his fidgeting rhythm section that was wild to begin again; and as Wing and Walden left, there he was, grinning shyly at the eager crowd, clear-eyed as he uncapped his mouthpiece, ready to call them all together one more time, announcing with his fat-toned song: Who do I love, and celebrate, and covet? . . . All these: all shouters, dancers, boasters; all who turn the volume higher; all given to extravagant gestures, and impulsive kisses; all thigh-slappers, back-pounders, breast-touchers; those who weep, and laugh, and love easily, and hear God's joyful hands keep time to all their couplings. All these, and Edgar, too.

For Metro's God was still the God he'd thanked for morning all those years ago, when he had known the breath in Edgar's sleeping mouth as final evidence that all was one, pride or humility; and that the only sacrament was life, the very breath itself. And just because of this, Metro's God laughed, Metro's God loved; and Metro took his horn into his mouth to say in song, as he said it every night, his single, simple truth: Go, and do thou likewise.

They left him to it, and went downtown to end their search.

RIFF

In that corner of the Go Hole's kitchen that was reserved
for the musicians, where a few straight chairs (too broken
for the customers) and a scarred table with a large cracked
dinner plate for an ash tray stood, something was just beginning. Cleo saw it foggily through his drunkenness,
powerless to do anything but understand; saw Edgar,
through the haze of steam around the coffee urns, lift the
pint he had obtained somewhere, and take a long, drowning choke out of it, wincing, holding the liquor in his
mouth for a moment as if afraid to let the burning slice of
it pass his throat, only to swallow all at once, hurrying it
down into his stomach, and then lurch on his heel to shout
to the rest of the kitchen.

"Like, listen, can't you cats keep it *down!*", all but
stamping his foot. "I mean, how can anyone dig the

band!" he roared at the faces of waiters and cooks that swung on him curiously. "Now, *shush!*" cocking his head to catch the smooth, muffled hushings of a tenor sax through the clatter of plates and the barking of orders.

"Like I was saying, I figure I can borrow *his*," he went on, jerking his chin toward the sound. "I figure I can blow you two sets okay, only, look here, Samm, I wan' fifteen each set, an' choose my own tunes, an' another bottle when this one's run out, or I'll go round the corner to Paradise Alley." He smiled the bargainer's bleary, hungry smile.

"He can't even *walk* that far," muttered the young trumpeter, Kelcey Crane, much to everyone's surprise, for he was small-boned, with sensitive, gloomy eyes, and a fatalistic mouth out of which very little ever came.

Mr. Samm, who ran the place, a solid, rotund, argumentative little man—whose dark jowl and sulky, shrewd mouth said very clearly: Oh, no, you don't! Now you listen to *me*—laughed at Edgar as if he enjoyed audacity on certain occasions, secure in the knowledge that he could not be intimidated by it. "You're giving *me* terms? I love it. It's rich."

"Man, I got to have thirty for the night," Edgar repeated, taking another swig out of the bottle, "or what's the sense . . ."

Mr. Samm noted the bottle, calculated, and decided to say nothing about it at that moment. "Okay," he agreed evenly. "Only I want a full set, no funny business, no short choruses— You understand me? And I can't give you a bottle, you know that."

At this, Kelcey Crane sighed, balanced his trumpet on one knee, leaned forward slightly, looking at Mr. Samm imperturbably, and announced abruptly, "Look. *I* won't play with him."

"You won't play with him!" Mr. Samm shot back. "You're advertised. You got to play."

Kelcey continued to look at him with hot, quenched eyes, like a consumptive. "Look. He's already gotten our piano man so stoned he can't nearly stand up. Look at him," one limp finger indicating Cleo slouched at the table, trying to get down a cup of coffee. "You expect me to blow with a drunken kid *and* this goof! . . . Man, I don't play with goofs any more."

Mr. Samm's peevish frown perfectly expressed his weariness with trying to make a living out of art, and he sighed with ominous patience, and said, "Now, Kelcey, I want you to understand me, because you're young and temperamental, and that's okay. You're an artist or something, and that's okay too. But you'll blow tonight, or so help me you'll never work my place again. I mean, you're advertised, and they've come to hear you, and so they're gonna hear you— You understand me?"

Kelcey looked away, haughty and impolite, to study his nails sullenly. All the while, Edgar had been standing there, holding his stomach in a peculiar, unconscious gripe, his pale sweating face twisted into the half-mocking, half-disdainful expression that everyone always thought of as "Horn's sneer," but all he said was, "Why don' nobody ask me if I'll play with *him?* Man, I never even *heard* him before. Who is he? How do I know he can follow where I'm going? . . . Hey, man, le's hear your *tone* there . . . And, here, have yourself a choke," he added, holding the pint forward with a queer lop-sided, goading grin. "Go ahead. I ain't got no germs—"

"All right, all right," Mr. Samm broke in sternly. "You've had enough. If you're going to work my place, lay off the booze. You understand me?"

Edgar put the pint down with a somehow insolent docility. "Man, I understand you. It's your idea I had enough to drink already."

"That's right."

"And I guess you oughta know," Edgar murmured, but Mr. Samm did not hear it, because he was peering at his watch, tapping the face sharply as if to jog the time ahead, listening to the unhurried tick with a frown.

"Okay, you got five minutes," he said conclusively, "and no funny business, and no antics, and no goofing. You understand me?"

"Man, I really think we do," Edgar said with a snicker, reaching for the pint as Mr. Samm turned and hurried away after a waiter. "I understood you the day I was born."

He lifted the bottle toward his mouth, and then paused at a thought. "Here," he said, offering it to Billy James Henry, who had stood, plainly discomforted and just as plainly irritated, through the entire exchange. "Have a choke, man. Like it might loosen up your right hand so you can really *blow*."

Billy James turned away with a hopeless pout of anger. "We ought to run through at least the line," he said to Kelcey. "And what tunes are we gonna do, anyway?"

"*I'm* not gonna play I tell you," Kelcey said. "Are you serious? Look at him."

Edgar's lids were heavy half-moons of weariness as he coughed off his last swallow into a sodden and disreputable handkerchief. "We can do 'Heart Stood Still,'" he mumbled, "or 'Don' Blame Me,' or 'Lush Life,' or 'Outa Nowhere,' unless you got some goony ol' tone poems up your sleeve—"

"Are you serious, man?" Kelcey repeated to Billy James, his puritanical, doomed gaze unwavering.

"But you heard Samm. What are we gonna do?"

"Though, man, I don't want to do 'Outa Nowhere,'"

Edgar mumbled on, "cause I did that one las' night. I guess it was las' night."

Kelcey got up, hands caught low on his slim hips, and looked at Edgar coldly. "I'm not doing anything," he stated.

Edgar noticed him. "But you been doing that one for years, man," he drawled sarcastically. "Here, you wanta choke?"

"Now, look," Kelcey said, actually leveling a finger. "Let's face it. Man, you're so drunk, you can't blow. I mean, let's *face* it . . . I don't care, I'm hip, but *look* at yourself," the finger waggling up and down impatiently, "that crazy suit, you ain't changed it for a couple a days, and you spilled something on the shirt, and you're sick, man, so all right, but you got no horn, and you're lushed to the eyeballs. I mean, who cares, but let's *look* at it. You let yourself go completely."

Edgar stared at him stonily, coughing quietly in his throat, but he said nothing.

"See," Kelcey concluded, turning away. "Like he can't even hear me."

"But maybe if we do a whole set of heads, old ones—"

"Oh, come on," Kelcey said harshly. "Man, it's just another binge to him, he don't care, but why should we get mixed up in it? . . . I ain't gonna blow with him, I tell you."

"It's my *only* suit," Edgar said as a whole tray of dishes clattered into a nearby sink. "I could get it pressed— Jeesuss, will you please keep it *down!*" he hollered, half turning to the rest of the kitchen again, a wild fury livid on his face. "You bastards gonna *break* something!" he yelled. And then, all of a sudden, he grabbed a couple of plates off a stack at hand, and shattered them on the floor at his feet, kicking at the fragments and almost losing his balance.

193

"You gonna smash something," he repeated, sneering crookedly at the sight of the scattered shards. "Man, why not have a belt?" he said to Billy James' shocked face.

"Take it easy, for Christ's sake!" Kelcey snapped out with alarm. "They'll hear you out front—"

But Edgar only laughed—a low, bitter, careless laugh that was almost half a cough. "They won't know who it is," he said. "Man, not one of 'em'd know who it was, even if he heard me . . . And don't worry," he added, winking with giddy sagacity at Billy James, "they got lots a plates."

"That's what I mean," Kelcey said with a pout of annoyance, and he went back and sat down again without so much as a look at Edgar, who was now bending over Cleo unsteadily, the bottle tilted into the coffee as he spiked it generously, murmuring, "Come on, kid. Hey, come on. Cause I'm starting to hear it again . . . *You* have a drink with ol' Horn. Cause I'm gonna blow, man, and did you see me break them plates? Heh, heh . . . Hey, kid, come on, come on now—"

But Cleo only looked up at him with a great blank, vague gaze, thinking dizzily, "Which? Which is it that he hears?"

But Edgar had raised himself up once more, all the fume of that day's drink now flooding over his waxen features, eyes in an abrupt and perilous uproll, shoulders sloping forward with an exhaustion of the bone itself, which he could not even feel any more, one hand pressing his stomach in that same rigid, unthinking gripe. He suddenly murmured to himself, "Man, you'll never get yourself home—"

Billy James looked over sharply. "What d'you say?"

"I said— Man, like I said maybe I won' go home after all," Edgar stumbled out with a loose half-grin. "Come on. Have a choke. Really . . . But none of you *serious* cats booze, do you?" and so he finished off the bottle in one ghastly, chin-straining gulp.

"Stop it," Billy James exclaimed, shaking his head with an unbelieving wince. "Stop it now. Man, you got to stop."

But Edgar didn't even blink as he threw the bottle carelessly away onto the floor, among the jagged fragments of the plates. He only wiped his mouth with a saw of his sleeve across the lips, and stared fixedly at them all.

"Why?" he said. "Why do I got to stop?"

CHORUS:EDGAR (1)

"Endure!—no—no—defy!"

POE

". . . And in line with the Go Hole's policy of bringing you the very best in modern jazz, as a special, added, sur*prise* attraction—blowing for the first time with these swinging younger musicians—a classic in his own time, and still known affectionately to everyone as the Horn—the influ*en*tial, the in*comp*arable—Edgar POOL! Let's bring him on with a big round of applause!"

Climbing after Cleo out of the darkness onto the stand, he thought, "You can make it happen any fool time you want to, boy. You always could," knowing suddenly, nevertheless, that the last gulp in the bottle had been the one gulp too many, because though he clearly saw the bass right there in his path, lying on its side like an oiled, wide-hipped woman, he stumbled into it anyway, setting up a hollow, discordant whirr in the soundbox; and so lurching to one side away from it, only to bump into the standing microphone, which bobbled back and forth with a series of sharp, amplified whacks and almost teetered off into the front tables. "Whyn't you get it out of the way, huh?" he mumbled to Billy James, and then stood for a moment, holding on to the mike, wincing and grinning emptily in the light, his suit baggy in the knees, wrinkled at the crotch; his tie blotched with spills; his shirt clearly unchanged, or even unbuttoned, in two days; his hair as long and stiff as a dervish; and yet his whole face so arrogant and self-proud that the sparse crowd applauded him. /

The lights seemed brighter than they had ever seemed before, and he turned his back on them, squinting at the fine drops of perspiration that glistened down the part in the drummer's hair as he bent off the stool to adjust the pedal of the standing cymbal, already muttering his rhythmic nonsense to himself through a cheekfull of gum.

"Hey, H-o-o-r-n!" a gay voice called out. "Where you b-e-e-n!"

But he had noticed the sax, left for him propped against the taut skin of the big drum, and without a further thought he reached for it (miraculously not losing his balance, though at the bottom of his stoop he was afraid for a moment that he was going to pitch head-first into the drummer's lap), and brought it up with him by the neck, experiencing a distant, professional curiosity about the heft and the key action and the reed. Automatically he snapped it into the sling, noting with a drum of fingers that the stops needed oil, tasting the other man's mouth on the beak, and, for the first time, missing his own horn with a workman's private, unsentimental affection for the tool worn to his own particular hand. Feeling that, he had a momentary flash of lucidity in the haze of the liquor. He had said he wasn't going to blow, and sold away the temptation with the horn, and yet here he stood, getting ready to begin. How in the world had it happened? He could not remember, and then he did. He had gotten drunk, and foolhardy, and brave. And now it was too late to be afraid.

He could hear Billy James tuning his strings (plonk— pause for another twist of the key—plunk, plunk), as the drummer, ankling his bass-drum pedal in short, preparatory booms, sat up, his tackle's shoulders moving in powerful, limbering hunches, to find Edgar's incurious black eyes upon him. "Don't worry, pops," he said, quizzically shifting his gum, uncertain and good-natured the way some drummers are. "I know you don't like no bombs or anything . . . I'll just keep it light and tasty—"

Edgar stared and said, "Really, man, I been here before, you know," and then turned arduously around into the hot sheet of light, through which the lacy, transient shapes of cigarette smoke drifted in a stately haze. He squinted against the four unblinking spots converging on him there at the mike, starting to make out the bobbing tips of cigarettes, and off to the right the dim bank of bar lights, across which unclear silhouettes moved in a restless frieze. Gradually the front tables materialized out of the featureless glare, like a photograph slowly taking shape in the developer, and he picked out a drink on the nearest table, and fixed on it, waiting for the ice cubes to appear. But then the sudden drowning dizziness came up out of his stomach again, and he knew that he was swaying, and widened his eyes, despite the blazing lights; and felt that alien, unfriendly thing moving in his belly again—not quite a hurt, but not just drink: rather as if his intestines were remorselessly clenching into a vicious knot that would inexorably grow into a pain. Involuntarily, he touched his shirt front to make it stop, and for a moment actually felt the curious writhing right through the shirt, thinking,

"Man, that ain't no rock no more," and wondered if he was going to be sick again. He got out the grimy, wadded handkerchief, but coughed into it instead, bringing up a small stain of bright blood, which, for some crazy reason, reassured him. "Well, if that's all that's left," he thought dumbly, "you got to the bottom of it." But what would he do now, what would he play? A lifetime of songs had vanished from his head in an instant.

"Hey, Horn!" that same wild voice yelled from out there in the thronged darkness, "blow 'Jun's Sees 'Er'!" leaving a ripple of laughter behind it as it died, like an echo that did not match the sound.

"Hey, 'Ah Got Rhythm'!" another shouted.

He stared out blindly into the smoke toward the voice, knowing the room intimately even though he could not really see it yet; knowing where the speakers were located, and where the dead areas were, and how much interference you got from the bar noise, and even how small the crowd was, just by the sounds—exactly as he knew two dozen other rooms along the rhythm streets of a dozen other cities in as many states, and knew their peculiar problems, too.

He had stood, naked in the light, waiting to begin, a thousand other nights that still had their brief immortality in his head; and there had been worse times, he reassured himself, there had been close times: Benny times, pot times, junk times, mad times. It had been worse before. Yes. He was only a little drunk, and a little sick, and a little older. But a man's life didn't fail him all in a moment. It didn't. And his will was stronger than his flesh; it always had been. You didn't lose that, you didn't. And if it could destroy you, it could save you, too.

"Hey, man," that gay voice yelled again, "wail one! 'Jun's Sees 'Er'!"

"B-flat," he began telling himself automatically, "then

—" But he did not want to play. He did not know whether he could do it any more, and sighed suddenly with an exhausted pout. He did not know whether he could even remember it enough to get started, and all at once hated that goading, disembodied voice, imagining a face for it—smirking, oily, confident, white, finally ignorant of all it took for him to stand there. The hate came up into him for a moment with pure and savage clarity—hate for the drinkers, the talkers, the glass-tappers, the foot-pounders, the sing-alongers, the eager and the bored, the hip and square; all those who had paid their money and, no matter what their reasons, expected value in return. He had given them a vision once, and they expected him to have it still, like a birthmark or a scar that no amount of life effaces, and they would settle for nothing less. He was a victim of his own past excellence.

"Blow!" the voice insisted. "Come on, man, like play the music!"

"Creep!" he thought, searching the glare to find it. "Don't walk towards *me*, you creep! I'll blow b-u-r-p at you! I'll blow c-r-a-p at you!"

The old mocking sneer passed dimly, fleetingly, across his beaten features as, for a moment, the hate conquered the drink and the gripe and the anxiety that neither had subdued till then. He could go through it cold, he thought in a fierce, slow rant. He could do it without trying. Almost gagging, he hated everything there—the smell of bad breath and dried saliva that filled his nose from the microphone, and the smell of melted Italian cheese and dishwater that came out of the kitchen each time the door swung, and the smell of his own liquored sweat and damp clothes, and most of all the *feel* of the impatient crowd out there who could see every stain down his tie, and every sleepless hour on his face, but whom he could not see. He had never cared before that a jazz musician was condemned to utter his truth in the half-dark of dangerous, thronged rooms where everyone's breath tasted of alcohol and cigarettes, and everyone left something of the day behind him at the door. But suddenly he saw that he had spent his life like a moody fugitive among sensation hunters, enunciating what seemed to him just then (because he could no longer remember how it went) a rare and holy truth in the pits of hell.

"You stupid creeps," he thought with icy defiance, standing before them like an insult, strong in his contempt, knowing that he could pitch over into that audience with a wild giggle, and be carried retching, laughing, spitting, lost, from the place, and it would not really matter. They had told worse stories of him already; he had done worse things. And with an insolent fumble of thick fingers, he blew all the way from *blurp* to *wheet* on the horn.

"Man, is he high!" someone whispered. "Man, he's twisted! But on what? On what?"

"Oh, come *on!*" Billy James snapped out in a biting undertone. "That mike's open!"

But even the alert, one-Scotch faces of the A and R men along the bar, and the initiate faces of the musicians lounging near the stairs down from the street, and all the hot, pale faces in the large, low-ceilinged room, had turned to look now, for Edgar was leaning close to the mike and saying something that echoed in a hoarse, booming gibberish through half a dozen loudspeakers.

"Hey, man, bring it *down* a couple a decibels!" someone yelled, and all at once it cleared as he drew back, and he was saying, ". . . you'll hush-up, we'd like to blow a little tone poem that used to be called 'Out of *N*owhere.'"

He half-turned from the microphone, snapping two stubby fingers to set a beat, staring fixedly from Billy James' stiff-lipped, angry glower of dissociation from the whole thing, to Cleo swaying at the piano like a vacant-eyed somnambulist.

"Are you girls ready?" he said with a crooked smile. "An' let's don't get too ambitious, because, like, I don't want to have to straighten anybody out," failing to notice that Kelcey had not come up onto the stand at all, but was still leaning against the mirrored pillar to one side, with the sulky, hungry-to-be-insulted slouch of a young punk gunman in a Laredo saloon. But the drummer picked up the beat anyway, and Edgar took his reed into his mouth, feeling but not tasting it (like a sacrament), and they began.

He had trouble with the reed from the first few bars. It let out queer, whistling squeaks whenever he ventured into the upper register, and, gloomy and unhurried, he would break off to fiddle with it intently, and then come back right in the middle of a phrase, throwing Billy James off each time. He played on indifferently, not thinking about what the changes were, but only watching the drink out there and thinking, "I take two, and then the trumpet, and the kid is good for two, and then maybe reprise and out— Hey, what the hell're you doing anyhow! Hey," for Cleo's chords were falling further and further behind, coming in a fraction of a bar later every moment, as if the music was reaching him only after a lapse in time. Edgar turned, turning the horn too, and was confronted by Billy James' blunt, angry profile, limned with a sweat of shamed embarrassment, as he muttered in furious half-whispers over his shoulder toward Cleo's young and stricken eyes, which were full of that curious agony of hopeless concentration that all drunks know.

"What in hell's wrong with him!" Edgar thought irritably, and then of course knew, remembering the tilt of the emptying pint over the coffee cup, piqued by a strange and unwelcome feeling of responsibility. "But, man, he only had a few lousy beers is all," he thought angrily.

"For Christ's sake!" Billy James was seething, "catch up!", his large, fleshy face livid with humiliation. Edgar broke off his chorus short.

"Buster," someone yawned audibly over the summary prit-t-t *boom* of the drums, "this group's just not *speakin'* to me," and Edgar searched blackly out into the haze for the origin of the voice, only to become aware that nothing was happening behind him.

He turned crossly in Kelcey's direction, thinking, "If we gonna do something here, man, let's do it," and saw his implacable sloping shoulders still leaning, poised and impertinent, against the pillar, his sullen young face pointedly averted. He felt a flash of aggravated fury at the insane stubbornness on that black face, the very willful slope of those shoulders. But then he was unsure whether he had finished his chorus or had simply broken off when his mind strayed, and hurriedly took the reed back into his mouth again, thinking angrily, "Whyn't you let me do my work without cutting up back there, you bastards, so I can remember where I'm at!" turning back into the light out of habit, vaguely aware that the steady clenching of his innards had shortened his wind. He blew on, eyes level, with that hoarse, strained and unpleasant tone, his face streaming with cold sweat, the reed grown throaty with saliva.

But suddenly he noticed that the trills of the piano had dwindled and slowed and finally stopped altogether, like his old crank victrola running inexorably down; and, turning again, he saw that Cleo had swayed away from the keyboard entirely, and was slumped off the end of his bench, staring blankly down into the tables at his feet, both hands flopped on his knees like two stranded crabs, his eyes fixed on nothing, with the catatonic's unwavering, compass-like adherence to his mental north.

Edgar let the reed out of his mouth, hesitated just as someone gasped excitedly, "Watch this! Watch what old

Horn does now!" and then went over to Cleo, right across the stand in the harsh, almost shadowless glare, frowning and remorseless, only to notice (as he swayed over him) that Cleo had no beard at all, not even the beginnings of a soft black fuzz, and probably had never shaved, though already the hip night had given up so many of its secrets to him.

"And he blows pretty fair piano, before *I* even had myself a horn," he thought begrudgingly, angry with himself because somehow he could not be angry with that young and beardless face. And, abruptly, he reached down and took Cleo's hands, both of them, in his own, complaining, "Come on now, kid, come on. This ain't no goddamn lesson . . . Come on, no, all the way aroun'," actually turning Cleo on the bench toward the keyboard again. "Come on," laying the two dumb hands upon the uncaring ivories, "B-flat . . . No, no, now right here, and then there," finding, and pressing, and sounding the chords, "that's right, and just the changes . . . Dah . . . dah-dah . . . That's right," unconscious, for that moment, that Billy James was glowering at them across his strings, or that someone hissed, "Dig! Dig! Here comes the put-down!" for it only seemed important then that Cleo's frozen fingers resume their collapsing, boneless spidering over the keys, and once they did he stumbled back to the mike to croak into it: "He's a good piano all right . . . don' worry," and then took up his horn again, and went on with the chorus.

He finished up, coughing (an empty convulsion down in his throat that freed nothing, and brought up nothing but a rusty, bitter taste), knowing for certain that no one would come in to relieve him, and they would just abandon him out there all alone if he let them. "But you blow anyway," he raged on bewilderedly to himself. "You don't plead no five with *no* one once you get on the stand with him," and he spun on Kelcey again to find the trumpet still hanging by its coil from one slim black finger, and the poised shoulders still leaning against the pillar, and the prim pout still narrowing the arrogant lips. But just as he was about to snap out a sharp remonstrative word, something about the pose struck him with undeniable familiarity, and he remembered how once he had stood like that, feigning indifference with his horn, off to one side, just as obstinate, just as nonchalant, just as wrapped in his own tangled, dark ego as Kelcey—just like that, though he had *longed* to blow.

Then he was going toward the stubborn slope of those shoulders, and grabbed one of them and was urging it firmly toward the light, admitting gruffly, "All right, all right, kid, I'm hip, but you come on now—"

But Kelcey did a shocking thing at that (there was even a clearly audible gasp from someone nearby who realized that extent of the repudiation). He hunched his shoulder violently away from Edgar's hand, without even looking at him, and turned his back with the rash petulance of a child.

Edgar stared piercingly at him for the barest second with a withering look of last anger, and snapped out, "You goddamn fool, so you don't want to blow with me, but—" But then he broke off, realizing that that was exactly it, somewhat amazed by the lengths to which Kelcey would go, and then aware of the antics for which he himself was justly notorious (the whole array of put-downs and parodies and sulks, which had made playing with him a hazard in recent years), and so shuffling back into the glare, his face stonier, his eyes more unreadable than before. After all, there was something almost filial in Kelcey's very defiance of him.

"My God, did you see that!" someone breathed. "What's wrong with him anyway? What's wrong?" and he knew in a flash that they were speaking of him, and not of Kelcey, and that what Kelcey had done had seemed to them right in character, but what he had failed to do had not. It came home to him for the first time with the shock of recognition by which we finally admit something that we darkly know—only some subtle and ironical gesture or retort (as shaming as a blow from any other man would be) was typical of the Edgar Pool that haunted their heads. And he saw how they could think that, and why they did, and knew that they would never think to pity him, because he had never shown them anything but a murky, scornful smile.

He bent to his reed to stop his mouth, because he knew nothing else to do, and began to blow again, hurting and winded and enraged. "I can *make* it happen," he insisted, staring pitilessly out upon the dim faces, "because it ain't magic or accident or God, you goddamn creeps! It's your-*self*—it's *me!*"

But Billy James was muttering again in a ranting whisper, as Cleo's chords began to trail off once more, and before he knew it Edgar heard his own hoarse voice snap out over all the speakers, "Nobody *help* you do it, you know, nobody," and shut up with a wince, only to know, with crazy certainty, that everyone would think that he meant Billy James (for *that* was characteristic of him, oh yes, to say such things right out; he knew it—that was the Edgar they would recognize; and maybe there was no other Edgar any more) and so he smirked a sour, wicked smirk at Billy James' startled eyes, and shuffled toward him like a ghastly old queer exhilarated by the uncorrupted buttocks of a boy; playing it out adroitly; realizing, at the very moment that he did, that it had never really been a role before.

He capered up to Billy James in a madly dainty little dance. Feet together, forearms vaguely raised, eyes uprolled, he waggled his hips like an overpainted dowager in the toils of mambo; and then, just as ludicrously fetching, he backed away again, to pause and cock his head and listen to the bass' pulse with a grin that said, "Can you imagine! Listen *there!* Well, well, well—" But his small, fixed eyes, catching the light, were cold and wily and in deadly earnest—the eyes of a bored Zen master muttering his idiotic "Wu!" into his pupil's ear, then shouting, "*Now*, you silly fool, do you see the truth!"

There was a ripple of nervous laughter, which silenced Billy James, whose nightmare was (Edgar realized with a dizzy falling away of all veils) only the failure to be taken seriously. But it was also enough to distract poor Cleo from his arduous concentrations, and he broke off again, and turned and peered in dumb bewilderment at everyone.

But Edgar only swung his shoulders to the cymbal's splash, and went over and turned him back again, lecturing in a steady, heedless drone; and then padded back, drag-footed, winking grotesquely at Billy James as he passed, suddenly not caring anymore about his dizziness and his exhaustion and that thing in his stomach that had become a pain without his noticing. For he had realized that nobody knew him, and nobody had ever seen him, and he was a mask over a mask over a mask to them, and even he had not glimpsed his own true face for years.

Automatically he blew part of a sketchy chorus, finding an old idea and then losing it again. "You squares, you creeps, you bastards!" he raved on and on to himself. "I can still outblow you all if I want to, I had it *in* me once," knowing at that moment that it had been realer than anything else in his life; and was realer now than it had ever been before because it was so poignantly gone. "Oh, come on!" he begged them in a desperate rage. "Somebody come *in*, you goddamn fools!"

So he broke off willfully, running with sweat and gasping for lost breath, and clearly indicating Billy James to the crowd with a flick of his hand, he gave the melody to him. But what he saw in the frowning, self-centered face that bent over the bass' neck maddened him anew, and before he knew it he had pranced into the sidling little jig again.

Billy James tried not to look, communing tight-lipped with whatever solemn muse whispered to him secret praise, but when Edgar started toward him, dizzy with uncontrollable malice, a word forming on his lips, a shrewd word, a devious word, a word with a terrible half-truth inside it, Billy James abruptly, madly, laid down his bass, overcome with fury and mortification, and stalked off the stand to a shocked gasp from the whole room, slamming into the kitchen.

The drums went on and on, as if only some final, catastrophic thing could halt those tireless sticks, and Edgar stood there, dazed and blinking, the handkerchief held against the choking shudders of the cough that each time wrenched harder at that thing in his stomach which, all at once, he knew could tear loose.

"All *right*," he spat out aloud, not even looking at what he had coughed up into his handkerchief. "All right," and bent his punished mouth to the dumb beak of that alien horn, and all alone up there at last, began to blow once more.

"Oh, man, not *again!*" that same goading voice called out. "You're like bugging me!" followed by a burst of laughter.

But Edgar's drowned eyes flared at that, and biting down upon the reed, he blew a wild, defiant squawk toward that voice. Something in him seemed to catch for just a moment, and miraculously somehow held, and he plunged on after it recklessly, clenching his eyes tight and bending further back in his exertions, his two dumb feet planted wide and awkward as he pushed the big horn forward with his loins.

The crowd hushed all in an instant (so that the giggle of one inattentive woman twittered with forlorn hilarity in the silence), for the sloppy, laconic figure up there had now become as strained and grotesque and natural as a spread-legged woman giving birth.

He missed the beat, he blew three clinkers in a simple phrase, his reed kept squeaking shrilly, but he did not pause, even when the bass resumed again and he knew that ego (or Mr. Samm) had urged Billy James back to the stand. He did not hesitate, but sweated over it—impervious to shame or pride or even that paralyzing perfectionism that keeps a man from trying, lest he fail—because he was hearing it somewhere in his head again, that crude, formless, faint, rare music that he had not heard for years, and he struggled manfully to free it through the horn, and for a moment his tone grew soft and inexplicably sad against the doomed, rebellious group behind him. And just at the end he caught a little of it long enough to blow a hint, and then gave it to the drummer, who plunged into a final series of stuttering explosions and press-rolls, punctuated with the steady crash of cymbals, until, with a gathering clatter and cah-*boom,* it was over.

It was over, all except for the gruff voice with the whine barely hidden in it that he heard as he stepped down off the stand into the darkness again—Billy James' voice, clear and shocking, echoing through all the speakers: "Don't associate me with this . . . This isn't jazz . . . These people are sick, *sick!*"

But that finished it, that and the chagrined and imploring face he saw hovering over the microphone when he turned in amazement; the flushed face that did not even look in his direction, and could not even wait till he had gone to utter those words—just as if he had no more reality to it than a poltergeist once dawn has come.

All he knew after that was that he had to get out of

there, and he pushed his way past the jostling waiters and the dim, obsequious faces that thrust close to him, talking steadily to snag his attention, to snap out when he took no heed, "That old dinge nut! Who does he think he is!" not even caring that he heard.

He made for the stairs, eyes fastened on them like the eyes of a swimmer turned wildly up as he tries to surface from a smothering depth. He had forty-five minutes before the next set, his last set, and maybe by then— Rain, chill, night.

Each step up caused a funny little hitch in his guts, as of something giving way, but nevertheless he made for the door, and the canopy outside it, and the wet night beyond, without pause, longing for the splatter of rain down his forehead and into his eyes, the anonymous hurry of the swarming sidewalks, the methodical splash of taxis crawling through streaming lights; and reached it, and walked off away from the place.

The Broadway night enclosed him in its impersonal vast roar, and he passed through it like a gloomy misanthropic ghost, his head echoing with voices that were not there—"I ain't gonna play with no goof." "Oh, man, not *again!*" "Sick, sick!"—as clear and crazily dispassionate as only an overheard truth can be. "It's only another binge to him—" "This isn't jazz—" "Sick, sick, *sick!*" The old habitual fury choked up into his throat, dizzying him for a moment in its rush, only to evaporate with his thin breath upon the night air; and for the first time his anger struck him as an impotent and useless prevarication.

"What does it matter anyway! Maybe I can't play too good no more, but—" No, they couldn't understand him; they were too young and full of themselves; the night still held out its pulsating promise to them, and all their music was still ahead, like a woman they had never seen but knew would yield. No, they were as strong and thoughtless

as untried lovers to whom the inexorable waning of powers
had no reality; they could no more understand him than
boys can understand their fathers; but, then, he too, yes, yes,
had scorned understanding once, and gone his way uncaring in that same blind certitude of strength.

"But, man, I never pulled no five," he thought with a
crazy shred of pride, despite what it had brought him to.
"I never out an' out wouldn't blow with *no* one . . . So
you see what all this music school'll do? You see that?
Man, I could have told them—" and with this foolish momentary vindication easing the bitterness, he was carried
along down Times Square's great river (that was created
from nothing a few blocks uptown and would be dissipated
into nothing again a few blocks down), reminded of the
great Missouri of his corduroyed boyhood, moving past
even the most astonishing of cities with an ever accelerat-
ing premonition of its destiny further on—his first suspicion
that there was something else, something else, something
other than the life he knew.

"If I could get my *fare* is all," he raged out. "Why can't
I get my fare!" revulsed by that perilous and exhilarating
street he knew so well—all blacks and whites, all outlines,
run together in the rain. "And what the hell's New York
anyway! Who needs it!" The Big Town, the Apple (as jazzmen dubbed it, unconscious of the fatally accurate Biblical implications), the City that only the great men can impress enough to merit destruction at its hands. "I'd take
my face away so goddamn fast! You'd see—I don't *need* it.
Man, I don't *want* it!" once more full of the wild and
senseless longing (which only exhaustion awakens) that
had driven him all day; a longing for the oblivion of se-
curity, for the end of struggle, imaged to him in the land-
locked spaces of his youth, where the Great Unknown
(somehow always associated with the river in his head)
was held to its proscribed channel by the jealous land, and

not, as here on this doomed and blasphemous island, lapping malignly at the end of every street. And suddenly he thought of his mother's frail, bony back bent over her tubs, her pots, her brooms, in a perpetual, humble stoop to life —that small, frightened, lost little woman (dead now eighteen years) whom he had loved so angrily, so inarticulately once, having too much of her in him to ever show it. "Ma," he murmured aloud surreptitiously, trying the strange word on that unlistening night. "Mama . . . Mother." But she was irrevocably dead to him, her face and voice and love faded from his memory: only her weary, self-martyred back seen through the steam was left. "I can see why the old man was bugged, I guess," he thought, feeling for the first time (aged himself beyond any years his father had attained) a disquieting sense of closeness to those scowling eyes, that razored cheek. "Huh!" he grunted to himself pensively. "Well, if I can get my fare is all," he vowed again, "and not even beer money, I don't care," longing just then for even the bus traveler's queer, sleepless suspension from life, in which one state blurs into another, one mood into the next, Ohio's noontime meadows darkening to Indiana's eerie thickets, the despair of flight fusing with the hope of home. "And once you get to Terre Haute, man, you got it licked—"

He fingered the meagerly assembled bills wadded against his thigh, in ironic reminder of the distance he had come that day. "Just fifteen, Baby—" "I need five to get straight again, even part of five—" "*You* got any money, kid?—" "Give me forty for it . . . All right, thirty-five— Well, man, what *will* you give me for it then? There ain't no music in it any more—" Ironic, because there were still too few bills and still a treacherous and unknowable distance to go.

"But, let's see—two left from my ten, and Baby's old fifteen, and twenty-seven on the horn, make forty-four—and then I got thirty coming when—" But that reminded him that he had still another set to play (an impossible idea), and those other voices joined the chatter in his brain with their passionless, damning drone: "Play the music—" "Blow for *them*—" "Sick, sick, *sick!*" bricking him out, each one, into the ghastly knowledge he had fought all day with drink and mockery and self-delusion, that his life and his work had betrayed him somewhere, long ago perhaps, and he had gone on refusing to see it, his pride swelling like a boil around the dark suspicion of the truth, until there was nothing but the pride, festering upon itself, to burst with sickening abruptness when an earnest and respectful youth stood up, and loving him, opposed him too, because the truth belongs to no one.

"All right," he murmured, "oh, all *right*," as if to quiet his thoughts, as if to admit to them that he had accepted their pitiless logic. "But what am I gonna do? Them cats *won't* blow with me. And I ain't myself enough to just bull it through— I mean, I'm beat, and okay so I got too lushed somewhere, too. But, man, I'm sick," coughing as though to prove it, and surrendering to self-pity all at once, as if it would make someone or something relent. "Cause there's something wrong, and they keep yelling at me, and cutting up. And, man, I can't get that crappy horn to working— I ain't my*self* enough to—"

But he broke off again with a hopeless frown, remembering the reaction of the crowd. "You old, damn fool!" he spat out sternly, bitterly. "What're you talking about! You ain't been yourself for years! You been grinning and yawning and faking yourself since—" Since when? Geordie, the habit, when? "Oh, it don't matter. But you ain't blown anything for years you'd turn halfway 'round to hear! You ain't blown anything you *meant*—" as Walden had: that sudden, beautiful, almost wistful widening of his eyes last night, when something issuing from his horn in the heat of contest had

213

surprised and overjoyed him—the discovery and the creation of it one— And Edgar had heard, and only squashed it with an empty imitation. "But he don't know, he don't. What does he *know?* Man, he only knows the *truth*," stopping again, because inadvertently he had come out with it, and it was the innocence, it was the trusting assumption that truth itself would be enough, it was the purity that Walden had retained that maddened him. "Oh, I know, I had that kick, too, but—" the rare, faint, formless music, or rather the memory of having heard it once with that same astounded, joyous widening of eyes, coming back to him in a tumble of images and emotions that did not take a second to fall through his head . . .

. . . His buried years, his woodshed: the obsessed hours of listening in bars, in alleys, to records, always all alone, to someone whom now (because of him) everyone had forgotten, but who had then seemed to give a flawless rhythm to the night; the added hours, snatched in evening from the dreary days he paid the world for his obsession, in a Louisville warehouse and an Omaha stockyard and a Baltimore elevator—the hours of getting to know the beat as *he* (whoever it might have been—the current idol) knew it; the further hours, by now gigging with local week-end bands, during which rank imitation finally gave way to *knowing* as the idol knew, as well as playing as he played, until the other man's freedom had freed him, and he could listen for himself. He remembered being a wild nigger in the ugly back o' town sections of small factory cities, shunned by the respectable and the industrious, even of his own race, because he never got up till two, and wailed all night. And there was not one moment that was *the* moment it had changed—or just one, which at the time had not seemed cataclysmic (but merely the culmination of long thoughts, the fruition of many planted things); one quarter-hour all alone when he sat with an arrangement of "Cherokee" open on his bed, irritably running through it in his mind before sleep; and suddenly hearing, not the melody or even an idea on it, but a new, long-suspected conception of the line, which this one night became *sound* —though in his head only, having no idea then *how* to play it on the horn, but hearing nevertheless (the veer, the bend, the new accent), and puzzling over it, and even sniffing curiously to himself; but from that night on trying intently for it after hours, "Ool-ya-ya-be-ah!" That was all he could remember of the first pure, inward thrill, isolated entirely from the endless problems of lip and fingering and tone that had followed it—all too arduous and technical, and finally too dull to be remembered. That was all—for the first time hearing something that he knew was his: apt, original, something that seemed evident the instant he heard it.

"But, man," he insisted to the memory of Walden's eyes, exasperated by their clear, sad gaze, "that's *still* only the beginning. That's only a *part* of it," exasperated because he knew, nevertheless, that it was the most important part, the thing that had to be tirelessly recreated, night after night, if a man was to guard his own peculiar gift.

"Well, how can someone blow his best with a goddamn bunch of creepy, hung-up kids like that! What the hell do they expect, asking, 'What's *wrong* with him, what's *wrong* with him' that way? . . . But, *man*, anybody makes a hassle this next set, I'll show 'em put-downs if that's all they're after—"

But he could not believe in it, even enough to continue, and a terrible wave of hopelessness flooded over him. The thought of the set still to be played, and the bored and demanding crowd waiting to be diverted by it, and the other musicians to whom he was only a hateful nuisance, and, most of all, the baffling emptiness in himself, out of which he could seem to bring nothing, nothing—all this was suddenly unendurable to him.

"Somebody," he murmured desperately. "If I had somebody to listen, somebody who digs— Man, I'm used to playing for a mob. You can't work when there ain't *no*body"— he who had scorned the breathless and attentive crowds hanging on his merest note, in the giddy years, the dead years, giving them only his backside then at which to gape, purposefully not playing well. "There must be somebody around. It's only one-thirty, two o'clock . . . Man, it ain't *late* or anything! If I knew somebody was *out* there, that's all—sure, sure—"

And there ahead, as if conspiring with this last wild hope, was the canopy of Paradise Alley, gay with light, under which squealing girls darted from open taxi doors to stand, flushed and a-glisten with the rain, while their escorts counted change.

CHORUS:EDGAR (2)

*Ah, broken is the golden bowl!
The Spirit flown forever!*

POE

"Yes, man, it's Monday night," he said to himself, passing through the doors. "Everybody'll be here," unconscious, as he swayed down the stairs toward the sound of a trombone, that the hat-check girl eyed him warily and signaled to the captain, who started toward him with a scowl, only to recognize him as he got closer, and nod briefly to the girl.

"Hey, Horn, you got all wet," he said with an impersonal smile. "How about this rain?" touching his soaked sleeve, as if he had considered not doing it but had then thought better of it. "How're the nerves?"

"What? . . . Oh, groovy. *You* know . . . Man, you got a crowd, eh?" for beyond the captain's heavy, no-nonsense shoulders he could make out dark, thronged tables.

"You kidding? The weather bombed. You never make

more than salaries on a Monday anyway, but when it rains—" He shook his head with a tough fatalism, slapping the sheaf of menus against his thigh, and appraising Edgar with quick cynical eyes that had not been surprised for years, and knew just where to look in a man to find the weakness or the vice or the emotion that might develop into trouble. "Man, it looks like you been swinging. We sell a little booze, *too*, you know," conveying perfectly the saloon keeper's irritation with having to cope with people who have spent their money getting plastered somewhere else. "You want a table or something?"

"No, like I'm just looking for somebody—"

"Well, let's keep it down, you know. No one can hear this sissy group anyway."

"All right, man," Edgar said, "I'm hip," moving off into the darkness, and adding automatically, "I'm hip you're square."

His gaze skipped from table to table in the half-light, not pausing at the rollicking groups of Ivy Leaguers with their martinis and steak sandwiches, or the chic, expressionless Negro girls, staring down their noses and trying to convey by their hauteur that this was *their* place and not some college hangout. "There must be someone," he repeated. "Man, this here's Monday night," but he could find no face he recognized; only the young, cool, bright, unmarked faces of a generation he did not know, intent upon their own thing, full of their own life; a generation that revered his name, but was, at the last, somewhat impatient with his horn. "I guess you all of a sudden got old," he murmured aloud bewilderedly. "Man, you don't know these cats, any of them—"

But then, just then, just as he was about to relax the way a drowning man finally relaxes into the end of his breath, he saw Geordie. Her table was one of the house tables off to one side, out of the way of the waiters who hurried up and down among the jumble of chairs with the unerring ease of glum Indians following all-but-obliterated trails. The quick-eyed, good-looking white man sitting with her had just lit a cigarette, dragged on it deeply, and handed it to her as Edgar appeared at her elbow.

"Well, how about this for c-c-crazy," he got out with a flush of relief for which he had no words. "What are you doing *here?* There's nothing happening here, is there? . . . Who's blowing up there anyhow?" barely turning to look, a secretive smile glimmering for a moment on his face. "You following me around or something, Baby? . . . Seems like I been running into her all *week*," he explained to the alert, freshly-shaven face of the man, uncertain there was anything in that face to indicate whether it realized who he was. "Man, that's a real nutty tie, I dig that tie . . . Baby, you learned about ties yet? She got the *worst* taste in ties, you know—"

The first surprise had passed from Geordie's lips, leaving them moist and parted, and as he rambled on she looked up at him with an alarmed, clear-eyed expression of such instantaneous shock and understanding that his words trailed off all at once—his suit, his shirt front and most of all his drawn and ravaged face so clearly reflected in that look that he was nonplussed for a moment.

"Eddie," she began, one hand lifted in confusion toward him with a jingling of the complicated bracelets she had always hankered after, "I thought you were cutting out— And what have you done to—"

"I lost my overcoat, I guess I tol' you, and then . . ." red-rimmed eyes noting the expensive narrow-shouldered suit on her companion with a surprising dart of self-consciousness, "and then I didn't have no time to go get my *other* one . . . So I'm some fine mess now, ain't I? Because they finally conned me into sitting in over at the Hole. *You* know, at the last minute . . . But I'm cutting

219

out in a couple of hours anyway, so I thought why not, why not—" And all of a sudden he crouched down on his aching calves beside their table, dizzy and trying to snicker it away as he muttered, "Might as well let them cats back there see, I guess, and I only got a minute," to be suddenly confronted by the small alert face of Geordie's dog, nestled in her lap right there before his eyes—a little soft brown bundle against the black sheen of the dress that shaped, taut and wrinkleless, over the full curve of her thigh. "Hello, there, Buster," he mumbled, entranced and saddened and sobered by the bright, impenetrable eyes, the patient wet nose and the strange, sensitive animal mouth— all more familiar to her now than *he* had ever been. "What's his name again? . . . Yes, man, hello there . . . Yes, yes . . . hello—" ruffling its silky, delicate head against Geordie's belly, chuckling and coughing to himself.

"You soaking wet," she exclaimed as his sleeve brushed her bare arm. "Feel that. And what's that cough?"

" 'What's that cough!' " he chided her desperately. "Why, that's from cigarettes and booze and kicks. *You* know that . . . You think I'm trying to *kill* myself, or some silly thing? . . . Man, you better watch out," he said to that sun-lamped and attentive face, feeling the strange necessity to assure it not to worry. "She be dosing you with horse pills, and makin' you wear your rubbers if you don't watch out," laughing pointlessly. But the well-groomed white hand that closed over her brown one as he said that, as if to quietly assert possession, made him add before he could stop himself, "Although, man, like you don't really need nothing like rubbers when you with Baby, that's for sure," unable to stop even at her sudden hurt and embarrassed frown (out of which he clearly knew no retort would come, and all the more damning to him for that very reason) so that he stumbled on. "I fell by here looking for a chick, but where is she? You know her, Baby. Helen—

What's her name? Meaty girl. You remember it? . . . But, no, that's right, I guess that was later—" feeling the cold sweat gathering across his forehead, almost level with Geordie's eyes, and knowing it would start to run down his cheeks in a moment, but somehow unable to get out that dirty knot of handkerchief for fear the stain of blood would show. "But I don't see her nowhere," he drawled on help-lessly, turning to survey the nearby tables. "But you oughta fall by over there. You know, man? For the last set," speak-ing casually to the man, as if that might make up for the tasteless joke, and not sure he could last much longer. "They really swinging over there—"

"Well, we're due at this party," the man replied indeci-sively, looking at Geordie's wide dark mouth to gauge her mood.

"I mean, this new kid, this Kelcey Crane, is blowing goofy, *goofy* things, Baby," Edgar went on. "Have you caught him yet? . . . And that other kid, Cleo what's-his-name—"

"Well, I don't know," she hesitated, glancing down at him uncomfortably, confused by a powerful premonition for which she could not account. "We're supposed to meet some people, but— Are you all right though?" she added nervously, at the same time squeezing her escort's hand as if to say she would explain later. "Are you all right now? You look—"

"I'm lushed," he said, trying to laugh, "and I don't feel so good, I guess," unable to keep it up any longer under her eyes, and so staring at the bare inside of her brown fore-arm turned out as she allowed her hand to be held, "but I'm gonna blow this next set all right," he insisted, nod-ding his head steadily. "I feel plenty good enough for that, oh, yes . . ."

And all the time he was not even listening to what he said, because his glance had fixed on the clean, almost translucent skin right there where the vein lay close, finding no scars—the tiny whitish scars where once his needle had sought and pierced that vein—and then remembered that, of course, most often toward the end she had taken it up inside her thigh where it wouldn't show, remembering, too, the monumental trivialities of the habit that had dissipated drop by milky drop the tense, dark passion they had had together once; losing themselves separately because the drug brings no one close, but (like grace or like damnation) happens in a single soul at a time. The scars, wherever they might be, came to a sad and irreducible total, he suddenly thought, and they were *hers* alone, as his were his. He could neither justify nor expiate them, no matter what his guilt or his responsibility might be. She looked at him over a wall of weakness and pain and fantasy shared in connivance in the past, and it would separate them forever, as only knowledge can. She could not reach him over it; she could only grieve; and when he glanced up, for a moment their eyes met, and the way she looked at him, concerned and nervous but invulnerable, made him realize, all at once, that she was stubbornly intent on surviving the strong temptation of that past, and dared not succumb to its griefs, and would not; and so he looked away again, down at her arm, and when he said, "Please, though, whyn't you fall by? . . . Please, Baby—cause there ain't *no*body over there to listen. I mean, there ain't *no*body at all—" he almost whispered it, coughing under her large, troubled eyes.

"Well, maybe later we— But you sure you're not *sick* or something, Eddie? You sure you're—"

His head shot up at that hateful word, to fix her with an expression she had hoped never to see in him again—the old haughty and ironical expression that severed him from everyone in an instant, revealing how little of himself he had ever really shared.

"Sick! I ain't sick. You *always* talking about sick, Baby! I swear I get worried about you—" suddenly incensed and turning to the puzzled face of her companion. "Man, I'm telling you, these *Southern* chicks, all they talk about is food, and gettin' sick! She be starting in on you, you wait . . . And at sixteen she was just the goddamn same— I tell you it's that fever-air down there come up out of them swamps, them bay-*oos*," drawling grotesquely, eyes wild and sharp with irony, "and all that goddamn emanci*pation* pork they feed 'em night and day! . . . *Sick!* Baby, I told you and I told you," he pronounced with brutal condescension, somehow getting on his feet again, despite pain and hopelessness and anger, only hoping they would laugh at the desperate variation on the old joke that came into his head at that moment. "Didn't I never *tell* you, Baby? . . . I got to get *high* before I can get sick. I got to get *lifted* before I got the patience to go through it!"

And on an impulse, giving them an airy, sneering smile, he turned around and walked away, almost immediately dizzy with regret at having ruined it, and ruined it for nothing but his fatal, swollen pride that seemed to have no one left to wound any more but himself.

Sick, sick, sick: the word banged around his brain as he navigated the stairs again, thinking halfway to the top, "It's when you go up, man, it pulls loose that way." He made the street and the rain and the chill, and started back with the word bitter in his mouth: sick, sick, sick—

"But I ain't been sick since Cadillacville, you creeps, and *that* was only to throw my stupid habit," fastening upon his body because he dared not think about his mind (though it was something in his mind that worried him), fastening on the dead, cool, depthless white of everything in Cadillacville State Hospital—beds, sheets, uniforms and plaster walls—(which had not helped his mind any), but then it was his flesh, his black flesh, that was the trouble, he told himself; it was his flesh that screamed and revolted; it was his flesh they had protected when it shook with chills; it was his flesh they pitied with the diminishing withdrawal shots; it was his flesh they seemed intent on saving when he tore at it to make it stop, to make it stop. It was his black, hateful flesh, he told himself, knowing that he could remember nothing of that twelve-year-old agony, except that it had happened—for the body's experiences do not occur in time, and so cannot really be relived in age.

"But I *wasn't* goofy, I was only hooked from taking Baby's half because she went so square on me," he thought stubbornly, knowing nevertheless that it was something in his mind that had brought him out of the room he had not left for two days and into the smoggy canyon street that last dawn when the prowl car eased in, sirenless, beside him, and the officer (without even getting out) inquired pedagogically, "And where do we think we're heading, blackie? Muscle Beach or something?" and he found he had on nothing but his shorts and socks.

It had been something in his mind that two o.z.'s of ripe Pachuco pot had brought out into the shade-drawn, airless room where the bed-table lamp burned steadily for those two days. It had been something in his *mind* (because the thrice-daily fix kept his body quiet) that emerged as layer after layer of wrath peeled from him, and he kept the high just right, and solidified and nailed it down (as it were) before increasing it another notch, lying there through the urge to move and jump about, through the urge for people, into the moment when he started to smile gleefully at himself, and beyond that to when he first heard the giggle tickling in his throat, and right into the moment when he noticed the voice, his own voice (but almost breathless with laughter) saying to someone, "That's all right, Miss Letitia, that's all right, yes, heh, heh, heh . . . Oh, I know . . . You're in my dreams, and Ah'm in your

nightmares . . . I know, I know . . . Heh, heh, heh . . .
But that's all right, cause that just proves we both of us are
hip that in the *dark* we all the *same!!* . . . You see? You
see that, *ma'am?* Heh, heh, heh . . ." finally able to admit
that it was his black, sweating face, strained and contorted
as he blew (or some other face indistinguishable to them
from his), that haunted the bad nights of countless Southern ladies with the giddy horror of buck rape in a dark
alley; knowing it, but too high to care, and seeing around
it and beyond, to where it was only sad, only blind, only
silly: for him, hating them, to lust; for them, hating him, to
fear. It seemed so silly that he laughed and laughed—without rancor, softly. And then went out to look for Geordie in
his shorts, to tell her, but was picked up instead, and lost it
later when they brought him down.

So maybe it was *since* Cadillacville that he had been
sick, he thought suddenly, and something in his mind (that
ruinous pride that seemed to be his only heritage from the
age-old humilities of his race) had steadily soured everything around him—even Geordie, even the music, or at least
the clap-hands, jog-foot, shake-head rollicking music that
celebrated the wild joy of life itself, and always made him
frown out disgustedly: "What you got to grin and prance
about, Rastus? What? What? What?" Pride was his spur.

Born midway in the land, not truly North or South, born
midway in the relentless, painful change in prejudice, he
was nowhere, nothing, in between; and he stared with furious bafflement up into the American night as he staggered
along, as if it could tell him the secret of his bitter patri-
mony. "What do I have to *do!*" he felt like screaming out
to it. "What do I have to *lose!* . . . I been poor, cold, cruel,
loved, ignored, praised, hooked, mad, *black,* ain't I! . . .
But I played the music for you, you wild old Bitch, didn't
I? I blew the truth for you sometimes, didn't I? . . . Why
do you have to destroy something to create something

here! *Why!* And it's always yourself, it's always *you!*"

But he broke off short, knowing he could no longer afford this, and did not really believe it anyway, and only raged to ease himself—as always. "And everyone had it just the same," he thought. "Baby had it the same, and worse— And I ought to a said something to Baby just now," not knowing what exactly, a true word, a straight look, something relinquishing, a final armistice in the pointless battle of their wills—for now they were too old for war. "You ought to a said it years ago when you first thought of it," he told himself. But, foolishly, he had thought that he had time; cruelly, he had let her stew. And now, instead of the word, the look, all he had given her as valedictory was a mocking little speech, meant to injure and humiliate; and the only one he had hurt was himself.

"Well, maybe she's hip that that's the way it was . . . She always dug me more than anyone," feeling that thing choke inside his throat. "And I coulda said something nice to Walden, too . . . I coulda said, 'Close, man. You got close.' I coulda said *that* anyway . . . Cause I don't *hate* him, it wasn't *him* who bugged me," sniffing and getting rain up into his nose as he swallowed at the thing. "Man, what've I been *doing* anyway? And sneering at the kid, too —I been doing it all along like that . . . And he wasn't trying to put me down or anything . . . He was just sticking with me cause I was sick," able to admit it now, the whole thing, his mind, his belly. "Man, you *coulda* said something nice, but you never did . . . It's so simple, and it don't change nothing, but it don't *hurt* nothing either," glimpsing himself again with pitiless objectivity as the crowd saw him—all drawl and slouch, all layered over. "Just look at the mess you made of it—" And then he saw the Go Hole's canopy up the block, and automatically stopped there on the rainy sidewalk.

"Oh, man, just walk away," he murmured. "Yes. Just

walk on uptown, and make the bridge, and find a highway going west, and bum it till you get to someplace you
got enough loot to take a bus from . . . Yes, yes—"

But he did not believe this either as he said it. He was
too old to just walk away, he was too drunk to make it, he
was too sick to be afraid. And something indestructible in
his heart, that had nothing to do with his mind or belly
(perhaps pride, perhaps hope—who can say?), whispered,
as it had whispered to him from the very beginning,
"Maybe this time, eee-oow, maybe this time it'll be something no one can stand, it's so true . . ."

And there, right there where he stood, was Parker's Tavern, offering a temporary reprieve, and he muttered, "I'll
have me one last shot to pull me together, that's it. Yes,"
hoping to find somebody there to whom he could speak,
dumbly hoping for something that he could not name; and,
at any rate, having to postpone the stairs, the crowds, that
last unthinkable set.

Beyond the door the room was jammed, smoky, full of a
hubbub that jangled strangely in his ears. He got through
the shoulders to an open section of the bar, and ordered a
straight shot, leaning toward his lifted hand and letting
his eyelids flutter shut as he sipped at it, waiting for its
sting, its momentary gathering of the faculties, before he
looked around.

When he did, the first face he saw was the white, weary,
harassed face of Mr. Willy Owls a little down the bar, talking to a disk jockey. "Man, he don't never go home either,"
he thought as he pushed toward him.

"Hey, Owlie," he began, "ain't you got a bed somewhere?" unsteady with the drink, and feeling suddenly af-
fectionate toward the little, drawn-eyed white man: after
all, he dug; he could make more money, and have his days,
too, if he would represent an actor, a hand-painted tie, a
publicity-hungry oilman; jazz had hooked him, too.

"What— Oh, Horn," he said, obviously impatient at the interruption in his train of thought. "I thought you'd, well — But, look, man, hold on while I finish this— I'll be right there—"

"Like, Owlie, you got to come on over," Edgar blurted out immediately, too dizzy, too hopeful to be proud any longer, "to the Hole, man, cause—"

Mr. Owls sipped hurriedly at his seltzer to give him strength. "I'll be right with you, Horn, but let me—"

"—cause there's *no*body over there, and—"

"Now, come on, Edgar, I'm talking to this guy, all right? Haven't you kept me up long enough with your goofing already?"

"I guess I don't know what got into me," Edgar began to explain. "I coulda said something nice I guess, only—"

But Mr. Owls had turned back to the disk jockey, as he might have turned away from a bogus-derelict cadging quarters along Third Avenue.

Edgar swayed there for an instant, thinking with bewilderment, "But he got to understand, so he'll come on over," and found he had laid a hand on that small, humped shoulder facing him. "Man, wait, you got to under*stand*—"

"Come on, Horn, let go," Mr. Owls muttered, squirming under the hand and continuing to talk, as if burrowing his head in the conversation.

"But I don't know whether I can *make* this last set, you see," Edgar insisted. "You dig? What if I can't *make* it? . . . But if you'd—" and before he knew it he was trying to turn Mr. Owls around, thinking that perhaps he couldn't hear because of the noise. "Man, I'm talking," he said, as if it were a puzzling truth, "and you're not listening . . ."

"Let *go* of my suit!" Mr. Owls seethed out, bringing one arm up to hunch away that hand, his irritation turning into fury so abruptly that the gesture had more momentum than he intended, and caught Edgar off balance.

"Now, leave me *alone*, Horn!" he exclaimed. "I'm doing business here," his little, besieged eyes widening as Edgar stumbled backward hard into the bar just at the small of his back, to rock there for a moment, blinking and surprised.

"I'm doing business! Can't you understand!" Mr. Owls yelled almost plaintively to that face, and to the two large dirty hands that had come up to cover the stomach, as if in anticipation of a blow, or in response to one. "All right, all right, I give up— Here . . . here," he snapped out, "go get yourself a drink," throwing a dollar on the bar. "I give up—"

"Oh, no, man," Edgar breathed with a curious, soft croak, shaking his head slowly back and forth, staring oddly at Mr. Owls, and holding on to his belly. "That ain't it, that ain't what I meant at all . . ."

"Go ahead, go ahead, I said I give up," Mr. Owls repeated, although the faint wince around Edgar's eyes seemed to worry him. "You just don't know who your friends *are*, Horn, or you wouldn't pull this kind of thing. You don't *think*."

Edgar had half turned, in a daze, and started away, but he glanced back at this for the briefest moment. "I guess I know," he murmured in that strange, hoarse voice. "You my friend as much as anyone—" and then turned again and somehow reached the door.

The pavement swam in a hazy, treacherous blur before his eyes, and something had happened all right when Owlie pushed him (a snap, a kink, a sound almost, rather than a pain), and he went toward the Go Hole with dumb obedience, aware that somewhere inside him, in the wet dark of his belly, there was something like a leak.

"You went too far this time—you went too far—maybe you went too far," he mumbled, unable to finish the thought, but somehow getting through the crowd coming

229

up the stairs, and staggering in the crowd going down, so that they moved away from him and he heard, "Oh, some drunk." "Hey, isn't that the Horn?" "Man, they just *gotta* push you, don't they," but did not listen, moving into the dark throng, packed and curiously quiet, at the bottom of the steps, and into music, too, wondering, "Is that them others, or is that me?" able to think now only of such details.

He went on past the piqued, then startled face of the captain, into the dark, into the tables, drenched with sweat down his back and into his drawers, hearing the strange, loud hiss of his own breath in labored exhalation. It was a trumpet blowing, and was there a trumpet with that other group?—but then he stumbled over a woman's enormous handbag down in the murk at his feet, and paused, thinking he would pick it up, as a voice somewhere began, "Hey, watch it there, daddio," and then knew he dared not stoop, and had no room to do it, and that if he ever put his head down toward that dark he could never right himself again, and so pushed on, mumbling, "I'm sorry, man, I'm *sorry*." But then he could go no further, his knees melted, his breath was gone, and his eyes fluttered shut, hot and dry under the heavy lids, and he swayed back, thinking, "If I can only hit something solid though, cause I can't pay for no more dishes," and came up against a wide, mirrored pillar, still on his feet, quickly stuffing one hand into his jacket pocket, with crazy nonchalance, to cover the fact that he had almost fainted. He stood there, blinking and dizzy, peering out over the sea of tables toward the stand, muttering, "Who *is* that? Who *is* that anyway?"

But it was all a shimmering blur, and he struggled to focus his eyes, and was suddenly frightened for the first time. He had never thought about his body, he had never cared about it, he had never stepped aside for anything because of it; but leaning there, trying to tell whether he had

Four Seasons Hotels

missed the beginning of the set or still had a few minutes
to work some magic in himself he could not even think
about, he felt his body revolting, he felt something in it
that was not *him*, and he grew alarmed.

"Man, man," he groaned under his breath, searching the
nearby dark for a face he knew, someone to speak to,
someone to ask. But, curiously, everyone had drawn away
from him: the people at the tables there, and there, dili-
gently looking away toward the music, and even the standing crowd, for which there was no room, keeping their distance from him—as people instinctively turn or keep away
from a drunk, a madman, someone struck down helpless on
the sidewalk.

And so he turned back, trying to concentrate on the
trumpet, trying to blink the foggy shapes up there (far
away on the stand) into perspective, and managed it, and
saw Kelcey's small, spare shoulders gathered forward, and
the gleaming gold bell of his horn held close into the mike
as if to charm it, like a snake; hunched and intent, the
smooth, lean planes of his face burnished in the light;
blowing well.

And for a moment, with the clearing of his vision, his ears
seemed to clear, too, and the music came to him with such
startling reality that even the doubling of the bass was
distinctly audible within it. Something had pulled them all
together, and they were swinging now, and Kelcey's trumpet had a savage certainty above the eager rhythm. Edgar
felt that quick lift in the heart that occurs only when
everyone, inexplicably, miraculously, has found the same
pure groove; the good, hopeful lift of jazz (which is always
deeply on God's side, after all); the lift forward and up.
And just as he felt it his eyes lit on two young white men
transfixed at a table right before him, their faces full of
ecstasy and music, and all at once, staring and shivering,
he seemed to *know* them, their very souls: the dark one,

who was probably the sort given to muttering with drunken frustration at four in the morning, "Jus' give me a piano and a drum. Man, I'll make the bass, doom, doom, doom. But, oh, let's jump"; the one with glasses, listening a little too intently, as if he did not quite trust his ears or heart— one of those sad, somehow crippled young Americans whom jazz alone has reconciled to his country . . . And probably their fathers had Charlestoned indefatigably to Louie, and felt more than a planter's itch for Bessie. And in the thirties he himself had watched their older sisters dance tirelessly past the stand in the grave dips and glides of fox trots, their wistful prom gowns half-mooned with girlish perspiration. And, yes, hadn't he seen these very two, perhaps, riffing exultantly on windy midnight street corners in stark winter, brandishing a sorrowful quart of beer, and imitating him?

"It's all the same," he thought, staring at them. "It's just the same for them as me," black or white—no matter how they shouted at him now, no matter what they said; in spite of bitterness and irony and scars. They loved the thing he loved, and it had spoken to all of them alike, and that generous, eager, joyful softness of anticipation in their faces had been in his face, too.

And then Kelcey was finished, backing out of the light behind his lowering horn, and for a moment there was silence, except for the clean swing of the insatiable rhythm. "What are they playing?" he thought in his confusion, imagining he was next, and that the dreadful moment had come. "What're the chords?" his hands groping limply up toward stops that were no longer there, on a horn no longer his. "If I can only get the *key*—" but then felt a hand on his arm, and heard a voice saying, "No, man, *no,* you don't have to any more," and turning in bewilderment, saw Wing's troubled eyes, and felt two hands take his dumbly twiddling fingers in theirs, but (like a miracle that nothing in his own prayerless soul could have wrought) heard his horn anyway; recognized it with a sharp, sad thrill, and knew the song was "Junius Sees Her," thinking in a foolish muddle that they must be playing the record. "But *I* could make it if I had my horn," he gasped out. "I could blow," suddenly half-angry and struggling against Wing's hands. "And are they gonna pay me anyhow? Cause—"

"Man," Wing said. "Be *good* to yourself, wait—"

And then, indefinably, the horn checked Edgar, distracting him, because a man knows himself no matter how he may pretend, and (though note for note that was his solo) it was not him. He turned back, and dimly saw someone up there at the mike, through the shimmering blur that had come up over his eyes again: middling tall, somewhat stooped, and standing flat, lips fastened to the beak of a horn that seemed to struggle like a throttled bird to get loose—himself.

"Man, what's happening!" he moaned, blinking wildly. "Man, I must a gone too far. Man—" but his eyes came into focus, and he stared forward crazily, and it was Walden up there, and Wing was saying as he held his hands, "No, man, listen. He's only working out your set—so you can get your loot."

Something in Edgar seemed to shrivel at that, something huge and unsubstantial in his spirit that had warred without respite, without quarter, without reason against the very limits of his life, and his hands went lax in Wing's, and he stood there heavily against the pillar, as Walden went into the second chorus, never varying by even a single note the solo Edgar had cut so many years before with Junius, but not having to think about it either, because it was part of his whole apprenticeship in jazz, after all; a tune as much as any tune he played; a true confession flung up bravely once against a world that had small use for truth; a fragment of a man, and of his life, and thus (to Walden) holy. The crowd heard, and sat in breathless silence, and Walden suddenly let the horn go up (cocking his head to snare the reed) until it stuck out sideways from his frame, and someone gasped, "A-h-h-h, Horn!"—remembering.

Edgar stood there motionless, shocked at last to understand what he had said to other ears all this time, listening dumbly as Walden paid to him, living, the sort of tribute that is usually only paid to those dead: the voluntary submergence of the personality in someone else's work; the loving, faithful recreation, one more time, of what he had to say.

But just then the knot that had become a pain and then a leak became something that the sheer will to endure beyond it could hold down no longer, and he felt himself collapsing inside, like a wall crumbling at last under the patient demolition of a big sea that has rolled all the way from some shipless, bleak center of the watery Unknown, where not even intrepid sea gulls scream. He staggered, gasping out, "Like, a-a-a-h, I got this funny bellyache—" eyes rolling uncontrollably, as Wing, catching hold of him and pulling him back (right there among the tables), exclaimed, "Come on, come on—" to help him in the stumbling, sleep-walking steps through the half-darkness of the aisle, toward the kitchen.

"It won't wait no longer, it won't *wait*," Edgar gabbled, wincing and slamming into the door, "and I only need that thirty to get me *home*—" shambling through it as it swung away, to find himself confronted by the alarmed and hazy faces of waiters, among the steaming coffee urns. "And if I could only get myself to Terre Haute . . ." he croaked out, "cause when you get to Terre Haute, man—" but then he fell, beyond Wing's desperately grabbing hands, forward and down, and did not even feel the floor when it struck him.

"But how did I know he was *sick?*" a gloomy, young

voice was complaining, as Edgar came to for a moment to see a smooth, smoke-blackened plaster wall, which (just as he recognized the voice as Kelcey's) turned out to be the ceiling of the kitchen, because, when he moved his head a little, Billy James' broad, stubborn back entered his blurred field of vision, and he heard him whine, "But didn't I *say* he was? Didn't I *say* it?"

He seemed to be lying on one of the marble counters, cleared of dishes, his feet unsupported off one end (from the pain around his ankles), and he was cold in his flesh, and could taste his own blood in his mouth, and thought that he must have smashed his lip in falling; but when he licked it, found no cut and felt no sting, and knew then that it was something else, thinking, "Oh God, oh God— maybe if I sleep real long, if I could sleep long enough, and maybe eat—" feeling it steady and remorseless in his stomach all the time, beyond the bribery of good intentions now. "Oh God, oh God—I shoulda stopped, I coulda stopped this morning—"

Vaguely, he heard the door creak, briefly letting in the uproar of the crowd beyond, heartless somehow to him, their night unchanged for all of it; and someone breathless said, "I called Bellevue, doctor, like you told me. They'll be right over." Wing. And then a face was hanging over him suddenly—a white face, flushed, unlined, not over thirty-two, but to make it look older, a large black mustache like a suede brush, one corner of which the grave thin lips were chewing. "It's just lucky I was out there, that's all," the eyes not looking into his, but at his mouth, and then drawing away. "What's this man been *doing* to himself anyway?"

And Edgar tried to speak, suddenly afraid, wanting to say, "No, wait, I'm listening, I'm listening. Don't say nothing bad, don't say nothing *terrible,* cause I can *hear!*" but could neither move his head nor make a sound.

And then another voice, Walden's, said in a worried undertone, "But will they take *him* there, man? The ambulance?"

"Sure," Wing snapped out, "this ain't Georgia . . . What is it, though? What do you think it is?" And that other voice, the white voice, nervousness clipping it just as the mustache aged the solemn, blushing face, was saying it anyway, the bad thing, the thing he was afraid to hear, knowing it already. "Hemorrhage. Stomach—" and then utter silence, and then Wing: "But what can they do? Can they—?"

"Well, maybe if they hurry—" breaking off, as though unused even to an occupational dishonesty. "In any case, they can make him more comfortable. If only I had my bag—"

But then he paused, for Edgar's lips were grinding now at words that would not form, his eyes flaring up like levee lanterns in a river gale's black shriek, and his nails began scraping in ghastly, powerless scrabbles on the marble, and just as he got halfway up, wild and teetering on his elbows there before them like a resurrected corpse, he saw Geordie coming through the door, and felt, all the way across the steam-fogged room, the terror in her eyes (perhaps the premonition of his death come back to her from earlier that night), and croaked out in an agonizing fury of reproach, "They don't even *care* that I can hear!! Baby, listen, they don't even *care*—"

But at that, a trickle of dark blood overflowed his mouth (torn open with the cry), and he swallowed grotesquely at it, choking and moaning somewhere down inside his throat, "My horn, my horn," his wide hurt eyes darting helplessly as he clawed inside a pocket with a desperate, fumbling hand; and then he fell back hard, his head thumping cruelly on the marble, the scrap of paper fluttering from his outstretched fingers, as Geordie gasped.

CODA:CLEO

Celebrate (Cleo thought some time later). What had he meant by that?—lying there, under the unflickering, cold lights, his bruised head vanquished and immobile on the folded tablecloth someone had thought to put beneath it; Geordie beside him, a wisp of her hair come stiffly loose from the combs in back, vaguely wringing the limp hand she held in one of hers, and sighing to him in an involuntary, ageless croon, as if to coax those waxen lids into a final flutter so she might see the eyes, the living eyes, they hid; her white escort standing off a ways, alarmed and ill at ease, and (most of all) trying not to stare at the faint wrinkles that grim light picked out upon her neck.

Celebrate. What had he meant by it?—when for a moment the lids did flutter (Cleo, awestruck that in that shapeless mass of soiled clothing, all askew, all heaped and uninhabited, there was still any stubborn ember left to glow), and the eyes opened, and he peered up at Geordie without surprise, as she murmured, "Honey, oh, honey, oh, honey," with all the pitiful, repetitive inadequacy of the living. Cleo stared openly, too young to be embarrassed, too moved to heed proprieties, because something was gone from Edgar's face already (elusively, undeniably gone); and he realized with a shock that the body and the features and perhaps everything but the eyes were only a husk housing a mystery; and that whatever *it* had been in Edgar once, it was ebbing from his face now: the rage ebbing from the stained and stricken lips, the irony ebbing from the flared nostrils, the animal urge that had pushed him on and on (and was ignorant of all but breath)—ebbing, ebbing.

He peered up at Geordie, looking at her eyes and at the two shiny streaks her tears had left in symmetrical curve from lash to chin; looking at her mouth and the hank of hair fallen rigid behind one ear; looking at her with a curious, unhurried, almost distracted glance that silenced everyone. "Geordie," he breathed thickly, the name strange and formal on his lips to those who heard (because he had never called her that to anyone, though all along, perhaps, he had thought of her as Geordie to himself), "I meant to say—" and then his voice trailed off, his flecked lips still twitching as she leaned closer.

Perhaps he murmured something more (though there was not a sound), because suddenly her eyes moistened, and she choked at a sob (a woman's sob, natural and unashamed), gulping and sniffling at it, as she methodically squeezed his hand over and over again. And Cleo knew that whatever he had said was something, not for the dark goddess Geordie was to his generation, who could be touched and moved and experienced only in the guiltless room of the imagination, but for the woman only Edgar had ever known that way: the woman with flaws somewhere beneath the dazzling dresses, with days when her stomach would not settle, with brown and awkward toes a man might tickle; what he said, something that only the Geordie who looked ungainly fastening her bra, or woke rumpled and human with the wrinkles of the sheet upon her morning cheek, or was bored sometimes, or sick, or shameless without pants, could ever understand; something trivial or commonplace that had remained complete and unimpaired in his memory (and hers), though love and passion and everything else that mattered between them was long done; something not dwelt on or argued over or thought about in their tumultuous years, so that now it alone remained whole, like a stray deck chair or cushion, bobbing up out of the spreading whirlpool where time had dragged everything important—just as she looked at him (weeping a little, but only because he hurt), and must have seen something other than that abused and aging face.

Who could say what it was? Who had the *right* to know?

And then those curiously unhurried eyes fell on the white, shamed face of her companion, who looked as if he had no place here, and wanted to bolt, but obstinately would not go without her; and for a moment Edgar actually smiled—wanly, encouragingly—as if to say (Cleo imagined): Don't worry, man, don't worry. I knew her once, colored; and you know her, white. And there's the wall . . . But all problems are abolished in the womb, or in the grave. Forget your skin, hers, make her forget . . . Go ahead, go on ahead anyway, no matter . . . Because the Rednecks are righter than they know, yes, yes, and the end of it will come, not in strife or legislation, but only when the two sundered halves are yoked again: the male, the female; the black, the white, yes . . . It's going to go on being silly, sad, tragic, *square,* until two creatures look into each other's eyes at the moment of inmost fusion, and see the miracle of their own reflection in another's hungering gaze . . . The womb, man, the womb, oh, yes—

But then he looked away from that white face, and from Geordie, too, a last horror contorting his mouth, moaning all of a sudden, "You bastards! you creeps! you squares! There's more, I know there's *more!*" as if, for a moment, life with all its rage and thwart and loss (like a malignant fever) had made one final shudder in his heart. But then it passed, and he was still.

But, celebrate? What had he meant by that?—after the eyes had wavered shut again, dimming the face until it was as lidded as a mask, and Geordie turned away from him unable to look longer, and the hectic siren (somewhere nearby in the uncaring streets) first reached their ears. What had he meant? Cleo had stood, staring at the large dead hands that not long ago had taken his and moved them sternly back to life and work, thinking, "It went and happened after all, and maybe nothing that I tried to do made any—" only to notice the scrap of paper there below the counter among the ragged shards of broken plates, and go toward it without thinking twice, to stoop (so close to all that was left of Edgar, he certainly would have heard him breathing had there been breath left) to pick it up, hearing the incongruous, muffled sound of the alternate group blowing just beyond the doors (for jealous life does not stop for death); only, as he rose, to hear the faint murmur, too, and—scared and superstitious —come up level with one dim and slitted eye, still stubbornly open in the ruined face, the lips barely moving as they breathed, "Celebrate," so soft that no one else could hear. "Celebrate, yes," no sign even in that eye that it saw him. "Listen, listen. Oh—"

What had he meant by it? (Cleo thought, still holding

the bit of paper and standing there alone after they had taken him away, out through the service entrance.) What had he meant, if not that his music, *theirs,* had always been a celebration of— Of what? The hard winter light on American rooftops? The great automobile graveyards behind dilapidated board fences on the grimy outskirts of red-brick cities, flivver piled on flivver, entrails driven out? The dank bars? The tenement ghettos? The sun-merciless highways? The radio that buzzes through the interminable afternoons in every furnished room across the continent? Of this? Of this? This was all that he had ever known.

Yes. But of the enigmatic beer can, too, that lies in the densest thicket, in the remotest glade, beyond the farthest country road, where someone has gone off (as Americans have always gone off!) into the leafy wildness that still waits just out of any town; where the arrowheads still lie, ages lost, under the ferns; to brood or carouse or make first love or fall tipsily asleep under the astonished eyes of birds, and then go on, go on. And of America that has always been bigger than any man, *forcing* him to think, to imagine, to create, just to keep from drowning in sheer, insentient nature, and that has made Americans slaves to rhetoric, abstraction and idealism, in an effort to match the manless Rockies always looming in the corner of their eyes. And of America where John Muirs lash themselves, sky-high, in towering spruces to ride out in shrieking ecstasy the roaring secrets of the Teton storm; where sad-faced bearded introverts (invoking God to justify the law) become the suffering Christs of national calamities; America that cannot admit that out of imperfection all perfection comes, but which, despite everything (the ugliness, the hate, the greed and the hypocrisy), has always been an infinite possibility to match man's infinite desire. Yes. Jazz was as much a celebration of this American reality (everything, *everything!*) as a protest against it. Yes.

241

And Cleo looked at the slip of paper in his hand, and saw the number, the broker's name and the address, imagining as well the horn already handed gingerly into the dreary pawnshop window to sit between a tooled leather wallet and a tarnished crucifix; and thought, for just a moment, that he would go and pay the money and redeem it, but then—

No, leave it there. I will go home, tonight, and chalk upon the unfeeling iron of the subway wall, "The Horn still blows," in grave, anonymous hand. And you will have another hero soon, America, to join the John Browns, Houstons, Poes. What matter that he was black in soul and skin and that sometimes he hated you and that, like all your heroes, he fell so far? A man is dead, the last fifth drained, the last girl loved, the last horn lost, and he is dead too young. You will have another hero, and it does not matter if the way you think of him is not the way he was. He will join the others who obsess us still: Bessie moaning in her blood as they carted her crosstown; King puttering away his days forgotten in Savannah; Bix coughing in his horn or glass; old Fats gone finally to sleep in the ultimate lower berth; young black Fats grown pale and thin; Wardell killed down hard in a snarling bar; Bunk finding he could still pick cotton; Tesche dead in an auto crash; Brownie dead in an auto crash; Bird dead, Horn dead—tuberculosis, narcosis, arteriosclerosis, neurosis— It does not matter what carried them off. Once they blew the truth.

No, leave it there. For somewhere at the suburb end of a subway line, where the wet streets glisten in the faint street lights, a gawky, awkward youth, black or white (or something in between), walks in a formless discontent, dreaming a new dream, hoping a new hope, loving a new love; and perhaps tomorrow he will begin his arduous woodshed, and (rank and living in armpit and in crotch) will give up his hoarded money, and go out carrying the horn, to fashion on it a new song—a further chorus of the one continuing song—as he, too, progresses inevitably down his own bleak street, toward his own blank wall, where all the music ends; for only the song goes on, continually creating the need to create it anew.

No, Cleo thought, crumpling the paper suddenly. No, he is dead, and we can love him now. Leave his symbol where it is.

ABOUT THE AUTHOR

JOHN CLELLON HOLMES was born in Holyoke, Massachusetts, in 1926. He grew up in New Jersey, New England, and the West Coast, and served in the Hospital Corps of the United States Navy during World War II. He studied literature, philosophy and religion at Columbia University and the New School for Social Research, and began publishing poetry in the literary quarterlies in 1948. Since then, he has published verse, fiction and non-fiction in a wide range of magazines. His first novel, *Go*, appeared in 1952. At various times he has worked as a law clerk, movie usher, ghost writer, and researcher for a public opinion poll. His other books include a novel, *Get Home Free*, and a book of essays, *Nothing More to Declare*. He and his wife now live in Connecticut.